"The Life and Times of Rowan Daly is an extremely well-researched historical fiction novel that takes us into intriguing and difficult decades in this country's history, beginning in the Great Depression and moving through the challenges of the home front during World War II and into the strife of the Civil Rights Movement. In particular, the details of the Pack Horse Librarian project were captivating and educational."

> ~ Valerie Biel,
> Author of the award-winning
> Circle of Nine series

"The Life and Times of Rowan Daly is an irresistible read. Drama, suspense, pathos, love, and a sense of triumph reigns in this story. Rowan is a character you will love along with her dear friend, Florence. It was a thoroughly genuine read."

> ~ Frank Peot,
> Retired school teacher

"Wonderfully written and meticulously researched, Rowan is a heroine to root for; Florence is impossible not to love. This just may be Owens' best book yet!"

> ~ Anna Taylor,
> Public Services Librarian
> Sun Prairie Public Library

The Life and Times of Rowan Daly

May 2021

National Get Caught Reading Month
www.getcaughtreading.org

Other books by
Rex Owens

~

The Irish Troubles Series:

Murphy's Troubles

Out of Darkness

Dead Reckoning

The Life & Times of Rowan Daly

Rex Owens

CKBooks Publishing

Publisher's Cataloging-In-Publication Data
Names: Owens, Rex, author.
Title: The life and times of Rowan Daly / Rex Owens.
Description: Belleville, WI : CKBooks Publishing, 2021.
Identifiers: ISBN 978-1-949085-45-7 (paperback) | ISBN 978-1-949085-46-4 (ebook)
Subjects: LCSH: Packhorse librarians--Fiction. | Librarians--Fiction. | Man-woman relationships--Fiction. | Women—Fiction. | Kentucky--Fiction. | Historical fiction. | BISAC: FICTION / Historical / General. | FICTION / Women. | GSAFD: Historical fiction.
Classification: LCC PS3615.W46 L54 2021 (print) | LCC PS3615.W46 (ebook) | DDC 813/.6--dc23.

LCCN: 2021905569

Cover images courtesy of University of Kentucky Libraries, Special Collections Research Center

CKBooks Publishing
P.O. BOX 214
New Glarus, WI
53574
ckbookspublishing.com

Acknowledgments

Beta readers: Lynette Owens, Anna Taylor, Val Biel, Frank Peot and Rob Straughn for their honesty.

Jason Flahardy ◆ Archivist, University of Kentucky Archives. For help with the image that became the book cover.

Valerie Biel ◆ Lost Lake Press for her marketing wisdom and guidance.

Christine Keleny ◆ CKBooks Publishing for her patience with me.

Every librarian I have worked with.

*You must do the thing you
think you cannot do.*

Eleanor Roosevelt

Part I

Chapter 1

*T*he June morning promised to be another smothering day. Rowan rubbed her sore back muscles. Since Eli left for the mine, she had been hoeing the garden in her relentless battle of weeds versus vegetables, which required daily attention. Suddenly, like summer lightning, the heavy morning air was pierced by the warning bell from the Hope mine.

"Eli!"

Rowan dropped her hoe and ran the two miles to the mine entrance as fast as she could; it felt like twenty. As she got closer Rowan was joined by other wives and children all with glazed-over eyes and the look of impending doom on their faces. Outside the mine Rowan bent over, gasping for air and saw her feet caked in blood and dirt. She looked at all the familiar faces of the women who lived in the company houses next to theirs.

"What is it, Hattie?" Rowan screamed.

"I don't know girl, but it ain't good. Never is when they ring the bell. I don't see the supervisor, do you?"

Rowan clawed through the crowd toward the man pulling the bell and found Jed Morgan, the manager of the company store.

"Jed?" Rowan stammered in disbelief. Jed didn't hear Rowan; the clamor of the bell was deafening.

Hattie came up beside Rowan and shook Jed by the shoulders. "Jed, where is Earle?"

Jed glared back and Hattie and noticed the crowd surrounding him for the first time. "Earle's in the hole. Something happened, I don't know what. When I saw Earle scurry down the mine shaft, I started ringing out the warning. It's my job."

Rowan felt faint and grabbed for Hattie so she wouldn't fall. Hattie held Rowan up with one arm and gathered her three children around her. "Grab my waist." The women shouted out names: Howie, Chester, Robbie, Walter, Darnell, Floyd, as they inched closer to the mine entrance. Earle Calhoun appeared at the entrance knowing there would be a crowd of terrified families there.

"Listen up, I only got time to say this once. There's been a cave-in. I don't know what happened so don't ask. We've got to start digging – now! The veins in Earle's neck throbbed as he blurted out orders. "I need every man in town, every one of them. Grab a pick, grab a shovel, grab a damn hammer."

"Is Eli in the pit, Rowan?" Lena, a neighbor, asked.

Rowan was still clinging to Hattie. "It's his week on the morning shift. What about Frank?"

"I left him at home asleep – he's on night shift this week. I heard the bell and had to find out what's goin' on."

"For the love of God, Lena, go get him up. We need him digging. Oh please, please," Rowan pleaded.

Lena took Rowan by the shoulders and looked directly in her eyes. "All the men will come, you'll see. I'll get Frank and then pound on the door of all the houses in our block. Stay with Hattie." Lena ran off with the speed of a deer to find help.

"Get back, ladies; the coal dust will kill ya," Earle shouted.

All together the women stepped back.

"Farther, damn it, farther." Earle waved his arms until the women were at least thirty feet from the entrance.

Rowan shut her eyes and held her hands over her ears, trying to stop the shouting. *Is it an explosion, a cave-in, a flood? This is a new mine; how can this happen in a new mine? Eli must be alive – he must.* Her mind raced with questions that had no answers – not now, anyway – soon. She was proud of Eli for having one of the most danger-ous jobs. He punched holes into the rock, shoved in the dynamite sticks, then ran like hell when the fuse was lit. He was good at it and eager for the extra pay every week. It bought meat twice a week and milk every day.

Rowan recalled the morning. It was like every other June morning. Rowan kissed Eli full on the lips when he left for the hole and handed him his lunch bucket with a biscuit, two pieces of fried chicken and a few of his favor-ite sweet pickles. "Meatloaf and potatoes for dinner," she hollered as he trotted off to the mine. Eli waved goodbye without looking back. Six mornings a week this was their life in New Hope. Eli wasn't a church person and Rowan was a lukewarm Christian so most Sundays they cuddled in bed until mid-morning, sharing their dreams for the fu-ture. In the summer they would go on a picnic next to the Red River. Rowan made egg salad sandwiches with sweet pickles and lemonade. Eli would spend afternoons fishing for small mouth bass while Rowan read Life magazines. With any luck Eli would catch their dinner. Life was good in New Hope. Even in the Great Depression they had steady income that provided for their daily needs and a roof over their heads, all that could be expected in 1936.

This isn't happening. It can't happen. Eli is good at his job. He wouldn't let this happen. Something went wrong. An icy shiver went up Rowan's spine and it shook her to the quick. *Oh God, what if he's dead? No, No, No, No. Not again. Eli would never abandon me, he promised – he promised.*

Chapter Two

$\mathcal{N}$o one wanted to leave the mine. The women and children milling around the mine entrance were tired and sat on the dusty ground talking, telling stories and entertaining the children the best they could. Rowan didn't want to leave either but everyone was getting restless. She ran home to collect a few magazines for the wives, a checker game and a game of jacks to occupy the children. The neighbors knew the Dawson home because Rowan hung a large bouquet of dried flowers on the door. A tear came to her eye as she closed the door, remembering how her grandmother taught her to dry flowers. *Has grandma been gone three years? Oh God, I miss her.*

Effie came around to where Rowan and Hattie camped on the ground trying to distract the children. "Hattie, when the sun sets it's going to cool down fast. Don't you think a couple of burn barrels would be a good idea?"

Hattie smiled and glanced at Rowan. "Oh Effie, always the practical one. Yes, I'm just not ready to admit we could be here all night."

Rowan piped up. "Kids, let's have a scavenger hunt for wood. I have some potato candy at home. We can make a blazing fire and eat candy together."

Hattie beamed. "Rowan Dawson, you are an angel. I'll watch after the kids while you collect the candy. We'll wait for you to get back before starting a fire."

Earle wanted to believe, but as dusk fell, Earle sent one of the wives into town to fetch James Birch, the local undertaker, and Jeremiah Hewett, the town pastor. Earle worried their appearance might alarm the families clinging to hope, but with each passing hour reality sunk in; the prospect of finding anyone alive was slim.

Earle's heart bled with hope but his mind told him the miners were most likely crushed in the first collapse. In a way he wanted it to be their fate so death came without struggling for breath. He knew it was unlikely they would have enough air to breathe until tomorrow. Crushed by stone would be God's gift for their sacrifice.

A host of stars pierced the clear black sky. Rowan lay on her back with the children gazing at all the constellations. "Who can find the North Star?" she asked. Several children pointed upward to their far left. "That's it. The bright one. That means north, doesn't it, Miss Rowan?"

Rowan recalled how her mother sat with her on their front porch pointing out the pattern of stars and constellations. "Guess you paid attention in school, Jeb. You're right. Now, look hard. Who can find the constellation Hercules – the great warrior?"

A few miners staggered out of the mine looking for Earle. They were careful to not call attention to themselves as the families began to doze off. "You got to see for yerself, Earle," one of them whispered. Earle looked around and took careful steps to the mine entrance. He grabbed a helmet from a man with a black, smudged face and bloodshot eyes and disappeared into the mine.

Hearing the commotion, Rowan raised her head. She saw Earle but kept quiet. She looked into the ashen faces of the women around her. Some were staring off into space and others crying. A few women dropped to their knees, folded their hands and beseeched the Lord to bring their men back to them alive. No one else saw Earle descend into the mine. Rowan's heart raced and felt like it would jump right out of her chest. She gulped, not able to get air enough into her lungs. It took a long time for Earle to return to the surface.

Earle appeared at the entrance to the mine, his head resting on his chest. Tears drenched his cheeks. The crowd stirred – the air drenched with anticipation. He tried to look at the women waiting for him to speak. He hid his face in his hands and his shoulders slumped.

"They're gone. All of them. Gone."

Rowan fainted.

Chapter 3

$\mathcal{R}$owan twisted in bed and realized she was lying on something hard with a green Army blanket thrown over her. She scratched her nose, blinked several times and rubbed her eyes. A woman with dark auburn hair pulled back into a ponytail walked toward her with a cup in her hands.

"Tea, dear?"

Rowan shook her shoulders to try and wake herself. She sat up and raised her hands from underneath the blanket to take the cup. The tea was so strong she wanted to improve it with a touch of milk but Rowan sipped the coffee-like tea and watched as the lady sat down on the cot next to her.

Where am I? Rowan wondered.

"Earle said my Eli was dead."

The woman smiled, although there was pity in her eyes. She pulled the blanket up around Rowan's chest, took the cup and tucked her in. "It's best for you to rest a while longer. There's no hurry. When you wake again, I'll bring you broth to help bring back your strength."

"Who are you? Don't touch me. I don't want the blanket – it scratches." Rowan looked around the room to see several other women lying on the same type of used Army cot she was on. She rested her head on the limp pillow, turned onto her side and pulled the blanket over her head. The rough material scratched her face. She felt lightheaded and found it impossible to focus her thoughts – everything was all scrambled in her mind. *Eli dead? That had to be wrong – a mistake – it was someone else. It had to be.* Rowan felt the same way she felt when her grandmother died a month before high school graduation – abandoned. Her grandma was the last living relative she knew about. If she had other family it was kept a secret from her.

"Whoever you are, go away. I want to be alone. I am alone – all alone." Only a few hours decent sleep was more than anyone could endure; her feeble body gave in to sleep. The woman left and closed the door behind her.

When she woke, light was streaming into the windows on her right. Rowan couldn't even guess what time of day it was. She looked around the room. All the other cots were empty. She sat up on her elbows, leaned forward and tried to sit up but her arms folded underneath her. Rowan heard a familiar voice close by.

"Here dear, as I promised, a mug of warm broth. Just sip now, it's very hot," the woman instructed.

"You're back? Why are you being so kind? What's your name?"

"My name is Florence, Florence Pruett." Florence puffed up the pillow so Rowan could sit up to drink the broth and sat at the end of the cot with a book. She began reading while Rowan took tiny sips of the broth. The first sip scalded the tip of her tongue. Rowan stared into the cup to avoid looking at Florence. She wanted to trust this stranger but was too deep in her grief to consider trusting any other person. She looked about the room; there were twenty cots. There were doors along one side of the room and Rowan's imagination couldn't fill in the blank for how the rooms might be used. Florence turned each page of her book with extreme care. In a few moments Rowan handed the empty cup to Florence.

"What did you say your name is?"

"Florence Pruett."

"Do you live in New Hope? I haven't seen you."

"No, dear, I live in Pikeville."

"Why are you here?"

"Because you are."

"Oh – why am I here?"

Rowan searched through her memories of that day. She recalled hearing Earle shout "There're all dead."

Rowan stared at Florence, not able to fathom why she had come from Pikeville to sit at the end of her cot and read a book.

"Do you want more broth, dear, or maybe some nice fried potatoes with onion and a hot dog. It's a favorite of mine. It'll fill your stomach for sure and, girl, you need to eat. In the next few days you've got to muster your strength. Vernon Dobbs will stop in later to talk with you, and then Mr. Birch will need to talk to you."

Rowan ran both hands through her hair and squinted at Florence. "Who...who...who are those men and why are they going to talk to me?"

Florence closed her book and scooted up toward Rowan. "Well, Mr. Dobbs is the Union Steward. You're at Union Hall now. And Mr. Birch...well, he's a...he's the undertaker, Rowan."

Rowan turned toward the walls and curled her back. "I don't want to see those men. Go away."

Florence moved behind Rowan, pulled her into her arms and rocked her back and forth. "There's no hurry. Let me get you the food. When you are ready, we can talk, or if you don't want to talk, that will be fine too. I'll be back with a plate for you."

"Don't come back. I'm not hungry," Rowan shouted after Florence.

§

Rowan picked at the plate of food and felt watched. She set the tray on the nearby table, lay on her side and curled up with her knees tucked in toward her stomach. In a few moments the pillow was wet with tears. She drifted off into a deep, dreamless sleep.

Miss Pruett peeked into the room to retrieve the tray. She was happy the valerian root in the tea worked well; Rowan would sleep through the night.

Chapter 4

The next morning Rowan woke to a ping, ping, ping on the tin roof. She pulled the blanket up over her head. The sound continued, just muffled. Curiosity drove her to sit up and listen, then look out the window. The rain was slow and steady and already there were little puddles dotting the ground.

"Well, good morning, Mrs. Dawson. Can I get you coffee, tea, a little breakfast maybe?"

The man standing in the doorway had a rough beard, like he hadn't taken the time to shave in a week. His hair was cut close with a flat top. He didn't seem to have a neck at all; his massive head rested on top of his shoulders. His eyes were sunk in with years of worry yet he impressed Rowan as a kind person.

"Who are you?" she asked.

"Vernon Dobbs is my name, or Vern, if you like, or just Dobbs. It doesn't matter much to me."

"Miss Pruett mentioned your name; you're the union steward?"

"Yes, Mrs. Dawson, I am. This is Union Hall. Are you ready to talk this morning or would it be better to have breakfast first?"

Vernon stood in the doorway; he didn't want to make Rowan feel uncomfortable. "When you're ready, come out into the hall. We can at least have a cup of coffee. The bathrooms are at the end of the hall, if you want to clean up."

Rowan looked at her rumpled dress and dirty feet. She could imagine how awful she must look. "Yes, that would be fine, thank you Mr. Dobbs. Coffee would be nice."

Rowan took her time washing herself, then pressing her dress out with her hands as best as she could. There was a towel, wash cloth, a bar of Ivory and a hair brush in the bathroom next to the sink. It surprised her that warm water came out of the faucet when she turned the knob. The only warm water in her home came from heating a pot on the stove. After washing and drying her face, she held her breath and looked into the mirror – frightened at what she saw. Her hair was a mess and there were dark circles under her eyes. Several creases crossed her forehead that were not there a week ago. She brushed the tangles out of her hair, then filled the sink with cool water and buried her face in a wash cloth.

§

"Feel better, miss?" Vernon asked as he pulled out the chair at the table for her to sit down. He placed a cup of coffee on the table for her, pushing containers of sugar and cream toward her.

"Just black. Black like coal."

Earle shuffled the papers and checked his notes on things to share with Rowan. "You can stay here at Union Hall as long as you want. I've collected two weeks' pay because the owner provides a little cash when things like this happen. After taking out for the rent and the coal, there's $154.60 left. If you had a balance at the store, we have forgiven it. Later today Mr. Birch will stop in for your instructions on the…a…you know, the burial. Father will stop by this evening. The ladies said they thought you are Catholic. If not, well, I can fetch the Reverend Jeremiah Hewett. The company will want you to move out of the house by the end of the week. I can get the ladies to help you pack and bring all your stuff here. They said you don't have any kin around here."

Rowan listened to every word Mr. Dobbs said. She looked around the sizeable room where a few days ago there were cots set up. Now, half the room was filled with tables. Four chairs were tucked under each table. Half the room was set with only chairs as if they were waiting for a meeting. At the end of the room opposite of where they were sitting was the kitchen and behind them a row of doors where Rowan guessed were rooms like the one she slept in. In the two years she and Eli lived in New Hope, he had not taken her to Union Hall once. Now, it was her temporary home.

"I'm alone! Abandoned!" Rowen cried out. "I don't have any family. Eli was my only family. This just isn't happening to me. It can't happen to me. Eli promised – he promised."

"Well, for now just take one day at a time. The truth is Eli has passed, no fault of his. He was in the wrong place at the wrong time. Mining is dangerous. Every man going down into the hole knows he may not be on the surface at the end of his shift. A man's got to provide for his family and learns to live with the risk – there isn't a choice. I guess you need to tend to Eli first. There are decisions you must make. Mr. Birch will want to know if you want him embalmed and if you want to buy a casket or use the pine one provided by the mining company."

"I...I don't know. I want to see him. I want to see Eli. I won't believe this until I see him."

"Well, I need to stay here to help the others. I'll go find Miss Pruett and ask if she will walk with you to the undertaker's office; it's not far."

"I don't need Miss Pruett to walk me anywhere. I can find the office. Just give me directions."

Vernon shook his head as he left the room. "Like I said, I'll fetch Miss Pruett."

$

"May I help you, miss?" Mr. Birch was dressed in a black suit, white shirt, a black string tie and boots polished so you could see your face. His black hair was parted in the middle and slicked straight back with hair cream, which gave off a sweet scent.

"I want to see my husband."

"This is Mrs. Rowan Dawson, Mr. Birch, her husband is Eli Dawson." Florence Pruett explained.

"Please follow me," Mr. Birch whispered.

Rowan wondered why he whispered.

The women followed him into a back room where ten or more pine caskets sat on top of saw horses. Mr. Birch walked between the boxes and read the names printed on each lid with a red crayon. He stopped at a casket a few feet away and tapped on the lid. "This is the one. Were you considering buying a casket for your husband, Mrs. Dawson? Do you want him embalmed, to preserve the body? I can make him look very nice, yes, very nice. Then there's the service...."

Rowan screamed, "I just want to see him! I want to see my husband! Lift the lid. I want to see my man." She grabbed Florence Pruett's hand so hard Florence's fingers turned red. Mr. Birch lifted the lid and leaned it on the pine box behind him. Eli's face had a gray sheen and he had blood-caked mud in his hair. His eyes stared toward the ceiling and his hands were covered in coal dust. The smell of death clogged Rowan's nose.

"What is that smell? Why didn't you close his eyes? He's staring at me, for God's sake," Rowan said between sobs.

"We undertakers refer to that as putrefaction, Mrs. Dawson; his body is decaying. He needs to be buried by tomorrow. The body will bloat soon and you don't want to see him like that. Mr. Aldridge, the mine owner, is providing a plot for all those in the accident; it's just a few miles out of town."

Rowan's chest caved in and her shoulders drooped. Her breathing was erratic, and she swayed back and forth. Florence wrapped her arm around Rowan's waist and let her lean on her. Mr. Birch put the lid back on the box without being asked. Rowan pounded the box with both her fists.

"What am I going to do, Eli? What am I going to do? I don't have nobody. Everybody is gone. I just don't know.

I can't go on without you. I'm lost, Eli, lost. Do you hear me? I'm lost." Rowan's knees buckled, then she fell on the floor next to the pine box. Florence Pruett crouched down beside her and held tight to her shoulders.

"We should go, dear. Nothing more can be done here." Florence said in a calm, soothing voice. "Mr. Birch, please help me get Rowan up. You can bury Eli tomorrow morning. I think ten o'clock would be fine."

Rowan wept and let Florence walk her back to Union Hall.

Chapter 5

Rowan asked to be left alone. She wasn't ready to go back to the house and pack up her things. Loneliness consumed her and grabbed her heart. She sat in the small room staring out the window without seeing. While Rowan was visiting the undertaker, someone had been to the room, made the bed and left a bible on the table. She wondered if leaving the bible was a hint or a not-so-subtle message. She picked it up and thumbed the pages. Her grandma taught her to close her eyes and let the bible fall open, then read the passage she saw first. Grandma Kelly swore it was God's way to talk to a person. Rowan placed the bible in her lap and stroked it. She had never tried Grandma's way of asking the Lord for help. She never felt she needed it until now. Her mind raced, wanting to know why Eli was taken from her with their entire lives in front of them. She knew Eli was a good man, a solid man. He loved Rowan and Rowan loved him. Their love was straightforward and simple. *It is wrong that he was taken from me, wrong, wrong, wrong.*

Rowan was so deep in thought she didn't hear the soft knock on the door. "Mrs. Dawson, I don't want to disturb you; maybe you are deep in prayer. May I come in?"

Rowan looked at the man standing in front of her. He stood with the door ajar like he intended to stand there until she talked to him. She didn't feel like talking to anyone. The silence between them was an impenetrable wall. Rowan put her hand on the front cover and the gold letters on top: H-O-L-Y B-I-B-L-E.

"I apologize, miss, I am Father Muldoon. I heard about the tragedy, and Mr. Earle Calhoun said he believed you and Eli were Catholic, so I am compelled to check in on you. Mr. Birch told me that Eli is to be buried tomorrow morning. You might want to give me some instruction on the service."

Father Muldoon inched his way into the room and sat in the chair next to the table. Rowan set the bible back on the table next to him. Rowan had never seen Father Muldoon. He had thin gray hair that he combed from one side of his head to another. His hands were thick and calloused.

"Did Eli ever mention me?" he asked.

Rowan shook her head.

"Well, I work in the mine myself – several days a week. It's my special time with the men. I came from a family of miners and decided that God's call didn't mean I had to give up mining. Over the years I learned the men were most comfortable talking with me while working in the mine. Deep in the bowels of the earth they could talk about their fears and doubts and know whatever they shared would not go to the surface at the end of the shift."

He shifted in his chair as if not sure how to continue.

"I knew Eli. He was a fine, strapping man with his head screwed on straight. He talked about you. That man loved you, Mrs. Dawson. I know you will miss him."

Father Muldoon reached out toward Rowan to take her hand, but she jumped back, not wanting his touch or anyone's touch. She stared at his shoes and noticed they were scuffed and worn. Rowan wondered why he either didn't understand or didn't care that she just wanted to be alone. Her heart felt the sting of abandonment. From somewhere an urge to speak welled up in her.

"How the hell is this God's plan to take Eli away? He's dead. Dead!"

Father Muldoon leaned forward and put his face in both of his hands. After a moment, he looked back up at her. "I don't believe we can know God's plan, Mrs. Dawson. I am too simple of a man to understand. You have a right to be angry. You can be angry with Eli for being a miner. You can be mad at the miner that goofed up and maybe caused the accident. You can be angry with Mr. Aldridge for opening up this mine to steal the coal from the earth. You can even be mad at God."

Rowan looked into his light blue eyes and noticed a tear trickle down his cheek. *Here was an honest man, a man who has grieved with more mine widows than I can imagine.* She picked up the bible and threw it against the wall. The book split open to reveal Psalm 23, which Rowan didn't notice.

"What do you want from me, Father Muldoon?"

"I need your instructions on the Rite of Committal, my dear. As a Catholic priest and servant of God, I must tend to Eli's soul. It is my duty, and as his widow, your obligation, to bury him following the church's directions."

Rowan doubled over and sobbed into her hands. Father Muldoon patted her on the back with a soft, caring touch.

"Yes, tomorrow I bury Eli. What is the...what did you call it, Rite of Committal?"

"It is our fate to return to the dust, and the church has provided us prayers to say at the gravesite to properly return the body to the earth and help speed the soul back to the house of the Lord."

"Prayers?"

"Yes."

"Eli flies to heaven?"

"Yes."

"Ok." Rowan reached out to Father Muldoon, her hands wet with tears. She leaned on his shoulder and felt his hand on the back of her head.

"Let us pray, my child.

"Our Father..."

Chapter 6

*J*uly came with the kind of relentless heat and lack of rain that causes plants to wither. Rowan's garden patch sat neglected for weeks. With her heart bruised, tending to the plants only reminded her of Eli. The Fourth of July came and went without Rowan noticing the fireworks or the parade in downtown New Hope. Howard Leach, the housing manager, visited Union Hall the day after Eli's burial and ordered her to move out by the weekend because on Monday another family would move in. Rowan had no one to turn to. The other wives had their own problems, she didn't have the courage to ask for help. She was alone.

Florence returned to Pikeville the day of the burial and Hattie was busy trying to make a life for her three kids without the income from her husband's job in the mine. Rowan didn't have the courage to ask Father Muldoon or Vernon Dobbs for help.

On a Saturday morning she struggled with nausea but forced herself to go to the house and pack. She hadn't been home for over a week. Nothing was familiar. There were two scratched, leather suitcases on the top shelf of the closet in the bedroom. She took her clothes hanging in the closet, folded each item on the bed and stacked them in the suitcase. She stared at Eli's clothes for a few minutes them grabbed them all at one time with her arms and threw them on the floor. She went to the dresser and slung his clothes into the air, not caring where they landed. She threw her clothes toward the open suitcase. Some landed in the suitcase and others didn't. She walked through the kitchen to discover that nothing there belonged to her and Eli, it all was in the house when they moved in. Rowan slapped her suitcase closed and dragged it with both hands toward the door. She walked a few steps toward town and put the suitcase down to rest. It took until past noon to get back to Union Hall. Rowan plopped on the bed in her room, not wanting to move a muscle.

"Oh, good, you have your things. You should have asked, I would have helped you, Mrs. Dawson," Vernon Dobbs offered.

"It was something I needed to do myself, thank you."

"I don't mean to get personal but there is a need for men's clothes. If you wouldn't mind donating Eli's, it would help a great deal."

Rowan's mouth opened but no words came out. She sat back on the bed, pulled her knees up to her chest and wrapped her arms around her legs. She looked at Vernon Dobbs for a few minutes as he stood in the doorway.

"Ok, you can get them; they're at the house. They smell of Eli. I can't stand them."

Tears gushed from Rowan's eyes as she buried her head in her arms.

Vernon Dobbs left without saying goodbye. He took

several paper sacks and collected Eli's clothes. There was a room in Union Hall where any miner could come and get donated clothes. Vernon asked a miner's wife to sort through the bags and decide which were rags and which could be folded and put on the shelves.

Vernon wanted to show Rowan respect so most days he went about his business without talking with her. She stayed in her room but did offer to sweep the hall and cook meals for Vernon. Vernon accepted her offer even though Rowan did not have the reputation of being a cook. He knew Rowan offered to do chores in order to stay in Union Hall.

§

One morning Rowan was sweeping the floor of the hall after the meeting the night before. Vernon came out of his office and flipped a page on the huge calendar on the wall. Rowan walked up behind him, her mouth fell open.

"August!" she yelped.

Vernon turned toward her and took a step to the side so she could see the full calendar. He couldn't find words to express his surprise that Rowan was just now learning it was August; Eli was buried six weeks ago.

Rowan's eyes widened to the size of walnuts. "Impossible, Impossible," she shouted.

Vernon dropped his head to his chest. "It is Mrs.; this is the first day of August. This may not be a good time but I have wondered if you have any plans? Friends you could live with or if you've thought about a job? Lordy, I know jobs are scarce but the Union could help you. It's our solemn duty to help."

Rowan's shoulders slumped, and she leaned on the wall. "Oh, Mr. D., I don't have nobody. My Ma died from the pneumonia when I was in ninth grade. My Dad took off soon after I was born; I've never seen his face. I grew up with my grandma and grandpa. Grandpa had a railroad accident when I was fourteen, then it was just me and Grandma Kelly. Right before my high school graduation Grandma came down with the pneumonia, just like Ma. The Lord took her from me too. Eli proposed on our graduation day, and I was the happiest girl in the world. We were lucky when we heard about the Hope Mine opening. We were together just two years the month Eli died in the mine."

"Go have a seat at the table. I'll get you a glass of water." Vernon returned in moments with two glasses of water and took a seat opposite Rowan.

Vernon gulped down the water and set the glass back on the table. "I am sorry, Mrs. Dawson, I did not understand. Well, I need to go into town for a meeting this afternoon with Earle Calhoun and Stanley Aldridge. The repairs to the mine are about finished. I'm hoping the mine will re-open next week. Would you like to know what caused the accident?"

"No...no...no, no. He's gone – that's all that matters," Rowan mumbled.

Vernon stood to leave. "Would you like me to ask Hattie if she would stop by to see you?"

Rowan's hands trembled and she couldn't hold on to the glass. "No, I have things to do around here. There's always cleaning to do, isn't there? What do you want for supper?"

A smile crossed Vernon's face. "Yes, please, some of your fried chicken with buttermilk biscuits and maybe a few green beans. Oh my, just thinking about that supper makes my stomach growl. I should be back no later than five."

Chapter 7

$\mathcal{F}$lorence walked into the empty Union Hall. She didn't understand why all the windows were closed on a day you could fry an egg in a pan. The doors were closed on all the rooms along the far wall. "Rowan? Rowan, are you here?"

"Hello?" a whisper came from the room at the far end of the hall.

"Rowan, Rowan Dawson, it's Florence Pruett. I have wonderful news for you. Come on out now, girl."

Rowan opened the door to her room just enough to peek out. *Why would Florence Pruett be here? She's a long way from Pikeville.*

Florence saw Rowan hiding behind the door and rushed over and pushed the door open, knocking Rowan back onto her bed. "Oh Rowan, why were you behind the door? I am so sorry. Are you hurt? I am so excited. I have news. I have fantastic news."

"News? Ok, sit down, I guess." Rowan pointed toward the chair in the corner.

Florence sat on the edge of the chair and fanned herself. "Well, President Franklin Roosevelt has decided it's time to help the women in our country who need jobs. He also wants to make sure that everybody gets to use a library, if they need one. Here in Kentucky a lot of folks can't get to a library because there are no roads and most people don't have a horse or a mule, so they walk. It might be an entire day's walk just to visit a library, and that isn't right. The Workers Progress Administration is starting a program to hire women to deliver books to the hill people. The WPA has put thousands of men back to work and now they want to put women to work. I have been authorized to hire four women. I want to hire you, Rowan. Today."

Rowan pulled away. "What are you talking about? You've been kind to me, but I don't know you at all. Why should I trust you? Why should I trust anyone again?" Rowan's voice choked with tears. Rowan sat silent for a few minutes and breathed in deeply to calm herself. Florence gave her all the time she needed. Rowan thought about Florence's offer and out of curiosity asked, "How are the books delivered?"

"Well, it's too far to walk, so it would either be by horse or mule. Can't use a wagon; the hills are too steep."

Rowan shook her head from side to side. "I've only been on a horse twice in my life, never for a long ride. I...I...don't know if I could do it. I don't want to leave Union Hall. I feel safe here."

"Mr. Dobbs is a kind man but you can't stay here much longer. It's time for you to venture into the world again, find a place for yourself. I'm offering you a new start. You can take care of yourself."

Florence leaned toward Rowan and took her hands into her own. "There's plenty of hill women who can teach you to ride; it won't take long. The pay is going to be twenty-eight dollars per month. Can you imagine that? Now, there's a lot to do. We need to begin training next Monday. You will need to move to Pikeville. You can have a room at the boardinghouse where I live. Miss Perkins, the owner, is holding a room for you. I am on my way to visit my aunt and uncle in Elkhorn City. I'll be back on Saturday afternoon, and I can drive you to Pikeville."

Florence stood and took several steps toward the door. "Oh, this is so wonderful. I'm sorry. I need to go now if I'm going to get to Elkhorn City by supper time. I'm sure you will have questions. We can talk on our drive up to Pikeville Saturday afternoon."

Rowan stiffened. "You're not listening to me. I'm not ready. I appreciate you've been kind to me. Why should I turn my life inside out again and move to Pikeville with you? Pikeville is a huge city. I've never lived in a city – never. I don't want to live in a city. Bless you for wanting to help me but no."

"Don't make a rash decision, Rowan, think it over." Taking long strides across Union Hall she was out the door in a flash.

Rowan rubbed her eyes and then pinched her arm hard to make sure she hadn't dreamed the entire visit. She took time to catch her breath. Rowan felt a cup of tea would help her regain her balance.

She sipped the hot tea and thought about Florence's offer.

§

Vernon Dobbs returned to Union Hall and was relieved that Rowan was enjoying tea, although he wondered about his supper.

"Mrs. Dawson, you look as though you've seen a ghost. Is everything ok?"

Chapter 8

$\mathcal{R}$owan sat in the empty Union Hall with her suitcase on the floor beside her. After Florence left she took the time to calm herself. She knew there wasn't anything in New Hope for her, and it only reminded her of living with Eli. Rowan didn't understand why Florence took such an interest in her or offered her a job. She realized she was in a pickle and had to take a chance to trust Florence. Rowan did feel she had to close the door behind New Hope. Living in a city would be a challenge but it could also be exciting. *Mrs. Perkins must also be a wonderful woman willing to hold a room for me.* While Rowan was afraid, she was determined not to let fear stop her.

She couldn't sleep and got up early, hoping Vernon would appreciate having fresh coffee ready to start his day. Rowan found two biscuits left over from last night's supper, slathered a tablespoon of honey on each for her breakfast. As she sat eating the biscuits, Vernon walked into the hall without her noticing.

"Good morning, Rowan. Packed and ready to go, I see. You must be excited. I would be if I were you."

Rowan dropped her biscuit on the table. "Oh, Mr. Dobbs, you're up early for a Saturday morning. I got the message, you know, that it's time for me to be on my way. I told Florence I didn't want the job she offered but after thinking about it, I'm stuck; I don't have anywhere else to go. I called Florence and asked if she would give me another chance. I hope this is the right thing for me. I'm scared to death – or I shouldn't say that.

"I want to make breakfast for you this morning, Mr. Dobbs."

"I'm meeting Earle Calhoun at the café for breakfast this morning. After the report on the mine accident, we have a few changes to discuss. Thank God Earle is a reasonable man and will do anything to prevent an accident like we had in June. Say, Mrs. Dawson, I'm going to miss having you around here. It was nice to have you cook and clean up around here. I wish the best for you in Pikeville. For what it's worth, I think you've made the right choice. Florence Pruett is well respected in our county; you can't go wrong by her. When I'm in Pikeville, I'll look you up."

Rowan blushed and hid her face in her hands. "I can't honestly say I mind leaving. You have been gracious and understanding but it has been lonely here. I have a chance again, thanks to Miss Pruett."

"Oh, that reminds me. I have something for you." Vernon rushed into his office, shuffled through the papers on his desk and walked back to Rowan, waving a piece of paper in the air. He handed it to her.

Rowan looked at the fancy writing with her name in bold letters in the center of the page. Sterling Aldridge, owner of Hope Mine, signed the paper. She laid the paper on the table and smoothed it out but could not focus on the words. "What is this, Mr. Dobbs; it looks official or something."

Vernon rubbed his hands together. "Well, it's a certificate, see. It's a plot, right next to Eli."

"Oh, I see. A plot. What kind of plot, Mr. Dobbs?"

Vernon pointed to the paper. "Well, it's a cemetery plot. If you want to make your final resting place next to Eli, well, that piece of paper guarantees you a plot. It's a gift from Mr. Aldridge. He's trying to be kind, in his own way. He wants to make sure you could rest next to Eli for eternity."

Rowan opened her suitcase and placed the paper on top of her clothes, looked at it one last time before snapping the lid closed. She brushed her hair back and sat up straight. "Tell Mr. Aldridge that is thoughtful. Not sure if I will ever use it, but thoughtful."

Vernon Dobbs shuffled his feet and glanced toward the clock on the back wall. "Well, it's best I get going. I wish the best for you, Mrs. Dawson. If you come back for a visit, you are always welcome here. Have you said goodbye to Hattie or any of the other wives?"

Rowan stood up, nodded her head and stuck her hand out for a handshake. "I said what goodbyes I needed to say yesterday. Thank you for your kindness, Mr. Dobbs. I will not forget it. Goodbye. You make sure you fix that mine. This should never happen again to any wife."

"Yes, ma'am." Vernon turned on his heel and walked out the door.

§

Florence Pruett never mentioned a time when she would collect Rowan so Rowan thought the best plan was just to sit tight in the hall until Florence arrived. She busied herself with cleaning the coffee pot and her cup and putting everything away in the kitchen. She pulled a favorite book, *Gulliver's Travels*, from her suitcase and read until mid-morning.

The door of Union Hall crashed open. "Rowan Dawson, I hope you are ready!" shouted Florence. Startled, Rowan dropped her book on the table.

"Good way to spend your time – reading. I can tell, you are going to make a fine librarian. Suitcase packed and ready to go. Ok, let's head north. We have about a four-hour drive. My aunt packed sandwiches and a thermos of lemonade; we can stop along the way for lunch." Florence reached for Rowan's suitcase. "Let's say goodbye to New Hope, Kentucky."

§

Rowan sat still in the car. As the sun climbed to the top of the sky, it warmed Rowan's cheek. Without rain the past few weeks the wheels of the Ford kicked up dust as they drove down the road. Florence held the steering wheel with both hands and kept her eyes glued on the road in front of her. Rowan wasn't sure if she should talk with her or not since Florence was so intent with her driving, so Rowan kept quiet. She didn't want to distract her and cause an accident. After a short time, Florence rolled down her window. Rowan took that as a clue that she should do the same. Dust flew up from the front tires and surrounded them, but the breeze helped with the heat in the car. Rowan watched Florence's pony tail blow in the wind. She had never seen Miss Pruett wear her hair in any other way than a pony tail pulled straight back with a different color ribbon tying her hair every time they met. Rowan wondered if she should let her hair grow out and pull it back into a pony tail too. Florence was the first librarian Rowan had met. Her high school couldn't afford a library or a librarian.

They drove for a while, then Miss Pruett took her eyes off the road to look at Rowan. "Lunch?" Rowan nodded her head. Her stomach ached, reminding her she had a small breakfast hours ago. Up ahead there was a gigantic oak that shaded part of the highway, and Miss Pruett pulled over to stop the car under the shade.

"This will be fine. Are you hungry, Rowan?"

"Yes, ma'am; I only had biscuits for breakfast."

"Ok, good. First, drop the Miss Pruett. My name is Florence and I would much prefer you call me Florence. There's a basket and a thermos in the back seat. You can get them out while I check the map." Rowan reached around to the back seat to grab the basket and thermos. "I'm guessing we have about another two hours to get to Pikeville. That means we'll get there by mid-afternoon, which will give you a chance to move in and take a little nap before dinner where you will meet the other women at Mrs. Perkins' boardinghouse. How does that sound?"

Rowan leaned over and gave Florence a hug. "That sounds like a new life to me."

Florence opened the basket to find two sandwiches wrapped in wax paper tied with string. She handed one to Rowan and untied the string on her sandwich.

"My guess is that they are both the same. Oh, it's Aunt Tillie's famous homemade pimento cheese sandwich; you are in for a treat, Rowan." The basket also contained cut carrots, two juice glasses and two chocolate chip cookies. "I'm definitely Aunt Tillie's favorite niece. She's won awards at the county fair for these cookies." Florence poured each of them a glass of lemonade. "The lemonade might not be cold but it's wet and made just before I left."

Rowan's stomach wouldn't let her talk as she took large bites out of the sandwich and chewed with zest. She finished her entire sandwich before Florence was half done. Florence threw the carrots into Rowan's lap and motioned for her to help herself. Rowan counted ten pieces, took five and handed the package back to Florence. When her stomach was full, she leaned back against the tree, grasping the glass of lemonade with both hands. Rowan looked out across the rolling hills shimmering in the midday sun.

Rowan looked over at Florence. "Why did you hire me to deliver library books? I can barely ride a horse, I don't know the country and I don't know how to be a librarian."

Florence finished her sandwich and drank half her glass of lemonade before answering.

"Fair question. You are alone after Eli's death. Why else would you stay at Union Hall? Mr. Dobbs called me one day and worried that you were just drifting from one day to the next with no direction and didn't know who to ask for help. Vernon Dobbs is a smart and observant man. I told him I would visit my aunt and uncle, and could stop by to see you. I may have a job for you. I asked him not to tell you because I had to confirm a few things first."

"Like what?"

This is a brand-new federal program. I wanted to know

how many women I could hire, what the salary would be and exactly what is expected. The biggest problem was to make sure we have enough books to take around to folks. The most important question was what I expected the librarians to do if you found hill people that couldn't read."

Rowan's eyes widened as big as silver dollars. "People can't read?"

"I will expect you to read to them. I don't expect you to teach them to read. Others can take on that herculean task. You are young, strong, alone and need to support yourself financially. I will find someone to teach you to ride and learn a delivery route, and if you are interested, I will teach you how to become a librarian. I've been thinking about a name for our group, to give us our own identity. What do you think of Pack Horse Librarians?"

Rowan moved closer to Florence and reached out to touch her hand. "I'm going to be a pack horse librarian." Rowan's eyes glistened, and she sat straight up. "I promise not to disappoint you, Florence. I will work very hard and listen to every word. I like the idea of learning to work in a library; I've always loved reading."

Florence leaned back and grinned from ear to ear. "I hoped you would have that reaction. You see, a few years ago I received a gift. I was accepted to study Library Science at Berea College. It is one of the few colleges that enrolls both men and women. You don't have to pay to attend, either. A very generous man created an endowment that pays the tuition for all the students. Each student must work twenty hours a week on campus. For me it was easy; I worked at Frost Library."

"Free? What is an endowment?"

"I love your curiosity, Rowan, and your eagerness to

learn. An endowment is a large sum of money that is invested and dedicated to one purpose. People contribute to the endowment, and the funds earned are spent to help people."

Rowan leaned back against the tree, finished her lemonade and closed her eyes. "Maybe someday I can go to Berea college."

"Maybe you can, Rowan."

"Before we get back in the car, I have to tell you something important, Florence. Eli and I were never married. He refused to marry me until he could afford to buy a proper wedding ring with diamonds or rubies or other fancy stones. That's why he volunteered for the blasting crew. He put all the extra money in a tin box and hid it on the top shelf of the cabinet. He made me promise not to count it. When we moved to New Hope, everyone called me Mrs. Dawson and I liked the sound of that. My maiden name is Daly. My surname, I mean. I took the money the mining company offered me; they thought I was Mrs. Dawson too. That's everything I have, except the money from the tin, that is.

Rowan handed the tin box to Florence. She pried the lid open and a lot of crisp bills flew out. "Oh, I didn't mean to do that, Rowan, I'm sorry."

Rowan picked the cash up, folded it and returned it to the container. "I'm starting a new life. I must be honest with myself and the world. Rowan Daly." Rowan extended her hand in greeting and Florence shook it.

Florence sat up straight and stared at Rowan. "Some people would say you lived in sin."

Rowan let out a heavy sigh, tears rolled down her checks and onto her skirt. "It didn't feel that way."

"I said 'some people,' Rowan; I'm not one of them. I have loved – too." Florence stared off into the distance. "Nathanial and I attended Berea together. He was a man of vision. He majored in agriculture and had a life goal to find a way to get profitable crops out of Kentucky's lousy soil. His father lost the farm in '31 and went to work on the railroad. Nathanial attended Berea because of the scholarship program."

"In our junior year we became engaged on my birthday. He was the most thoughtful man you could imagine. After being engaged, I felt it would be ok to know love in all ways. He kept an apartment off campus, and I would spend a few nights every week with him. He was so tender with me." Florence shut her eyes drifting off into lingering memories.

"I didn't notice you wearing a ring, Florence."

Florence stood and gathered the picnic things in the basket. "No."

"You can't stop now; you've got me hooked. What happened?" Rowan insisted.

"Like you, I lost him. He would spend weekends asking farmers to let him use a patch of land so he could experiment with crops, different ways to till, all sorts of new farming ideas. He was working on how to till around a hill and he misjudged the slope he was plowing. The tractor rolled on top of him and crushed the air out of his lungs." Florence wrapped her arms around herself and hugged herself so tight she struggled to breath.

Rowan's mouth fell open. "We are sisters in grief."

"But I didn't feel that Nathanial abandoned me. It was an accident pure and simple."

Florence stood up. "We should get back on the road. Help me clean up."

Chapter 9

They pulled up to the side of the street. The hand painted sign in the front yard read "Perkins Boardinghouse 55 Lexington Ave." with a smaller sign dangling by two chains below the main sign "No Vacancy." Florence pulled the parking brake, tugged the ribbon out of her hair and shook her head. "Whew! We made it. I'm tired of driving. It's time for you to meet Mrs. Perkins. You've not said a word since we had our picnic."

Rowan leaned toward Florence, grabbed her shoulders and began shaking her. Rowan held her breath, unable to utter a single word. Her eyelids fluttered. "I feel like God brought you into my life. I have someone to share my life with. We are going to be great friends, aren't we Florence?"

"Yes, I believe we are."

Rowan let go of Florence. She doubled over and covered her face with her hands as she sobbed. The world felt like such a strange place to Rowen. Inside Union Hall was safe and no one bothered her. Mr. Dobbs was kind.

He appreciated the small chores she did to give herself something to do. In the days after Eli's funeral, nothing changed. Every morning when Rowan woke, Eli was dead. She retreated into her own world where nothing could hurt her. Thinking about working as a pack horse librarian, Rowan's legs felt shaky. She wasn't sure she could get out of the car. *Why did I say yes? I can't ride horse. I've never even visited this part of Kentucky; I don't know anyone but Florence. I should have stayed in New Hope. Now, I can't see Eli's grave every day. Oh God, help me.*

Florence turned toward Rowan and rubbed her back. Her heart opened and swallowed Rowan's loneliness and fear. She lowered her voice to a whisper and said, "I understand, dear. Of course you're afraid. This is all so new. It will take time to adjust. Time is your friend. Let's go meet Mrs. Perkins and get the grand tour. You don't need to worry about unpacking. We can have a cup of valerian root tea, and you can take a nap."

Florence lugged both their suitcases into the boardinghouse with Rowan following behind her in silence. "Hello! Mrs. Perkins?"

A woman in her early sixties with hair as white as cotton balls opened her arms to give Florence a hug. They held each other for a moment, then Mrs. Perkins opened her arms toward Rowan. Rowan stood in the hallway, her head bowed and shoulders slumped. "Rowan, this is Mrs. Lillian Perkins, the boardinghouse owner. Your new boarder and my most recent hire is Rowan Daly from Marion County."

"I am so happy to meet you, dear. Florence has already told me a little bit about you but I'm eager to get to know you so much better. I am so sorry for your loss. I am a widow too. I lost Mr. Perkins in a railroad accident over five years ago. I miss that man every day but having a home full of young women living with me makes it bearable."

Florence smiled with relief with Mrs. Perkins' warm greeting. Florence intentionally didn't share very much with her about Rowan Dawson's life, except that she was deep in grief from losing her husband in the Hope mining accident. She felt Rowan was so young to have one door slam behind her and another open. It was clear to Florence; Rowan wasn't prepared for living alone and being a widow at this age.

Rowan looked down the robin-shell-blue painted hallway and through the two pocket doors into the parlor on her right. The room to her left didn't have a door and had a huge dining table with at least eight chairs and a vase filled with flowers she didn't recognize. Florence pointed toward the parlor. "Rowan, go have a seat and make yourself comfortable. I'll drag our luggage upstairs while Mrs. Perkins makes the tea."

Rowan took small, hesitant steps into the parlor. There was a light-orange glow in the room from sunlight reflected from a large mirror hanging at the far end of the room. In the corner was an upright piano with a small wood stool. In front of her sat a large sofa with two end tables and an oval table in front. The tables glistened as if they had been polished with oil just that morning. To her right there was a large bay window with two wing chairs and a small round table covered by an Irish lace doily. Behind Rowan sat a velvet love sofa with another wing chair beside it and an oak rocker in the corner. Rowan guessed the room could hold at least fifteen people, maybe more. There was an oil lamp on each table and two lamps on the piano.

Rowan jumped from hearing a voice from behind her. "Now, Rowan dear, why don't you sit on the sofa. I'll put the tea tray on the table. This tea will sooth your nerves. Florence should be down in a few minutes. After tea I can give you the grand tour. I am so happy you are here. At a time like this a person needs to be around other women. There are four of you. Florence, then there is Emma Wallace and Selma Rutledge. I believe you all work for Florence."

Rowan took a seat on the couch as she was instructed, smoothed her dress and smelled the fragrant tea. Mrs. Perkins poured them both a cup and pulled over one chair near the bay window to the sofa. Mrs. Perkins never asked Florence about Rowan's age. Seeing the forlorn expression on Rowan's face reminded her of the day she learned her own husband died in a train accident in Mississippi. It took over seven days to have his body shipped back to Pikeville for his funeral and burial in the Methodist churchyard. Watching the plain pine box taken off the train and put on a four-wheel cart is one sight Mrs. Perkins would never forget. She didn't ask the mortician to remove the lid of the box. The mortician didn't offer to remove the lid because he knew the sight would frighten her.

Florence walked in to join Rowan and Mrs. Perkins. "So, I'm all unpacked and ready for tea. I guess you two haven't talked yet. Maybe to get started we can discuss the business of living here, Mrs. Perkins."

Lillian Perkins scratched her head and gave Florence a quizzical look. "Oh yes, the rules and rent and so forth. Well, I have a pamphlet on rules. The lodging includes two meals a day, seven days a week. Linens are changed once a week, on Mondays. The cost is eleven dollars and twenty-five cents per month due the first day of the month. Since its past the first of August, your lodging this month will be ten seventy-five, and I would like it today, if you can manage."

Rowan finished her cup of tea while listening to Mrs. Perkins and nodded her head to acknowledge she understood. The tea did its job to relax her, and she fell back into the couch. She didn't understand the expressions on the ladies faces. They both appeared to be worried about her and she couldn't imagine why.

Florence walked toward the couch and put her arm around Rowan's back and lifted her up off the couch to stand up. "This has all been too much for you, dear. You must be exhausted with another sudden and dramatic change in your life. Trust me, all for the best. Now, let's get you up to the room to lie down until dinner."

"Remember, dinner is at five-thirty this evening. You can bring me your lodging money then."

Rowan didn't hear Mrs. Perkins because it was all she could do to concentrate on the stairs and put one foot in front of another. Florence opened the door to her room, sat Rowen on the edge of the bed, slipped off her shoes and let her lie down, helping her put her feet on the bed. Florence shut the drapes and the room went dark. She set the pamphlet of rules on the pine table next to the bed with a note to pay Mrs. Perkins ten seventy-five for August.

Chapter 10

When Rowan woke, she took a few minutes to steady herself and recall where she was. She pushed herself up on her elbows and looked around the room that was now her home. It was just large enough for the single bed, a table, a wardrobe and a dresser with a mirror, a porcelain wash bowl with a white wash cloth and towel folded beside it. The window was at least six feet tall covered by a heavy cream-colored curtain that opened in the middle. The oak wardrobe sat opposite the bed, leaving about six feet between them, enough to open the wardrobe doors. *Simple, but this will be fine.*

Rowan picked up the pamphlet and read the rules:

1. *Breakfast at 7:00 a.m. and supper at 5:30 p.m. daily.*
2. *Personal laundry is your responsibility. Provide your own laundry soap. Laundry is on the main floor at the back of the house.*
3. *Linens will be changed once a week on Mondays.*

4. *No men allowed on the second floor.*
5. *Parlor is open until 9:00 p.m. every night.*
6. *You may play the piano when the parlor is open.*
7. *You must take turns using the upstairs bathroom with other lodgers.*
8. *You may use the bathtub in the lodgers' bathroom once a week.*
9. *Rent due on the first day of the month.*
10. *All rent is in cash.*

Rowan found comfort in living in a boardinghouse with easy-to-follow rules and a daily routine. *Ten rules to live by is the magic number and easy to memorize,* Rowan thought One part of life she missed most after Eli passed was a daily routine. Her routine at the Union Hall was whatever she wanted it to be, which meant she did just a few chores and stared out the window most days. She wanted to remember to thank Florence again for giving her a chance at having a new start.

Rowan opened her suitcase, hung her clothes and put her shoes at the bottom of the wardrobe. From the packet of money from Eli's last pay, she removed twelve dollars. Mr. Dobbs never asked her to pay for the room or the food at Union Hall so she had a nest egg of about $142 dollars left after paying Mrs. Perkins. Rowan clutched the money in her hand, went downstairs and found Mrs. Perkins working in the kitchen. She promised herself not to spend the money from the tin unless she was desperate and didn't know how she would get her next meal. She hid it on the top shelf of the wardrobe behind a few cardboard boxes.

Before going downstairs Rowan plopped on her bed

and stared at the ceiling. Out of nowhere fear clutched her throat. She clenched her fist and threw her legs to the side of the bed, stood up and stiffened her back. *I am doing this!*

§

"Here." Rowan smiled and thrust her hand out to Mrs. Perkins with the rent money.

"Let's see, eleven dollars and seventy-five cents. I will get you change, dear."

"No, you have been so kind to take me in without meeting me. You have such a fine home. Is that fried chicken with buttermilk biscuits you are making for supper?"

"Yes. Around here I'm known for this dish." Mrs. Perkins stuffed the bills into her pocket and returned to the kitchen to finish dinner.

"Everything will be ready in about thirty minutes. I hope you are more rested now. Florence and the other girls will come down soon. Why don't you go wait in the parlor and you can get acquainted when they come down."

Rowan sat in one of the wing chairs next to the window. When dressing for dinner Rowan made sure to put on shoes. She placed her feet together flat on the floor; she was still getting used to wearing shoes every day. Folding her hands in her lap, she focused on breathing.

A woman with red hair, tied with a red ribbon, wearing brown pants and a blouse filled with sunflowers walked to where Rowan sat.

"You must be the woman Florence has been talking so much about. Emma Wallace is my name. Glad to meet you."

Rowan looked down. "Same."

"I don't recall what Florence told us. What is your name, dear?"

"Rowan D...Daly."

Emma covered her mouth with both hands. "Oh, the widow."

Rowan winced, unable to look Emma in the face. "Yes, the widow. Maybe Florence has shared too much all ready."

Emma sat in the chair next to Rowan and leaned toward her. "Please, please. I meant no offense. Sometimes things just pop out of my mouth. Florence shared a little bit with us – not much. I want to get to know you since we will live at the boardinghouse together."

Where is Florence? Rowan wondered.

"Hello, Hello, Hello. You must be Rowan. We have expected you for several days. Florence was not kind enough to share with us which day you would arrive. The pack horse librarians are now all assembled and ready for work."

Rowan looked in awe at the tall woman with raven hair. It fell over her shoulders in long curls, and she had on ruby-red lipstick. She wore a red and white striped skirt with a red V-neck blouse. Her smile spread across her entire face. She held herself like she had just graduated from finishing school.

"Oh, forget my rudeness, my name is Selma Rutledge of the Floyd County Rutledges. I just graduated from high school a year ago this past June. My pleasure to meet you."

Rowan bowed her head. "Thank you."

Rowan looked into her eyes and found kindness. "Pleasure, I'm sure, Selma."

Emma turned toward the parlor door. "I guess Florence must have dozed off after your long car trip."

Emma and Selma sat on the couch.

Florence walked into the parlor wearing khaki pants with a pink blouse and a matching ribbon with her hair pulled back into its usual pony tail. The women fell silent as she walked to the middle of the room, turning around to survey the three women. No one greeted her. Florence guessed that she was the topic of their conversation before she came downstairs for dinner. Florence decided not to challenge the women and ignored their silence.

"Well, it looks like everyone has met the newest lady librarian, Rowan Daly. Rowan, have they greeted you appropriately?"

Rowan kept her hands folded in her lap and didn't look up. "Yes ma'am."

"Good. It smells like Mrs. Perkins has one of her delicious meals ready. I'm famished; let's eat."

Just then, Mrs. Perkins shouted from the dining room, "Ladies, supper is ready."

Florence took the lead and each of the women followed her like ducklings swimming in a line after their mother.

Mrs. Perkins had a large plate of fried chicken, an enormous bowl of mashed potatoes with a pat of butter swimming in the center sitting on the table with a plate of buttermilk biscuits and a bowl of canned, French-cut green beans. Two pitchers sat on the table, one with water and one with ice tea. The women giggled and exchanged small talk as they passed each dish around. Rowan had not seen so much food at one time in months. The meal reminded her of her grandma's home cooking. As each woman filled her plate, the chatter stopped and everyone dug into their food.

Mrs. Perkins cleared her throat. "Ladies!" Everyone

put their utensils down and bowed their heads. "Thank thee O Lord for the food we share together and welcome our new boarder Rowan Daly. Amen. We pray at all our evening meals," Mrs. Perkins explained.

Rowan tried to control the amount she ate, trying not to give the impression she was undernourished. She finished the food on her plate before the other women and listened to herself asking to pass the plate of chicken to get a second helping. Then all the plates were passed again, and Rowan took another helping of mashed potatoes.

Mrs. Perkins looked around the table and smiled with satisfaction. She took joy in cooking for these independent, hard working women. "I have peach cobbler cooling in the kitchen. Maybe we could let it cool a bit longer and I'll serve it in the parlor about seven o'clock with a dab of cream. Is that ok?"

"May I be excused?" Rowan asked with wide eyes.

Mrs. Perkins hands flew to her chest. "Oh dear, we are not so formal in this house. You don't need to ask to leave the table."

"Thank you. I would like to spend the evening in my room. I still need to unpack, and I'm feeling tired. Mrs. Perkins, it was a delicious meal; I'm stuffed. Living here may not be good for my waistline."

Florence stood up as Rowan left the room. "Rowan, tomorrow I'll give you a walking tour of Pikeville. Ladies, if any of you would like to join us, you may."

"Thank you and good night." Rowan shuffled out of the dining room.

Rowan's suitcase still sat at the foot of the bed, waiting for her to unpack. She slung it on top of the bed and popped it open. It only took a few minutes for her to put her clothes away in the dresser, hang a few blouses and dresses in the wardrobe, and put two pair of shoes next to each other on the floor beside the dresser. She looked around her new home, which was both warm and lonely. It hadn't been two months since Eli died deep in the earth, and her grief was as intense and unsurmountable as the day she saw his mangled body in the funeral home. She wondered if he suffered or had the rock crushed out his life in an instant. These days she felt like life was trickling out of her a drop at a time. Staying at Union Hall, one day was much like another, no one bothered her. After the other women buried their men, they went on with life filled with responsibility for children and making enough money to keep food on the table. For them there wasn't time for grief. Rowan was only responsible for herself, and most days she didn't have the strength or will to go on. Tears grew in her eyes and slid down her cheeks. She curled up in bed. She had never lived in a city before and wasn't sure it would suit her. There were so many people and all of them strangers. She didn't miss New Hope; there was nothing there to miss. She had put her life in the hands of Florence Pruett.

Rowan heard muffled voices floating upstairs from the parlor. The women were savoring Mrs. Perkins peach cobbler and cream. Rowan wasn't ready to make new friends or idle chatter on a Saturday night. Her loneliness felt comfortable, for now, at least. Her mind tried to reassure her she had made the right decision to move to Pikeville and take the job Florence offered. She did not understand how to be a librarian and was not an experienced rider. She hoped Florence had someone in mind to help her improve her riding skills.

Rowan draped a towel and washcloth over her arm, grabbed her toothbrush and powder to clean up in the bathroom before the others came up stairs.

She changed into her nightgown and tucked herself into bed. It had been a long day with many changes. The new experiences swirled in her mind. It took Rowan more than an hour to conquer her raging thoughts and fears and go to sleep. Someone was playing music she had never heard before on the piano in the parlor, but it lulled her to sleep.

Chapter 11

$\mathcal{R}$owan rolled over, opened one eye, and saw a shaft of light through the window. She heard voices downstairs so she thought it must be breakfast time. In a few minutes she was in the dining room. The table was cleared and the room empty. She rushed into the parlor to find Florence and Emma talking.

"Well, good morning, Miss Sleepy Head, so glad you could join us." Emma said in a sarcastic tone.

Florence jumped up and gave Rowan a hug. "Emma, enough."

"Evidently, someone needs an alarm clock," Emma said.

Florence turned toward Emma with both hands on her hips. "Emma, that is enough. You must have plans for the day, this would be a good time to leave."

Emma left as she was ordered.

Several w-shaped wrinkles crossed Rowan's forehead. "What was that about? What did I do to her?"

Florence smiled. "You missed breakfast, dear. Emma

is a little high strung. Just forget about whatever she says. She sometimes thinks too much of herself, but her heart is good. Now, Mrs. Perkins has kept a plate warm for you in the oven. After your breakfast, meet me in the parlor and we will talk about your day."

Rowan stretched her arms wide for a hug. "Thank you for watching out over me. What time is it anyway?"

"A few minutes past eight a.m., dear. Maybe we should get you an alarm clock today. Let me help you in the kitchen."

§

Florence waited in the parlor with a tablet and pencil. Sunshine drenched the parlor floor, and she wondered how warm it would be outside on this late August morning. Florence flicked the pencil on the tablet as her thoughts drifted off to her days at Berea College. Florence wrote herself notes in slow, cursive writing:

Map out routes for Emma and Selma
Make list of family names for Emma and Selma
Take Rowan on walking tour downtown
Give list of tasks to Rowan

The Pack Horse Librarian Project was just a week old, and Florence was eager to get Emma and Selma started. Last week they completed beginning library training – just enough so they could begin visiting families this week. Florence wanted to devote this week to training Rowan with the goal of having her start her route by next Monday.

Rowan stood at the entrance to the parlor watching

Florence write on the tablet. Rowan didn't know what to expect on her first day but knew Florence would guide her. Rowan shuffled her feet. "Hello."

A smile swept across Florence's face. "Well, that was quick. You didn't need to rush. Now, sit beside me here on the sofa and we can plan your day."

"Where are Emma and Selma?"

Oh, they're at the library sorting books. They didn't want to join our walk. We'll stop in to chat with them later. They both started last week. Monday they will both go on their first delivery route. It gives me goose bumps, I'm so excited."

"They work on Saturday?"

"Just this once I asked them to spend the morning at the library so everything is ready for tomorrow morning. Don't worry, it won't be regular."

Rowan cleared her throat. "When will I make my first delivery?"

"I was just thinking about that. I would like you to ride next Monday. You have a lot to learn but you are intelligent, take direction and are enthusiastic. This is the start of your new journey, Rowan."

Rowan clutched Florence's hands. "I'm ready."

"Ok, take this pencil and pad and take notes. First, today I'll take you on a tour of downtown, show you the department store, post office, county offices, the livery stable and the library. This afternoon I want you to shop at the department store."

"For an alarm clock."

"Yes, and for any toiletries or similar things you might need. Soap for laundry, for instance."

"Next, you need to visit Gus Mattox, owner of Gus's Livery Stable."

Rowan wrote the list on the paper. Florence put her hand on top of Rowan's to have her stop writing.

"I think I should visit Gus with you to help explain how much help you will need. There is no better person in Pike County to teach you how to ride in those hills. Yes, we'll go together. Now take down a few more tasks."

Rowan printed in small letters so she would only use one sheet of paper.

"Monday morning, Alexander's Tack Shop; Tuesday afternoon visit the stable – not over two hours, then library training. Wednesday, Thursday and Friday will be the same."

"Whew, I'm going to be busy, Florence."

"Now for the tour. Are those good walking shoes you have there?"

"Yes, ma'am."

They left the boardinghouse and were downtown in a few minutes. It was a fresh summer morning, and Rowan breathed in the sweet sunshine and felt her spirits lift. As they walked, Florence explained Pikeville was founded as the center of county government in 1899, and the county was named for General Zebulon Pike. The city was named Liberty by Zebulon Pike. Folks didn't care for the name and they voted to change it to Pikeville after the General. They remodeled the courthouse in 1932 as part of a special work program started by President Roosevelt. During the remodeling, a library was built in the basement, the first library in the county.

Their first stop was Alexander's Tack Shop just a few blocks from the courthouse. The shop smelled like leather, had saddles hanging on the wall, racks of clothes in the middle and in the back corner, riding boots. "Millie, is Mrs. Alexander in?" Florence asked.

"Yes, Miss Pruett, she's working on the books in the back office. Should I get her?"

"Yes, please."

A tall slender woman with dark hair streaked with strands of white walked toward them. Her stride was long. She walked with confidence, a woman who knew who she was and her standing in the community. Her eyes filled with curiosity as she gazed at Rowan. "What can I do for you?"

"Mrs. Alexander, I would like to introduce Rowan Daly. This is her first day working for the library. Rowan's going to deliver books to the folks in the hills, along with the two other women you met last week. She's going to need riding clothes for many different kinds of weather."

"I don't believe I know any Dalys in Pike County."

"No, ma'am, I'm from Marion County."

"Have you just moved to Pike County, then?"

Florence didn't want to waste time chatting with Mrs. Alexander. "Well then, Rowan will be back tomorrow to be outfitted. If she needs credit, I will vouch for her. She is going to have a respectable monthly income, but her first paycheck won't be until next month."

"Oh, I have savings. I'm sure I'll be able to pay."

"Thank you, Mrs. Alexander. Rowan, we need to visit the five and dime store. We also have a brand-new Walgreen pharmacy just one block from the library."

Mrs. Alexander moved to behind the counter. "Getting the grand tour then. Where are you living, Rowan?" Mrs. Alexander couldn't control her curiosity.

"She's with me at Mrs. Perkins' boardinghouse. Now we must say goodbye, Mrs. Alexander. Until tomorrow."

Florence took Rowan by the elbow, turned her around and walked out the front door. "Next, we need to visit Gus Mattox's Livery Stable. It's at the edge of the city. It will be about a fifteen-minute walk."

Florence walked at a steady pace and pointed out other stores Rowan may need to visit from time to time and the churches in town. They walked away from the courthouse on Main Street until the street ended. Rowan's eyes were as wide as a silver dollar. She couldn't find words to express her amazement at such a large city. Along the street were enormous two-story homes and a few three-story homes. Every home had a swing and huge flower pots and a little table where the owners would set their sweet tea in the evenings to catch the cool breeze.

Gus Mattox's Livery Stable began where Main Street ended. The livery stable had once been painted white but now most of the paint was chipped away and exposed gray weathered siding. There was a large corral to the left of the stable with tin water and feeding troughs. A thin man with scrappy hair that had not seen a comb in days lugged a bucket of water to fill the troughs.

"Mr. Mattox!" Florence shouted.

He set down the bucket, waved and walked toward the fence. He propped his arms on the fence, put his boot on the lowest fence rail and wiped his face with a red bandana. "Howdy there, Miss Pruett. This must be the new librarian you were telling me about."

"Mr. Mattox, let me introduce Rowan Daly. This is her first day working for the library."

"Ma'am. I suppose Rowan Daly wants to rent a horse?

Ride much, Miss Daly?" Mr. Mattox squinted into the sun and couldn't quite make out Rowan's face.

"I rode barback just for fun on my grandparents' farm. Yes, I need to rent a horse."

Gus was in his early sixties and looked every year of it. Years of working outside made his face leatherlike with deep wrinkles. His hands were calloused and as tough as nails. He had been on his own since his wife passed seven years ago. The horses kept him company, is what he told the folks down at the Baptist church who worried about him. At the beginning of the Depression he sold two horses just to put food on his table and so he could give the remaining horses grain twice a week. He worked hard to keep three mares and a gelding. The business Miss Pruett brought him was a godsend.

"Well, I have a five-year-old Kentucky Mountain horse mare that is a sweety. She's a perfect ladies' mount and knows these hills. She'll take care of you, miss."

Rowan looked past Gus Mattox into the paddock and didn't see any horses. She couldn't hear horses in the barn either. Why would Gus fill water troughs if the horses weren't there? She had not asked Gus what it would cost to rent a horse, and Florence didn't mention the price either. "Where are the horses, Mr. Mattox?"

Gus Mattox broke out into a deep belly laugh. "You don't see'em, do you? Well, today they're off on pasture. When they're stabled, I have hay, and I can only afford oats twice a week. I won't bring them back in until Thursday or so. Call me Gus; I haven't been Mr. Mattox for years."

Both Florence and Rowan nodded. Rowan, uncertain about asking the price to rent a mare, kicked dust at the fence and tried to think of other topics.

"What is the mare's name?"

"She's a beautiful gray so I've named her Ash."

"Well, I just have to ask, what does it cost to rent Ash for a week, Gus?"

"Miss Pruett is giving me a lot of business with you librarians. Good steady income for me. I want to be fair and charge all three of you the same. Let's say fifty cents a week plus food. With this income I should be able to give them oats three times a week. Riding those hills they will need the extra feed. I'd guess food will cost you another twenty-five cents a week so that's seventy-five cents a week. I'll need the money on Monday, when you pick up the horse. Fair enough?"

Florence reached out to shake Gus's hand. "That is fair, Gus! Because of you we are going to have a pack horse librarian project in Pike County. You get paid, the girls get paid and the folks in the county get books and magazines. Everybody wins. We're going to make it through this Depression, I'm determined. Now, Rowan, isn't there one more thing you need to talk with Gus about?"

Gus broke out his bandana again to wipe the sweat off his face. "To ride these hills you're going to need lessons, Miss Daley, I'm not judgin', you see, but these hills are tough even though the horses know their way. Gus rubbed his chin. Let's see now. How about ten cents a day for lessons? You can start tomorrow morning – about nine o'clock."

Rowan grabbed the fence with both hands to steady her wobbly legs. A smile grew across her face. "You are a godsend, Gus, but I don't have any riding gear yet."

"No problem, miss. I have my own way with the horses. You won't need gear for several days. Tomorrow

I'll give you a list of what you will need from Alexander's Tack Shop. Be prepared, there's a price on gear but good gear is worth it – will last you years."

"God bless you, Gus." The insecurity that nagged at Rowan all day evaporated. "You know, Florence, I could use lunch."

Chapter 12

Rowan turned to the first page of the notebook, smoothed it out and wrote at the top of the page in perfect cursive:

Sunday, August 24, 1936 Pikeville Kentucky, Perkins Boarding House

Monthly Expenses

Rent per month $11.25 (almost half my income)

Horse rental $0.50 + $0.25 food = $0.75 per week, $3.00 per month

Other expenses

Craddock riding boots $23.50

Riding breeches – 2 pair $10.00

Riding shirts (5) $5.00

Riding socks that come up to knee $2.00

Leather riding gloves $1.75

Canvas bag for books (2) $0.25

Incidentals (toothpaste, alarm clock, tablet, pencil, chocolate bar) $3.25

She got up and pulled the tin with the money from Hope Mining company and dumped it out on the bed. She separated the paper money and coins into little piles. At the side of the pages she wrote all her expenses in a column so she could add it up. The total was $142. The pencil dropped from her hand. She gasped and held her breath. The first month she needed sixty dollars, and she still had eighty-one dollars and seventy-five cents left. Rowan felt rich – money wasn't going to be a problem while she waited for her first pay check. She pondered getting a hot fudge sundae tomorrow after her shopping. She thought back on the day she accepted the money from Mr. Dobbs and the secret she kept to survive. Secrets are always bad in life but sometimes circumstances reduce a person's choices to zero. Rowan couldn't decide if her secret was a lie or not. She and Eli lived together in love for two years. Just the piece of paper from the courthouse was missing. *What does a piece of paper mean anyway?* she thought. *The paper has nothing to do with love.* She needed the money to live. Rowan was sure Eli would not mind she took the mine company money – the mine killed him. He also would be ok with using the few dollars in savings if it was for her well-being. She brushed her short brown hair back with her hand and looked at her face in the mirror. It was not the face of a liar; it was the face of a woman lost to the world without the man she loved.

She took several deep breaths to calm herself and put her fingers on her neck to wait for her heartbeat to return to normal. Rowan stared at the page and figured out her regular monthly expenses. Every month she needed ten dollars and seventy-five cents for Mrs. Perkins and three dollars for Gus. She thought fifty cents a week for spending money was fair – a total of fifteen dollars and seventy-five cents per month. The library job pays twenty-eight dollars a month, so she should be able to start saving, maybe open a bank account. Eli's last pay saved her from complete desolation. She scooped up the money and dropped it into the tin box and returned it to the hiding place in the wardrobe.

Rowan stretched out on the bed to think about everything that had happened this week. Her stomach groaned and felt empty. She didn't include needing to buy lunch every day. She hoped that thirty cents a day would be enough – that would be a dollar and fifty cents a week. Rowan grabbed the tablet to figure all her expenses again. Her numbers were perfect. Rowan bent over, holding her angry stomach.

Rap, rap, rap "Rowan, are you there, dear? May I come in?" Mrs. Perkins asked.

"Yes, ma'am."

The door swung open and Mrs. Perkins strode into the room. When she turned around, she was carrying a tray with a sandwich, an apple and a glass of milk. Rowan jumped off the bed to take the tray from her landlady. "I thought you could use a sandwich, dear. Just peanut butter but it will stick to your ribs until supper tonight."

Rowan's legs felt wobbly. She walked backward to the bed and plopped down, making sure to not spill the milk. "Oh, Mrs. Perkins, you are an angel. I was just trying to figure out my expenses every month. Florence insisted I have a plan for using my salary. I had to buy a lot of things, like all the riding gear before getting a paycheck. I'm going to make it. I'll review my figures with Florence tonight."

"You have friends here, Rowan, soon you'll get to know

Emma and Selma better, and Florence is already a dear friend, I'm sure. Now, enjoy your lunch and do me a favor and bring the dishes to the kitchen when you're done."

Rowan set the tray on one side of the bed, leapt up and gave Mrs. Perkins a bear hug. "You're my friend too, Mrs. Perkins."

Rowan gobbled down the sandwich in a few bites and washed it down with milk. The apple was crisp and sweet, the perfect dessert. She propped up her pillow and lay back to think about everything she learned the past few days.

Gus proved to be an expert at giving riding lessons. The first day all she did was walk Ash around the yard with a rope and talk to her in a slow soothing tone. The second day Gus gave her several apples and after the walk, she fed them to Ash. The horse's teeth were so large it frightened her when Ash snatched the apple from her open hand. On the third day Gus put a wood step stool next to Ash and Rowan climbed up into the saddle. Gus spent a lot of time adjusting the stirrups until they were perfect. He took the reins and led Ash around the yard while Rowan hung onto the pommel, trying to get Rowan used to the horse's gait. The next day Gus showed her how to hold the reins and give Ash instructions by pulling the reins and using a gentle nudge with her feet. Ash was gentle and seemed to be aware that Rowan was a novice rider.

"On Friday a friend of mine, Lucas Tate, will take you out to teach you to ride in the hills. Lucas was born and raised in Pikeville. He reports for the *Pikeville County News*. He's a smart boy."

"Boy?"

"Well, he must be about, now let me think, he must

be 26-28, something like that. He's kinda shy, especially around the ladies like yourself. It surprised me he agreed to do it after I told him you were a woman."

A smile crossed her face as she remembered their conversation.

§

The women walked into the parlor after another of Mrs. Perkins famous fried chicken dinners. She had won the fried chicken dinner contest at the Baptist church the last three years. "Rowan, did you work on your budget today?" Florence asked in a stern tone.

"Yes, ma'am."

"Go up to your room and I'll be up in a few minutes to review it with you. There's no use to share your situation with Emma and Selma. Ladies, do you have something to occupy yourselves?"

"I thought a walk down the river would be pleasant. Emma?"

"Perfect, I will be ready for bed after our walk. I have my first long route tomorrow. I need to get started by seven, and I don't expect to be back until five o'clock."

"I'll say goodnight, now," Florence said. "Rowan, upstairs with you now. I need to speak to Mrs. Perkins. I'll be up in a few minutes."

§

Florence took the tablet and reviewed Rowan's figures. "Mmmm, fifty cents a week for spending money, that would be two dollars a month. You plan on spoiling yourself?"

"Eli always made sure I had money every week to spend on myself. He loved me so."

"How much did he give you?"

"Oh, I don't know, it varied. The important thing was that I had something – even if it was only for a five-cent candy bar."

"Well, this looks fine – I just want to challenge you. Gus told me you're riding tomorrow in the hills for the first time with that good-looking Lucas Tate."

"Good looking?"

"Extremely. He's about my age, twenty-five." Florence laughed at the surprised look on Rowan's face. "Don't worry dear, I'm not interested."

"Neither am I."

"After each lession, I want to spend the afternoon at the library teaching you library science – or as much as I can teach you in that short time. I also want to review the records you will need to keep on your routes. I want you to be ready to go on your first route the following Monday. I have changed Selma's schedule for next week so she can ride with you. I feel it would be best if either Emma or Selma ride with you the first week. Afterward, you'll be on your own."

Rowan set her jaw and looked into Florence's eyes. "I will make you proud, Florence, cross my heart."

Chapter 13

Walking to Gus's livery stable was no way to break in new leather riding boots. The boots were heavy and stiff and not designed for walking. The walk was only about a mile from Mrs. Perkins' boardinghouse but when Rowan opened the gate to the livery workout area, her feet were sore and sweaty.

"That's what I like, right on time." Gus said as he led Ash out of the barn. "You look exhausted all ready and we haven't even started."

"It's the boots. I should have known better than to walk here in brand-new riding boots. It's a mistake I won't make again."

"That's why mistakes are so important in life – it's the primary way we learn, at least it has been in my life. I imagine life would be unbearably boring if we never made mistakes."

Rowan stood with legs spread apart, arms crossed in front of her, working hard to choose the right words. "Gus, that is brilliant. Just brilliant." She tried mounting

Ash without the steps. Gus held the reins as she threw her leg as high as she could and jumped at the same time.

"Grab the pommel," Gus shouted.

Rowan followed Gus's order and pulled herself up into the saddle. Ash stood without moving. Rowan leaned over to pat Ash's neck. A wide smile crossed her face. *Learning to mount without so much effort will take time.* She tapped Ash's sides to let her know it was time to practice. "Walk on Ash." She circled the yard many times, learning to shift her weight with the horse's gait.

Rowan concentrated on riding and didn't notice the young man sitting on a black stallion just inside the gate. He was thin, with brown hair brushed back and a part in the middle. As Ash walked on, Rowan turned her head, staring at the attractive man. He waved. "Hello, you must be Rowan Daly." *The girls were right; he's good looking. Damn, what am I saying? So shallow of me. Eli, don't worry, you are still deep in my heart.*

"Hello, Lucas, thanks for helping. Rowan, this is Lucas Tate. He's going to guide you on a ride into the hills this morning."

Rowan held her breath. Lucas sat tall in the saddle of his black mount. He looked like an athlete, and Rowan guessed he was in track and field. She hoped he would be a good guide.

"No hills today, Gus. Thought we would go up Levisa Fork, maybe cross the river to show her how horses react to water."

Gus opened the gate and held it open. Lucas looked at Rowan. "Ready?" Not waiting for an answer, he turned his horse and rode out the gate toward the east. "Just follow me," Lucas shouted without looking back. Rowan's fists tightened around the reins, and her knees hugged Ash's sides. "Walk on, Ash."

They rode several miles on the dusty road, which turned north when they reached the Levisa Fork. There was a dam at the far end of the Levisa Fork river, which transformed the river into a long, shallow lake. Small wooden rowboats dotted the lake with men fishing for their supper. Many families learned to rely on the river for at least one meal a day. The path they rode on narrowed as they rode east. Lucas never turned around to check on Rowan or give her any additional instruction. Rowan concentrated on her posture and feeling Ash's muscles as she walked along the path. She wondered how many times Ash had walked this path. The hills surrounding the river were steep and wooded, and there were no paths up into the hills that Rowan could detect. Rowan couldn't imagine what it would be like to leave the worn route near the river to forge up into the hills.

The forest was untouched, filled with big leaf magnolia, American beech and American linden. The woods were preserved from logging because the inhabitants of Pike County preferred to make their living digging out bituminous coal, which supported generations of families. There were no cabins along the path but several makeshift piers where the locals kept their boats when not fishing. Today there wasn't a single boat stored, everyone needed to eat. The river turned right at almost a ninety-degree angle and the sun was on Rowan's back as they rode west. The woods retreated and the dirt path widened while the river appeared to shrink and become more narrow, not over fifteen feet wide.

Lucas pulled the reins to the right and lead his horse

into the water. Rowan pulled the reins to stop Ash. Lucas stopped mid-stream, turned around and shouted "Come on!" Rowan tightened her grip on the reins. She pulled the reins to the right, and Ash stepped into the stream without hesitation. The water swished around Ash's hoofs. Once on the other side, Lucas turned right and headed back toward Pikeville. The sun climbed in the sky and Rowan guessed it must be close to noon. During their ride the only conversation was the few instructions Lucas gave.

Gus was putting out hay in the yard and opened the gate when he saw Lucas and Rowan. "Well, how was it?"

"Fine. I need to get to work." Lucas answered. He turned to speak to Rowan "Tomorrow?"

"Yes, thank you."

Gus watched Rowan dismount. She lost her balance and ended up sitting on the ground. She hid her face in her hands. Her body shook with embarrassment. Gus turned to add water to the troughs; he wasn't looking at Rowan. Rowan jumped up, brushed herself off and led Ash to the water trough without saying a word. She wanted to get back to the boardinghouse and grab a snack for lunch before meeting Florence at the library. Other than her less than graceful dismounting, she felt her first lesson went well. Luckily, Lucas was not there to witness her clumsiness getting down from Ash.

§

The steps down to the library in the courthouse were dark. Rowan clutched the handrail to not fall. She looked up to see a single light fixture that was missing a bulb. She went directly to Florence working in the library to report the hazard.

"I know, I know, there's no bulb in the stairs light fixture. I told Mr. Weston two days ago but I guess it isn't a custodial priority. Today I'm putting my request in writing. When someone falls and breaks an ankle, I will have proof that my request was ignored when the county gets sued for doctor bills."

"How was your first ride in the hills?"

"Lucas was kind to me today. We didn't go into the hills, just around the river fork. Tomorrow we head for the hills. I guess it will be the first route you are giving me."

"That's right. The first route will have only ten stops and a few hills. It will help relieve Selma and Emma; I'm sure you have noticed they have been riding until near dusk. Mrs. Perkins has been holding their dinner and then they go straight to bed. Now, take a seat at the table. Here is a paper I wrote on the history of the library. I need to work on packing books for tomorrow's routes. Later, we will start with the Dewey Decimal System."

Rowan sat in the wood folding chair at the end of the table. The library was small with no windows. The ceiling fan was also a light and the blades turned so slow Rowan couldn't feel a breeze. Florence kept a small, black oscillating fan on her desk that provided some relief from the August heat. The back wall was a bookshelf from floor to ceiling. There was a ladder on a metal track like the ones at the five and dime store to get the books high on the shelf. Bookshelves that must have been at least six feet tall were behind and in front of Rowan. On the wall next to the door was a large cork board that had a variety of notes, public notices, and posters announcing events in the community like the pie contest next Sunday at the Baptist church.

Florence watched Rowan study the room. "It is small but adequate. That bulletin board is going to be your responsibility. You will need to check it every week to make sure everything is current and when the date for an event passes, take it down to leave space for more postings. Now, girl, read the history paper."

Rowan put the paper on the table and smoothed it out.

A Short History of the Pikeville Library

In 1932 funding became available to build a new county courthouse. Jobs were scarce in 1932 and building a courthouse provided many good-paying craftsmen jobs. The Reverend Dr. Chester Lamar of the Methodist church proposed to the Mayor that space be created in the new courthouse for a public library run by a college-educated librarian. To help lessen the burden on the county, Reverend Dr. Lamar donated 612 books from his private collection. Coming from a family with some means, he also promised to pay one half of the librarians' salaries from the sale of his tobacco crop. Even during the Depression there was a high demand for tobacco products.

They completed the building in 1932 with a 15' x 15' room without windows in the basement for the library. A local carpenter Fred Thomas was hired to build custom pine bookshelves. They scavenged furniture from other county offices in the building since only a desk, table and a few fold-ing chairs were needed.

The Reverend Dr. Lamar was in charge of a committee to hire a librarian. The committee visit-ed Berea College, known for its excellent program in library science. The committee offered the job to Miss Florence Pruett. Miss Pruett graduated in June and was pleased to have a job right away. Once the books were delivered and organized by Miss Pruett, the library opened its doors on Monday June 6, 1932.

Since that time, Miss Pruett has added maga-zines to the collection and made a study of what materials are most popular to ensure they are available. She has also solicited donations for books and other materials and the collection has grown to 779 books. In June, 1936, the Works Progress Administration started the Pack Horse Librarian Project to deliver books to folks living in the hills of eastern Kentucky to improve literacy in the region. Florence hired three pack horse librarians.

Submitted: Florence Pruett, August, 1936

"You just wrote this?"

"I've updated it. Had to borrow a typewriter in the clerk's office. We don't have a budget for equipment. I plan on asking for a small amount in next year's budget for things that we need. Well, are you ready to learn the Dewey Decimal System?"

Rowan slumped in her chair, the warm room and

morning ride taking its toll. "Dewey Decimal System – that's a mouthful. What is it?"

Florence sat in the chair opposite Rowan and reached back to her desk to pick up a complex looking chart. "In school we called it the Dewey Classification System. It is a way of organizing the books in the library and was created by Mr. Melvil Dewey in 1876. This system has been around for quite a while and has proven useful. Before Mr. Dewey, library books were usually organized by the most recent addition to the library, which wasn't very helpful when looking for a specific title. If, for example, you want a book about Kentucky history, you would search through all the books to find the one book you wanted to read."

Rowan took the chart and stared at it for a few minutes. "It's a puzzle to me, Florence."

"Well, let's begin with the classifications. There are ten classifications: general works, philosophy, religion, social sciences, language, science, technology, arts and recreation, literature, history, and geography. Let's say you want to read a book on the history of Pike County. How would you find a book on Pike County?"

Rowan took the chart again and glanced at it. "That's easy; I would go to the shelf that had a number 900."

"But Rowan, how would you find a book specifically about Pike County, Kentucky?"

Rowan scratched her head and took a few minutes, searching for the right answer. "I guess I would look through all the books in the 900 section."

"That could take a very long time. There is one more step I need to show you. We have boxes with three inch by five inch cards. There is a separate box for each category."

Florence got up and looked at a group of boxes sitting

on the work table in the corner of the room.

"Ah, here it is." Florence returned to the table and set the box down in front of her.

"Now, there is a card for each book in the 900 section. Within the 900 categories, books are further divided into more specific categories. I have separate charts to show how each category is further divided, but you don't need to worry about that now. You can either glance at the 900-category chart or check the cards in the box. Each card has a specific number in the upper left-hand corner, then the title of the book, the publisher, year published and author. For now, why don't you review the chart on the 900 section; it will be quicker."

The chart was complex. It started with 900s, then divided into subcategories: – 990, 980...Within each group there was a single digit – for example, 995. There was a category listed for each. The number 995 said "History – United States – 1700 to 1900." Then there was a decimal point with three numbers to the right. Each book had a number on the spine. Rowan used it to find a book on the shelf on Pike County History – 995.040 History, Kentucky, Pike County, 1821 to 1901, University of Kentucky, Arnold Waters. "Here's one, here's one."

Florence smiled at Rowan's quick learning and enthusiasm. "Ok, young lady, now go to the shelf and find your book. Since it is a history book, it's probably not checked out."

Rowan used her finger to look for a book with the specific number 995.040. "Here it is!"

"Rowan, one of the most critical jobs in the library is to correctly catalog every book before putting it on the shelf. The Library of Congress has taken on the job of assigning the Dewey decimal number to all published books and printing it on the inside cover. Our job is to print the number at the bottom of the spine of the book. We then fill out a three by five card and put it in the right order in the cardboard box."

"Spine?"

Florence laughed out loud. "I am so sorry, dear – librarian talk." She picked up the book on Kentucky history and pointed to where the catalog number was printed in white. "This is called the spine of the book."

Rowan leaned back in her chair and wrapped her arms around herself. "So much to learn."

Chapter 14

The three women sat at the small work table in the library.

"Are you helping any of them learn to read?" Rowan wanted to know. Emma and Selma shrugged their shoulders as they looked at each other.

"Well, yes, we do. Florence knows which families they are and on the day we visit, she allows time for us to stay with them for an hour. God knows they want to learn, but many of them left school by third grade. Can you believe, they were working in the mines by nine years old. I don't think it would be right to share any names with you. I'm sure Florence would disapprove," Emma explained.

Rowan covered her mouth with her hand. "Oh, I don't want to know any names. I didn't mean to pry. I want to know what to expect, that's all."

§

The three women walked up the steps to the board-inghouse. "Rowan, you should be prepared to work with at least one family on reading for every route you have," Selma said.

When you load your bag, Florence will give you a copy of the New England Primer with a sheet of paper in the front cover with the name of the family needing help. Work with whatever member of the family is there. Florence will also give you a book to leave with them to practice reading out loud. At your next visit family members will compete to show you how much they can read. It's both sad and exciting but you end your day knowing you have changed a person's life. When is your first route, Rowan?" Selma asked.

Rowan cleared her throat as she opened the screen door for Emma and Selma. "Florence wants me to start next Monday. I still need a lot of practice riding in the hills."

"You must tell us what Lucas is like. I wouldn't mind spending an evening with him on the dance floor, I want to tell you." Emma stopped mid-step. "Come to think of it, I've never seen him at one of the community hall dances. Don't you girls think that is odd?"

Rowan had a wide grin. "Ladies, I'm not surprised. I would say he's the most shy man in Kentucky. I've been riding with him for a week and other than instructions I don't think he's said ten words." "I need to lie down before dinner. See you soon."

Selma stood quickly. "Rowan, wait. There's a dance this weekend; would you like to join me and Emma?"

"No."

"Don't be standoffish." Selma pouted.

"I'm not. I'm tired." Rowan walked toward the stairs.

"Turn around and talk to us, Rowan Daly. You are so rude. We're trying to be friendly but you always find a way to avoid us," Selma blurted out.

"Have it your way, ladies, I'm tired. Good night." Rowan pulled herself up the stairs to be alone.

§

Friday routes had fewer stops, and Florence let Emma and Selma off early so she could have a private conversation with Rowan. She learned from Lucas that Rowan was just an "ok" rider, and he wasn't sure if she was ready for some of the more challenging hills north of Pikeville. Florence spent some of the day Friday looking at the current routes to spread the work among the three pack horse librarians. Emma and Selma accepted bearing the extra workload; *they are so sweet*. She thought maybe Sunday afternoon she would treat both of them to a chocolate soda. Florence also studied a map of Pike County. She had to admit she was still learning the layout of the land herself. She decided she could create a route for Rowan to the east of the city that she could handle. She limited the route to ten families to begin with and only one family needing help reading. To make sure she picked easier routes, she walked to Gus's livery to have him check out the routes and help her draw a map for Rowan to use.

"Yup, I've seen her ride – she can get through that one. I don't have any idea how long it will take her; don't know if that matters to you."

"Well, it may take her all day."

"Let me see that list of names. I don't want her to have any rough characters – if you know what I mean."

Gus studied the list and gave it back to Florence. "All God-fearing folks."

Florence and Rowan met Friday afternoon. Florence explained the route and how she selected the books and magazines for Rowan to distribute. "Many of our patrons prefer magazines because they can finish them in one sitting. I would say the most popular magazines are *Women's Home Companion* and *American Detective*. Both can have very engaging stories."

"Maybe I should read a few over the weekend to become familiar with them," Rowan suggested.

"Excellent idea. Also, I've decided that next week I will ride the route with you until you are confident, instead of one of the girls. Emma and Selma have agreed to split their time between keeping the library open and riding their routes. While few patrons visit the library, there is always work to do."

Rowan buried her face in her hands to hide her tears. "You are all so good to me. I will do my best. I promise. I promise."

Part II

Chapter 15

It was over a year since Rowan had started riding her route. Selma, Emma and Florence sat munching breakfast without talking.

Mrs. Perkins said, "Ladies, I'm worried about Rowan. This is the second morning she hasn't come down for breakfast; I hope she isn't ill. We're having such a fine June spring; she shouldn't miss it."

"Well, it took her long enough to learn her route. She seems like a loner to me, or extremely shy – I can't tell which." Emma said.

"I may work with her but I don't like her. She's a loner or stuck-up or something," Selma complained.

"Ladies, you are being judgmental. Rowan has her own ways as both of you do too," Florence said.

Emma picked up her plates and walked into the kitchen. "Another delicious breakfast, Mrs. Perkins, thank you. I don't know what you all think but Rowan has been aloof all week – more aloof than normal – at least for her."

"I have been worried too. She told me she was preoccupied with organizing the children's collection," Florence offered.

Selma held her coffee cup with both hands and sipped without making a sound. She was looking forward to her day with her boyfriend, Rodney. He hinted he had a surprise for her today. "Well, I'm off. Not sure if I will be back for supper; don't count on me, Mrs. P."

"All right, dear. Have fun.

"I think I'll take breakfast up to Rowan. That girl needs to eat."

§

Mrs. Perkins balanced the tray with one hand and knocked on Rowan's door. She couldn't hear anything inside the room. She wondered if Rowan had sneaked out with no one seeing her. Mrs. Perkins knocked again so that anyone would hear it. Again, not a sound came from within the room.

Mrs. Perkins turned the knob and opened the door a crack. "Rowan, dear?" Mrs. Perkins heard a muffled sound that could have been crying. She opened the door wide to see Rowan lying face down on the bed still in her pajamas. "Oh Rowan, dear. I have what you need – my award-winning buttermilk biscuits with apple butter and an egg."

Rowan raised her head just enough to speak. "That is so sweet. You're like my grandma. Just set it on the dresser."

The landlady set the tray down and left the room, closing the door with great care.

In a few minutes there was a firm knock on the door. "I haven't finished yet, Mrs. Perkins. I'll bring the tray to the kitchen when I'm done."

The door opened. Florence stepped in the room with a look of determination on her face. "I think I know what this is about."

"You do?"

"Yes, the accident was one year ago this week." Florence sat on the bed next to Rowan.

"Oh God, I miss Eli. I hate this week. I always will. Without you I...I..."

Florence rubbed Rowan's shoulders and back. "You hide your grief well, Rowan. It's very normal to grieve the person you loved most in the world for as long as you want. In many cultures the traditional period of grief is a year. You can read about it in the Encyclopedia Britannica. What I'm trying to tell you is that it's ok to let go now. You should be proud of yourself for learning to care for yourself this past year. You are a natural librarian. You can have a career, if you want to."

After a few minutes Rowan turned toward Florence and took her hand. "You are my guardian angel. Working for you has saved my life. Working at the library feels like a natural calling. I can't imagine a career. I don't have a college degree like you do. I can never afford college so I will learn to be content with my job."

Rowan shuffled her feet. "It's not fair, it just isn't fair. Eli gone, and I'll be a library worker the rest of my life. I'm stuck. Some days it makes me so depressed I can't get out of bed, and other days I'm mad as hell because I can't do anything about it."

Florence recalled her astonishment when she received her acceptance letter from Berea College. She only applied because her high school librarian insisted she had the talent to attend college.

Florence stood still. Rowan was face down on her bed. "Rowan, it's a beautiful day. It would be tragic to stay cooped up in this room all day. Take a nice warm bath and in an hour we can take a walk. Maybe we can get a chocolate soda downtown after. I want to plant a little seed in your very fertile mind. Berea College is very unique. Remember, there is no tuition – there is a twenty-hour-per-week work requirement for each student."

Rowan sat up but didn't seem to hear what Florence told her about Berea. "I'll be ready when you come by."

$

Rowan opened the window to let the warm spring breeze flow into her room and warm her body and soul. She picked a plain, button-down blouse and tan trousers with matching sandals. Since working she saved enough to buy herself something new to wear every month. She looked at herself in the mirror and smiled at her reflection. Rowan brushed her hair, counting just twenty strokes as she did every morning. Her hair was stubborn this morning and needed something to tame it. She ruffled through the dresser drawer and found a red barrette, then parted her shoulder-length brown hair on the left, the barrette kept her hair from falling in her face. Glancing again in the mirror, she smiled.

Florence knocked and pushed the door open to find Rowan staring at the mirror. "You look lovely, dear. Let's go before it gets too warm."

Rowan turned toward Florence; her cheeks were flushed pink. "I'm very plain; I always have been. I like my hair down to my shoulders, and it saves me a quarter for a haircut. I typically only need to only have my hair cut four times a year."

"Oh my, you are so frugal."

Mrs. Perkins greeted the women at the bottom of the stairs, holding a brown paper bag and a thermos. "I thought you ladies would enjoy a picnic. I've made egg-salad sandwiches, carrot slices and snickerdoodle cookies with a thermos of milk."

Florence took the bag and Rowan took the thermos. "Thank you," they chimed in unison.

They walked from the boardinghouse to Levisa Fork, strolling at a slow pace and basking in the late morning sun. A flock of geese flew overhead and landed in the water. The geese opposed their presence by slapping their wings on the water. "I guess we should move along. Maybe we can find a place for our picnic at the edge of the woods." They walked a few hundred yards and found a fallen tree to sit on.

Florence set the bag on the ground, and Rowan followed with the thermos. Rowan leaned back and bent her face toward the sun; it was almost overhead. She closed her eyes and listened to the symphony of bird song. The sadness that burdened her when she woke, lifted and disappeared into the clear, blue sky. Rowan sighed and reached out to touch Florence's hand. Florence appeared deep in thought.

"You have been my guardian angel. I would never be here today without you. I have been so busy this past year, learning to ride, learning how to be a librarian, meeting wonderful families in the hills. I have tucked my grief into a closet."

Florence patted her hand. "Sometimes, being busy, especially learning new things is the best remedy for grief, at least in my experience. Watch the river Rowan, notice how it always flows – never stops – water flowing, flowing, flowing. It is mesmerizing. I have read the Greek philosophers. They teach us that time is like a river because you cannot touch the same water twice, because the flow that has passed will never pass again."

Rowan leaned back, kicked off her sandals and ran into the river. She leaned down and splashed water toward Florence with a gentle laugh. Florence jumped up to avoid the water but wasn't quick enough. She leaned down and threw off her flats and ran to the edge of the river near Rowan. "You're going to regret that, missy." The two women splashed each other until their blouses were soaked. "Now we must bask in the sun until we're dry," Florence said.

"I'm hungry, let's eat lunch and then just stretch out here and take a brief nap. I needed this, Florence. I still have my memories of Eli, always will, but I'm alive – very alive."

Chapter 16

$\mathcal{T}$he next day Selma turned in her resignation. She had no intent on working after being married and she wanted a June wedding; she refused to wait a whole year. She set the date for June 30th, which gave her just three weeks to make all the arrangements. For Emma and Rowan it meant they would have to divide up Selma's route between them. Selma's route went south from Pikeville, through the old forest area with some of the most dense woods in Kentucky. The families living there had been there for generations and were not inclined to move, no matter how harsh the living.

Rowan and Emma spread out the map on the table to review the route Selma had outlined. It took Selma at least eight hours to ride the entire loop and the number of families she visited ranged from twelve to eighteen. She rode three times a week and worked in the library twice a week. Florence would take care of the slack in the library, which gave both Emma and Rowan an extra day to ride a route.

"What do you think, ladies, can you split this up?"

Emma scratched her head and glanced at Rowan. Rowan stared at the map and hunched her shoulders. She slapped the map and announced, "We can do it."

Emma shook Rowan's hand.

Florence watched the women work out their compromise without intervening. "Well, if this works, maybe we can get by without hiring another librarian. I just don't know where I could find another woman to ride. You have become quite the organizer, Rowan, thank you. Now, when do we start?"

Emma and Rowan looked at each other with broad smiles. "Today, of course," Emma suggested.

Florence walked to her desk to find a pencil and two pieces of paper. She wrote each woman's name at the top of the page and then the names of the families for Emma and Rowan to visit. "Bring the map over to my desk, Rowan." She marked an X on the map for the families Emma would visit and an O for those Rowan would visit. "Now, make a copy of the map and make sure you take it with you. Why don't you wait until after lunch to start your new routes. Who wants to ride this afternoon?"

Emma and Rowan looked at each other. "Oh, let's flip a coin. I call heads," Emma said.

Florence flipped the coin and Emma won the toss.

§

That evening Rowan studied the map and memorized the names of the six families she would visit. It was impossible to tell from the map the distance between homes, but Rowan felt that making six visits in just four hours was ambitious. Her regular route had fourteen families and it took her an entire day to complete the circuit. She hoped she would not have to read to children or help someone learn to read on the new route. Selma left her job so quickly there wasn't any time to ask her questions about the families she visited.

The next afternoon Rowan pointed Ash south to begin the new route. The day before Emma returned in a little over four hours. Rowan decided her portion of the route would be about the same. Not quite two miles after leaving Pikeville, the forest closed in and formed an umbrella overhead. Rowan bent over Ash, searching the ground for a trail. Selma made this trip for a year and Rowan expected there would be a horse path to follow. As hard as she looked, she couldn't see the tell-tale sign of horses' hoofs. At one point she jumped off Ash and walked in front of her to search for a trail. No luck.

Rowan didn't notice the sky darken. Thunder clapped. Ash jumped and her nose flared. Rowan held the reins tight, and Ash bucked and ran off into the woods. Rowan ran after her shouting her name. About twenty yards into the woods Ash stopped under the protection of a huge magnolia tree. Rowan rumbled through her bag to find an apple for Ash. In a few minutes the rain lightened and Ash was willing to walk. Rowan and Ash wandered in the woods until dusk. She saw a cabin clinging to a steep hill with a lean-to in the back. Rowan didn't want to disturb the family in the cabin so she made herself at home in the lean-to. *At least we are out of the rain*, she thought.

Rowan smelled the familiar scent of maple wood burning and peeked out. Smoke meandered to the top of the trees. Ash was calm now, and Rowan decided she needed to meet this family even though the cabin wasn't on her map. She pounded on the door.

"Hello, hello. I'm soaked, can I come in?"

"What?"

The door opened a crack. A woman in her fifties with gray-streaked hair pulled back into a bun, stared back at her.

"Oh child, come in, come in."

"I hope you don't mind but I put my horse in your lean-to. The thunder and lightning frightened her so much."

Rowen heard a voice from a bed near the fireplace. "Oh, that's fine. That's ok."

"I should introduce myself. My name is Rowan Daly, and I work at the library in Pikeville. I deliver books and magazines and things to folks like you. Maybe you knew the other woman that rode this route, Selma Rutledge."

Rowan looked from face to face around the room. A man with a stubble beard lay on the bed. The woman stood in the center of the room with three children hiding behind her, taking a peek at the stranger.

"My name is Sadie Teel and that lump stretched out on the bed is my husband, Leland. He's been laid out for months, and we don't know what he's got. This is my oldest, Ella; she's twelve. Next is Maddie; she's ten, and then we have Wyatt; he's eight. There ain't been no other woman like yourself stop at our cabin – we're a bit off the beaten path here." Rowan began to shiver. "Look, you got to get out of those clothes or you'll be sick like old Leland. Ella, fetch a big Army blanket and one of my quilts. Rowan, stand in the corner and get out of all those clothes. Ella and Maddie will hold up the blanket for you. I'll hang your clothes by the fireplace to dry. In the meantime, just wrap yourself in the blanket and quilt. You can sit in the rocker by the fire. I'll make a fresh cup of tea for ya."

Rowan did as instructed even though she was embarrassed beyond words wrapped up by the fire. There wasn't another choice. The rain pounded the shake wood roof, and the wind rattled the loose shakes. In the far corner there was a dribble of water forming a puddle. Sadie threw a rag on the floor to stop the water from flowing into the cabin.

Rowan held the teacup with both hands, taking smalls sips because it was boiling. The three children stood at the edge of the room glaring at the stranger. None of them wore shoes. Ella wore a soiled dress that might have been white once. Her light brown hair hung limp like it might have not been washed. Maddie was just about two inches shorter than Ella. Her hair came down to the bottom of her ears and was parted in the middle. She looked as though she wanted to say something. Little Wyatt had brown eyes that sparkled and a broad smile with crooked teeth. Leland Teel propped himself up on one elbow to get a good look at Rowan's face. In the back corner of the one-room cottage, Sadie stood at the sink cleaning cups. She walked toward Rowan with the tea pot and tripped over the wet canvas book bag on the floor.

"What in the world is that, and why is it on the floor?"

Rowan bent down to pull the bag in front of her. "I'm sorry, Mrs. Teel, that's my book bag. I have books and magazines you can borrow, children's books too. Can...can the children read?"

Sadie's back straightened. "They can read. We're not hillbillies out here. We just like to be on our own. Whenever we can, me and Mr. Teel send the kids to school. They can read seed labels."

"I can still hear the rain beating against the roof. After my clothes dry, I would be happy to read to them," Rowan offered.

"You can stay the night," Mr. Teel shouted from his bed.

Rowan looked around the room. There were several mats on the floor where she guessed the children slept. *Mrs. Teel must crawl in next to her husband.*

"I know it looks slim. You can just stay curled up in those blankets next to the fire for the evening. Of course, that means you need to tend the fire all night. I can send Wyatt out to the shed for more wood before any of us fall asleep. Now, we were about to have supper. Cabbage soup tonight. I hope that suits you, Miss Daly. Besides, it's all we got."

"You are generous to a total stranger. I'm sure it will be delicious."

"Mmmm." Sadie brought a large pot to the fire to warm the soup.

Rowan reached down into her bag and mumbled to herself so that everyone in the room could hear her. "Now let's see, what surprises do I have in my bag?" She pulled out a copy of *Western Story Magazine* that was damp. She hung it on the line stretched across the fireplace where her clothes and undergarments were drying. The canvas bag didn't pass the test of standing up in foul weather. Rowan decided that before the end of the week she would visit the tack store and buy a decent leather bag from her savings.

The Teel family listened to Rowan read after everyone finished their cabbage soup. Ella washed the dishes in the tub, making sure she didn't make noise to interrupt Rowan's reading. Wyatt curled up on the mat on the floor and was asleep right in the middle of the first story. With Leland being ill, he was asleep by the end of the first story. Ella begged for another story as soon as the first was finished.

"Now Ella, Miss Daly must be tired, she had a long ride today from town."

Rowan waved off Sadie's concern. "No worries. Growing up with my grandma I often fell asleep in a rocker next to her fireplace. I'll probably dream of her tonight. Ella, one more story and then we will all go to bed."

A huge smile blossomed on Ella's face. "Oh yes, yes! Maybe you can leave some of those magazines for us. I'm teaching Wyatt how to read."

Rowan's eyes widened. "You are a great big sister. Before I leave tomorrow morning you can pick out three magazines to borrow. I have a copy of Robinson Crusoe I think is perfect for you. Now, let's read the story of a Kansas farm boy, from the *True Story* magazine."

After everyone was asleep, Rowan recovered her clothes from the line stretched across the hearth and dressed. She wrapped the blanket and quilt around her and stretched her feet toward the fire. She thought about everything that happened during the day, and in moments her eyes were drooping and she fell asleep with her chin on her chest.

§

Sadie woke up to a chill in the cabin. She looked toward

the fireplace where only embers smoldered. Rowan had collapsed and didn't add wood to the fire during the night. Sadie tiptoed around Rowan to add several maple logs to the fire and used the bellows to get flames flying high so she could make breakfast and a strong pot of coffee.

One by one each of the Teel's woke up to watch Sadie make breakfast. She had to work around Rowan, who finally woke with the sound of the bubbling coffee pot over the fire.

"We have hot oatmeal this morning for breakfast. I hope you like oatmeal; it's all we got. No milk for it – just water. Coffee's ready. You want a cup?"

Rowan looked around the room. She was the center of attention. "Oh yes, coffee. Do the children drink coffee too?"

"Ella can if she likes. Maddie and Wyatt drink water or milk when we have it. The coffee hurts Leland's stomach so he drinks water, don't ya Leland?"

Leland propped a pillow against the wall and leaned back. "Yup."

The oatmeal was thin but it was hot. Rowan promised herself a hot roast-beef sandwich at the pharmacy counter when she returned to Pikeville. After breakfast she opened the front door to peek out. There were a few clouds high up, big, puffy marshmallow clouds. She took the map to Sadie and asked her to mark where their cabin was located.

"It's kinda hard to tell – I'm not so good with maps. Leland, take this and mark it for Miss Daly."

Leland studied the map for a long time and marked a big "X" in the bottom right-hand corner. It was at least three inches from where the trail was marked. "Well, when a girl gets lost, a girl gets lost. On my ride back to town I'll mark the map so that I can come back here next week. Sadie or Leland, is there a book or magazine I can leave with you?"

They looked across the room at each other. "Well, we ain't what you would call good strong readers."

"I understand," Rowan said in a gentle tone. "I can help when I come next week, if Ella promises to practice with you between visits."

Ella's chest stuck out. "I would be honored."

"That's a plan. I need to get back to Pikeville. Miss Pruett, the head librarian, probably has the sheriff out looking for me. I will have quite a story to tell her. Thank you for all your kindnesses. I will see you all one week from today – in the morning."

Rowan rode so she could mark the map. She rode into Gus's where she was greeted with hurrahs.

"Damn, Miss Daly, we thought the worst happened to you," Gus blurted out.

Rowan jumped off Ash and led her to the water trough. "When she's done quenching her thirst, give her a big bucket of oats. I will pay for it. She must be starved and she got me back safely."

"Will do, will do. Now, you scurry off to the library. Miss Pruett is getting gray hair worrying about you."

Rowan tried to picture Florence with gray hair but couldn't.

Chapter 17

Saturday morning was another overcast day and there was little hope the sun would appear; there was a fifty percent chance of rain today. Rowan read the paper in the parlor after breakfast. Reading the paper made her think of Lucas, and she admitted to herself that she missed his company. Lucas was promoted at the paper and now had the title of Managing Editor. Once her horse-riding lessons ended she had not seen Lucas for more than a year. Pikeville was not such a big town that you wouldn't see someone at the pharmacy or in the courthouse. *For a man in the news business, he was aloof,* she thought.

Some Saturdays she worked at the library a few hours in the afternoon. She ran up the stairs two steps at a time, grabbed her raincoat and was at the library in less than ten minutes. There was a stack of magazines the Boy Scouts had brought in Friday afternoon sitting on the work table. Florence required that all donations be accepted, no matter their condition. The donors had big hearts even if they didn't take care of their magazines and books. In the past year Florence had taught Rowan how to repair books so they were almost like new. The collection grew mostly from donations. There just wasn't money in the city budget to buy new books and magazines.

Rowan spread out the magazines and separated them into two piles. One pile was for those in good enough shape to put into circulation right away. The second pile was those she would try to salvage. She stared at the second pile, racking her brain to come up with what to do with them. At that moment she recalled a conversation she had with Sadie Teel. Sadie wanted a book with quilt patterns. Rowan scoured the library's collection and couldn't find a book devoted to quilt patterns.

She leafed through several of the magazines in front of her that were falling apart and each one had two or three patterns in it. From nowhere an idea burst out of Rowan's mind. She found a pair of scissors and cut out the quilt patterns from each of the magazines. She had a stack of about twenty-seven pictures. Next, she searched through the supply cabinet for construction paper. There was only one size of cream-colored construction paper. Rowan took one piece of construction paper and then laid the quilt pattern on top. She could fit two or three patterns on each page. She brushed the back of each pattern with white glue and put it on the construction paper, then placed several books on top to make sure the magazine page didn't curl up. Once the glue dried she used the hole punch to make three holes on the left side of the paper. She bound twelve pages together with butcher's twine.

Rowan placed her first scrapbook in the center of the work table and turned each page. In this little scrapbook there were thirty-two patterns. Rowan sat straight up in the chair, her eyes shone and she felt a sense of pride.

"What are you doing working on a Saturday afternoon, Rowan?" Florence asked.

"Oh my, I didn't hear you come in."

A faint smile grew across Florence's face as she looked at the pattern scrapbook. "What do you have there?"

Rowan puffed out her chest. "This is a quilt pattern scrapbook. The magazines the Boy Scouts dropped off yesterday afternoon were in terrible shape. I just couldn't throw them away. With my luck someone would see them in the trash can and wonder what was happening. Several of the wives on my Monday route have been asking for quilt-pattern books and I just couldn't find a single one. So, I made one myself by cutting patterns out of these magazines."

"Looks like you're using butcher's twine to bind the pages together," Florence said.

"That's right. I'll hand out the scrap book this week and learn how the ladies like it."

"I give you credit, Rowan, you are a resourceful young woman. I am amazed that you spend your free Saturday afternoon working on a library project. You are passionate you are."

Rowan blushed. "Thank you, Florence. Do you want to help make another scrapbook? Maybe a recipe scrapbook."

Chapter 18

June soon became September and the start of the rainy season. After her first experience being caught in a Kentucky downpour, Rowan always carried a raincoat and hat with her on the route. She gave up the canvas book bag for a leather bag with a flap cover and buckle so the books would stay dry in the bag. Emma and Rowan were able to split Selma's routes without a problem and told Florence, in their view another pack horse librarian wasn't needed. It meant Rowan would work at least part of the day Saturday in the library. Rowan had no interest in socializing with young men in the city and didn't mind the extra work. Emma was determined to be married within a year of Selma's wedding so she spent every Saturday night at a local dance and every Sunday at some church event.

At least once a week Florence, Rowan and Emma would meet for about an hour to review how things were progressing. Florence assigned herself the job of seeking out donations. Emma and Rowan worked on restoring books, making scrap books and organizing the collection.

The three women had formed a close bond based on mutual respect and hard work. However, Emma was looking forward to the day that she didn't need to ride into the hills of Pike County to make a living. She took pride in teaching people how to read but tired of the long hours on her horse and fighting the inclement weather.

One September Friday morning the three women were working on their projects in the library when young Noah from the telegram office burst through the front door waving a small yellow envelope in his hand. "Miss Pruett, Miss Pruett, Mr. Skaggs told me to run over here right now. There's a telegram here for you all the way from Washington D.C."

Florence threw her arms up in the air. "Washington D.C.," she said, her voice almost a scream.

Noah handed her the envelope. Florence searched through her pocket until she found a nickel and handed it to Noah. "You have done yourself proud, young man, thank you."

Noah's eyes widened. "Oh, thank you, Miss Pruett." He turned on his heel and was out the door, forgetting to close it behind him.

Emma and Rowan stared at the envelope in Florence's hand. "Open it, open it," they shouted in unison.

Florence took so much care in opening the envelope that Rowan fidgeted. She pulled the single sheet of paper out and read out loud:

To: Miss Florence Pruett
From: Ellen Woodward
I am interested in learning how you administer
the Pack Horse Librarian Project. Stop. I will visit

you on Monday, October 7th between two and three
o'clock in the afternoon. Stop. I would like to meet
some of the ladies that ride regular routes. Stop.
Mrs. Roosevelt will accompany me. Stop.

The telegram fell from Florence's hand and fluttered to the floor. She gasped for breath and felt faint for the first time in her life.

"Mrs. Roosevelt, coming here? That's less than two weeks away." Rowan had to balance herself on the work table. "Who is Ellen Woodward?"

"I need a new dress and shoes," Emma said.

Florence stood up with care and balanced herself at the work table. "I need a glass of water."

Rowan picked the telegram off the floor and read it to herself several times. Of all places, she wondered why the First Lady of the United States wanted to visit an obscure Appalachian town like Pikeville. Rowan knew she had a reputation for traveling all across the country to see things for herself and report back to Mr. Roosevelt. Pikeville would now be on the map.

Florence took command and gave Emma and Rowan a list of jobs to do. "Ladies, we may need to work through the weekend to get our little library in shape so don't make any plans for the weekend. You can start your list now; I'm going to notify the newspaper and the mayor of our good fortune. I should be back within the hour."

Rowan looked at her list. The first item was to take the books from the shelf, dust the shelf and the books, and return them to the shelf. She stood in the center of the room and turned, looking at all the books. She guessed they had at least 700 books. "What's on your list, Emma?

I have to dust all the shelves and the books. It will take me all weekend for that one job."

Emma set her list on the work table. "Well, I have to sort through all the magazines, toss the ones in bad shape and then organize them by magazine and by date. Next, I have to go to town and find broom handles. Her note says she has an idea to display newspapers. Then I am to organize all the newspapers by date and find a place to display them." Emma held her face in her hands looking tired before she started. "Gee, I wonder what she's going do? I don't think I'll have time to buy a new dress."

Rowan folded her list and put it in her pocket. "I'm going to get started. My guess is that Florence will work on the card catalog. A couple days ago the Boy Scouts brought in boxes of books. She'll want to catalog them and check them for repairs."

The two women went to work and greeted Florence when she returned without complaining about their jobs. Anticipating meeting Mrs. Woodward and Mrs. Roosevelt put the three women into a giddy state. They laughed and joked as they worked. Emma took several piles of magazines to the trash. She hadn't been aware of how shabby their collection was. Florence put a box of books on her desk and inspected each one and made a catalog card for each. She didn't know the source for these books, but they were in horrible condition. Their collection was so sparse she saved every book donated, even if it meant she would spend the next three days on this one job. The women became absorbed in their work and weren't aware of the time. The chime on the courthouse clock startled them.

"Noon! I can't imagine," Rowan blurted out.

"Emma and Rowan, you have been troopers. Let's get lunch at the pharmacy. My treat."

$

All three women dedicated themselves to preparing the library for the Monday afternoon visit. By Monday morning the library was in the best condition it had ever been. Florence invented a way to put a newspaper on part of a broom stick on a rack to hold five newspapers. The newspapers hung straight down so they wouldn't wrinkle. The paper wasn't published on the weekend so the rack held one week's worth of papers. For older papers Emma found shelving to fit behind the rack that patrons could search. The question was how long to keep the newspapers. There wasn't a standard for newspaper retention. Florence decided that they would keep papers for one month as an experiment.

On Monday morning the last job was to mop the floor. Emma and Rowan moved furniture back and forth and Florence mopped the floor with sudsy water and had to rinse mop three times. The three ladies were exhausted when they finished just as the clock tower rang out one o'clock. They were so determined to make the library sparkle they didn't take time for lunch.

"We have just enough time to go to the boardinghouse and change clothes. Maybe Mrs. Perkins can make us a sandwich. I'm going to close the library until Mrs. Woodward and Mrs. Roosevelt arrive. Let's meet in the parlor at one thirty and walk back to the library together," Florence instructed.

Rowan was the first of the women to arrive at the

parlor, followed by Florence; Emma was last. Emma wore a silk green dress with matching shoes. Florence wore a blue suit with black pumps. Rowan wore tan trousers, a flower pattern blouse, and brown and white saddle shoes. "Don't you have a dress, Rowan?" Emma shouted.

"Trousers are modern, Emma, and Mrs. Roosevelt is very modern," Rowan replied.

"There's no time to change; let's go. Emma, don't be so judgmental," Florence said.

"I bet Mrs. Roosevelt or Mrs. Woodward won't be wearing trousers." Emma had to have the last word when it came to fashion.

The clock tower chimed two and then two thirty without Mrs. Woodward and Mrs. Roosevelt arriving at the library. The Mayor and Lucas invited themselves to the meeting because they wanted to meet the famous First Lady. Mayor Woolridge paced, and Lucas examined the newspaper collection. "Whoever came up with the idea to hang newspapers on a broom stick? It is brilliant. Simple but brilliant," he said.

Florence covered her mouth to hide her smile.

"All the credit goes to Florence," Rowan said.

Finally, at three-forty-five the door opened and the guests of honor walked into the library. "Good afternoon, I'm Mrs. Woodward, and I'm sure you recognize Mrs. Roosevelt. Is Miss Pruett here?"

Florence stepped forward and shook hands with both women. She thought to herself that both women looked normal, like they could live in Pikeville. Mrs. Woodward had short, brown-gray hair that looked like it had been permed. She wore a flower pattern silk dress with a hem just below the knee. Mrs. Roosevelt wore a wide-brimmed hat with a large flower in front. Her black silk dress went to the top of her ankles. She wore a large carnation corsage on her large dress lapel. Her oxford shoes had at least two-inch heels, which made her appear more than six feet tall.

"Let me introduce our pack horse librarians. This is Emma Wallace and Rowan Daly. We also have Mayor Woolridge and our newspaper editor, Lucas Tate." Mrs. Roosevelt stood several inches taller than both the mayor and Lucas.

"Oh my, you are both so young," Mrs. Roosevelt said to Rowen and Emma. "I suppose to ride in the hills you need a young person. Now, Florence, show me your library."

Mrs. Roosevelt and Mrs. Woodward displayed a keen interest in the library and asked probing questions to learn how the Pack Horse Librarian Project worked and how they might improve it. Florence explained the challenge of adding all materials to the collection. She explained how she developed routes for Emma and Rowan and divided their time between riding and working in the library.

"Rowan and Emma, is the twenty-eight dollars per month salary adequate?" Mrs. Roosevelt asked.

"Oh yes, we all live at Mrs. Perkins' Boardinghouse," Rowan said. "And we rent our horses from Gus at the livery stable. I buy oats for my horse once a week because she's so special. Did you know we have horses bred to ride in the mountains? They are so sure-footed." Rowan was eager to share her story with Mrs. Roosevelt.

Both Mrs. Roosevelt and Mrs. Woodward scanned the shelves to learn what type of books were in the collection. "How did you get your collection started, Miss Pruett?" Mrs. Woodward asked.

"When Reverend Lamar of the Pikeville Methodist

church retired, he donated his entire collection to the library. We moved into this space when the county courthouse was built. Dr. Lamar said he intended to do a lot of reading with his spare time and needed to donate his books to give him more room in his home library. His collection amounted to over 600 volumes. We wouldn't have a library without him," Florence explained.

"Do you have a budget to buy more books?" Mrs. Roosevelt asked.

"No. I don't know when the county will afford to buy books. I spend most of my time pursuing donations."

Lucas stepped toward Mrs. Roosevelt with pencil and paper in hand, eager to interview the First Lady of the United States. "I'm sorry, young man, I am not taking interviews on this trip. I'm gathering information to share with Mr. Roosevelt on the success of the Pack Horse Librarian Project. If you like, you can write about the project here in Pike County."

Lucas sat down with a frown on his face. "As you like, Mrs. Roosevelt."

"Those trousers look very comfortable, Miss Daly. I should try them sometime," Mrs. Roosevelt said. "Now, how many miles do you ride on your book route?"

Rowan thought before answering. "I'm not honestly sure. Probably between fifteen to eighteen miles for each route, and I ride three times a week. I just keep track of how many families I visit. The bags hold about seventy books, so we limit each family to three books a week. There's not much to do in the hills so they have a lot of time to read. I'm also teaching three folks to read. People often left school to work in the mines and never learned to read well."

Mrs. Roosevelt smiled and shook everyone's hand. "Miss Pruett, I am very impressed. I will have a glowing report for Mr. Roosevelt. I am distressed about your collection. When I return to Washington D.C., I'm going to search through my library. I will donate fifty books to your collection. You can expect a box in the mail in about three weeks." Mrs. Roosevelt walked toward the door. "I have enjoyed meeting everyone. I must leave for Lexington. Goodbye."

Rowan felt light headed and leaned on the work table and her eyes glazed over. "Wasn't that amazing. We met the First Lady of the United States of America – right here in our tiny library. She's taller than I thought she was. People are right, her voice is kind of funny, but who cares?"

"You're right," Emma said.

"She's a role model for all of us," Florence offered.

"I want to be like Mrs. Roosevelt – a smart, independent woman. Did she have an education?" Rowan asked.

"Oh yes, she attended private schools in Europe and two colleges in New York State. She is a highly educated woman. I've done my research," Florence explained.

Rowan twirled around, landing in the chair behind the desk. "Well, maybe I'm going to find a way to go to college too."

Chapter 19

$\mathcal{A}$t the end of October Florence called a special meeting for Thursday afternoon. She asked Rowan and Emma to return from their routes no later than three o'clock in the afternoon. Florence refused to share the reason for the meeting with them except that what she would share was very special. Rowan spent the week trying to guess what the meeting was about by leaving hints and trying to trick Florence into revealing her secret. Her efforts were futile.

Thursday came and both Rowan and Emma promised to be back at the library by three. For Rowan it meant she would rush some of her stops and didn't take time for any reading lessons. Missing one reading lesson was not tragic, in Emma's eyes. She had her light route on Thursdays and didn't have to change anything to return to Pikeville by three o'clock.

Emma and Rowan walked from the livery to the library together. When they arrived, Florence was sitting at her desk with two large cardboard boxes on top of the desk. She looked up from reading a letter. "Hello, hello,

hello!" She greeted them with a broad smile and glistening eyes. "Pull up a chair and join me."

Florence stood up and took a long knife to slit open the lid of the larger of the two boxes. "You recall that Mrs. Roosevelt promised to send us books from her library to add to our collection. These boxes arrived from Washington D.C. earlier this week. I waited until we could meet to open them. Let's see what the First Lady has sent us."

Rowan and Emma jumped up and held the flaps of the box open while Florence took books out and stacked them on the top of the desk. Rowan's eyes widened when she realized how many books the box contained. "Can you imagine, the entire collection of Mark Twain books, even his travel books!" Emma exclaimed.

"They're in mint condition," Rowan observed.

"We are blessed," Florence said as she put the last book from the box on the table. She counted fifty books. "I think Mrs. Roosevelt deserves special recognition for her gift. What would you ladies think if we create an Eleanor Roosevelt collection and merge them into our collection?"

Emma and Rowan didn't hesitate. "Wonderful," they said in unison.

Florence sat in her chair. "I think it would be appropriate to write Mrs. Roosevelt a letter and all three of us sign it. Now, please sit down again, I also have a letter from Mrs. Perryman, our District Supervisor. Let me read it out loud.

"Dear Miss Pruett: I received a letter from Mrs. Woodward on behalf of Mrs. Roosevelt extolling your virtues and the outstanding work you have done for literacy in Pike County. Your library has been selected as one of four libraries in Kentucky to test the use of a visual device called the 'Tru-Vue.' We would like you to test it with your patrons for two months. The objective of the test will be to determine if they are easy to use, if the films are appropriate and we would like to know the general response of families in Pike County. Within several days of receiving this letter you will receive a box with the Tru-Vue, instructions and ten films. Please plan on sending me your evaluation no later than December 15th. Congratulations. Respectfully Ethel Perryman, District Supervisor.

"Rowan, would you open the box, please."

Rowan slit the box around the edges. Inside was stuffed with newspaper. She removed the paper to find the Tru-Vue. Underneath was a one-page instruction sheet and ten films. The device looked like a pair of binoculars with a slot on one side to insert the film and a handle at the bottom to advance each of the frames. Emma took the Tru-Vue from Rowan. "I've read about these. They are the newest rage. It helps people who can't read."

"This will be perfect for the Teel family," Rowan said.

"Hand it to me, Emma, let me see what films we have," Florence said. "Oh, here's one on the Rocky Mountains." Florence slid the film into the Tru-Vue like she had done it a hundred times. She lifted it toward the ceiling light and looked in. She gasped. "Even in black and white the mountains are so vivid. You can see a glacier. You're right, Rowan, this will be perfect for the Teel family. Take it to them on your route next Monday. Let them know they can only use it for a week. I want as many families as possible to use it before we write our report to Mrs. Perryman."

Rowan practiced with the Tru-Vue in her room. She wanted to insert the films with ease and become familiar with each of the films. She wiggled the first film in the slot and pushed it in too hard; the film bound up. She took it out and studied the slot. The film had to be inserted at the perfect angle. Rowan practiced inserting the film over and over until she could do it blindfolded. She held the Tru-Vue up to see pictures of the Barnum and Bailey Circus. There were lions, tigers, elephants, clowns riding unicycles – all pictures of a strange, fascinating world that would make a child giggle. There was a film on famous landmarks in America – like the Washington Monument in Washington D.C. – and a film on national parks, including the Great Smoky Mountain National Park with close-up pictures of black bears. It had been a long day and Rowan fell back on her pillow and drifted off to sleep with the Tru-Vue next to her and the films spread across the bed.

Rowan woke when she heard footsteps up and down the hall. She opened the curtain and greeted a sun-shiny Friday. She packed the Tru-Vue and films, and rushed to eat a small breakfast. Then she changed into riding clothes and walked to the livery to get Ash ready for the Friday route. Rowan worried that she may not make all her stops today because she was sure it would take some time with the Teel family to instruct them on using the Tru-Vue.

She urged Ash to walk on. The morning air had a tinge of cold and a few leaves covered the trail. Rowan looked forward to her route when the autumn colors reached peak, just before dropping to the forest floor when the trees went bare for the winter. Autumn also brought a smoky, musty fragrance to the air.

When Rowan rode up to the Teel homestead, all four children were stacking wood in the lean-to behind the house. Staying warm in the winter was always a challenge, and it didn't seem possible to have too much wood stacked up to fight off winter cold.

"Hello, children; take a break and come inside. I have a surprise for you."

Rowan jumped off Ash and let her wander to find fresh grass. The children rushed in front of her to find their places to sit on the cabin floor. "What's our surprise? What's our surprise?" Wyatt was eager to find out.

"Sadie, why don't you take a break from cleaning the kitchen. Leland, sit up now. I think you are going to like what I brought."

Rowan reached into her bag and used both hands to take out the Tru-Vue box. She sat the box on the floor in front of the children. "Do any of you want to guess what's in the box?"

"Oh, that's not fair. Just show us, just show us," Ella insisted.

Rowan opened the box with extreme care, pulled out the Tru-Vue and set it on her hand to display to the Teel family. They sat staring at it. Sadie put her hands to her mouth. Leland scratched his head. The children stared at the object with open mouths.

"What is that?!" Leland shouted.

Rowan broke out in an enormous smile. "This, Teel family, is called a Tru-Vue. It comes with ten films. You put a film in the bottom, point it toward the light and use this lever on the bottom to move the pictures. I have ten films you can look at. It is a special gift from the library office in Washington D.C. They want us to test it and find out if you like it. I can leave the Tru-Vue with you, but I will need to pick it up when I'm back on Monday. Now, who wants to be first?"

Wyatt jumped up. "Me, me, me. Oh please, me first!"

"I have a film of the Barnum and Bailey Circus that I am sure you will like. Let me show you how to insert the film. Before I leave today I want each of you to choose a film and learn how to insert it and look at the pictures." The family watched Wyatt thread the film like an expert in his first attempt.

The Teel family was so engrossed in watching films they didn't notice Rowan slip out the door to finish her route.

Chapter 20

$\mathcal{M}$rs. Perkins was just finishing up in the kitchen from Saturday lunch when a visitor arrived for Rowan. This was the first time in two years she had a visitor. She trotted upstairs, knocked on Rowan's door but didn't wait for a response and rushed into the room to find Rowan reading near the window. "Rowan, Rowan, Lucas Tate is downstairs – he's calling on you. Oh dear, you must get out of your room on this fine Saturday afternoon."

Rowan jumped up, and the book fell to the floor. "Lucas Tate?"

"Yes. Now take a few minutes to brush your hair. It wouldn't hurt to put on a little lipstick. I'll talk with Lucas for a few minutes."

Rowan changed into a dress, brushed her hair but decided against lipstick. Lipstick just seemed too forward to Rowen. Maybe he just wanted to get into the library. Florence allowed Lucas access to the library any time he wanted if someone was available to open it. *Why had Mrs. Perkins said Lucas was calling on her? That is presumptuous.*

Rowan stared into the mirror, her face was flushed – not a good look, she decided. She sat on the edge of the bed and took long slow breaths to build the courage to walk downstairs.

Lucas jumped to his feet when Rowan walked into the parlor. "Thank you for talking with me, Mrs. Perkins."

Lucas turned to Rowan. "Hello, Rowan. Sorry for the surprise but I had this great idea. I want to know if you're interested."

"Hello, Lucas, it's nice to see you too. I think it's been almost two years since our last riding lesson. Interested? In what?"

Lucas wrung his hands, "Well, *The Good Earth* is playing at the cinema this afternoon. You know, based on Pearl S. Buck's book. I'm sure you've read it. Everybody has. I have. I didn't want to go to the movies by myself. I just guessed that you being a librarian, you would have read the book and would like to see the movie." Lucas pulled a pocket watch from his trousers. "Well, look at that, it starts in just thirty minutes. We don't have to go Dutch. I can pay for your ticket. Well?"

Rowan looked back and forth between Lucas and Mrs. Perkins then stared at the floor, unable to look up. She couldn't find words.

"It's time for me to leave. Stop by any time, Lucas." Mrs. Perkins left.

Rowan and Lucas were left in the parlor standing less than three feet apart. They might as well have been on either side of the Red River gorge. Rowan shuffled her feet. She cleared her throat and looked at Lucas. "I accept your offer. I have read the book and enjoyed it very much. China is such a different place from Pikeville."

The couple walked to the movie house in silence. Lucas paid for their tickets, opened the lobby door for Rowan, then motioned toward the candy and popcorn counter. "Would you like some popcorn or anything?"

"No thank you. Buying my ticket was enough."

"Do you have a favorite place you like to sit in a movie theater?" Lucas asked.

"This is my first time going to a movie in Pikeville."

"Well, I like to sit in the back row in the middle. I don't know why, I just do. Would that be all right?"

"Yes."

"I read that Paul Muni is playing the role of Wang Lung. There is one Chinese actress – Soo Yong – she plays Aunt," Lucas explained. "I wonder what the movie will be like with everyone speaking English?"

"I'm impressed, Lucas, you have done a lot of research about this movie."

The lights went dark, and Rowan and Lucas sat in silence until the lights came back on.

"Well, I thought the move from book to movie screen went well," Lucas said. "Luise Rainer is a fine actress. I'm sure she'll get nominated for an Oscar. What do you think?"

"I agree. Rainer did a fantastic job. Although in both the book and movie, I felt sorry for her character; her sacrifice for her family was remarkable. You should write a review for the newspaper, Lucas, maybe then more people would see the movie. The theater is only half full this afternoon. What time is it?"

Lucas looked at his watch. "Oh, it's just four o'clock. Do you have time to stop for a phosphate or maybe a milk shake before we walk back to the boardinghouse?"

"I should get back. Mrs. Perkins serves dinner promptly at five o'clock on the weekends. She says she wants the evenings free for us girls to have some fun. Today is one of my favorite dinners: calf liver with creamed corn and mashed potatoes with a big buttermilk biscuit drowning in honey. Do you want to come? I'm sure Mrs. Perkins has enough food, and she would love to have you."

Lucas stopped on the sidewalk outside the boarding-house. He avoided eye contact with Rowan. "That's very kind. I'm not much of a liver person. I should go back to the office and write a review of the movie like you suggested. I hope you enjoyed it. Maybe we can do it again soon."

Rowan brushed her hair back with one hand. "I enjoyed it, thank you. I have a question for you, Lucas, was this a date?"

Lucas turned and walked back into town as if he didn't hear Rowan's question. Half way down the block he turned and waved. Rowan waved back, confused and disappointed he didn't answer her question.

$

October slid into November. Lucas and Rowan spent time together almost every weekend. Rowan had learned to love riding in the rolling hills surrounding Pikeville and often suggested to Lucas they take an afternoon ride. Some days they would leave mid-morning and take a picnic with them. Lucas always asked for egg salad sandwiches with lettuce, cold lemonade from a thermos and chocolate cupcakes. It was the same picnic every time. Rowan tried to get him to try something else, like maybe a fried egg sandwich. His view was that if you liked something, there was no need to change or try something else. Rowan found it a peculiar trait of his.

In the winter Rowan learned to dance the swing and the jitterbug. She felt the jitterbug was silly but had to admit it was fun. She and Lucas took lessons at the dance hall on Saturday nights for a nickel. The lessons started at six o'clock and the dance would start at seven o'clock. By nine o'clock each Saturday Rowan couldn't go on and asked Lucas to walk her back to the boardinghouse. Emma couldn't understand why Rowan was always back in her room early on a Saturday night. At least once a week Emma would tease Rowan that she was "square." Rowan didn't care what Emma thought.

One weekend in late November Rowan felt the need to be alone and told Lucas she wouldn't be available for any "fun" when he stopped by the boardinghouse. He shrugged his shoulders. "I can always go back to the office."

"You can ask, Emma, she's always looking for a good time," Rowan suggested as Lucas opened the front door to leave.

Lucas stopped and jerked his head toward Rowan, his eyes were dazed. "You'd let me take Emma out?"

Rowan crossed her arms. "Let you take Emma out? You don't need my permission to go out with Emma or any other woman in town. I don't own you, Lucas Tate."

"But...but...but we've been together every weekend for almost three months. That must mean something?" He opened his arms.

"I don't feel like talking anymore. Goodbye, Lucas." Rowan turned, walked to her room and slammed the door behind her. She had a long route the day before and soon fell asleep.

§

A soft knock on the door woke Rowan. "Rowan? It's Florence. I think we should talk."

Rowan sat up, rubbing sleep from her eyes. "Come in."

Florence sat at the edge of her bed. "I saw Lucas at the pharmacy. He was sullen and in a foul mood. I asked him what was wrong, and he said I should talk to you."

"Oh, Florence, I just told him I didn't want to do anything this weekend. I need some time by myself. That's not a crime. The new route tires me, and I need time to recoup."

Florence put her arms around Rowan's shoulder. "I have noticed you've spent every weekend with Lucas since July. I guess it would be normal for him to expect that you would spend this weekend with him. What do you feel for Lucas? Are you falling in love?"

Rowan pulled away. "Love? Eli is my only love."

"Does Lucas know? Well, is he seeing anyone else?"

Rowan puffed up her pillow and leaned against it, drawing her legs up to her chest. "I don't know. I've never asked. I told him he could ask Emma if she wanted to go out today."

"How did he react?"

"Like a wounded puppy; he pouted off."

Florence stood and paced the floor next to Rowan's bed. She struggled for the right words. She stopped and turned to face Rowan. "Are you really that innocent?"

Rowan stared straight ahead, refusing to look at Florence. "I don't know what you mean?"

"Well, young lady, it's clear to everyone in town that Lucas is sweet on you. Who knows, he may even be in love with you. Have you kissed?"

Rowan's eyes flared. "No.

"He's fun to be with. Kind. He can talk about any topic under the sun. He rides well. We've learned to dance and giggle. But I can't say I have feelings for him. Not like it was with Eli. Eli is the love of my life – period. Can't Lucas be my friend?"

Florence sat back on the bed and smoothed Rowan's hair. "I understand, I do. You need to take off your blinders. Lucas has developed genuine feelings for you. My guess is he loves you, and I wouldn't be surprised if he pops the question someday. You owe it to him to share your feelings. Remember, I have a lost love too. I know the hole it leaves in your life can never be filled. Does Lucas know about the accident in New Hope?"

"No. I don't talk about it. I still miss Eli every day." Rowan hugged Florence and buried her face in her shoulder. "What should I do? I don't want to hurt Lucas. I've been so dumb."

Florence pulled back and held Rowan's face in her hands. "You need to ask yourself what you need. Can you open your heart again? Eli isn't here. You can love him and learn to love another man. It doesn't mean that you are betraying Eli. Explore your heart and then share the truth with Lucas. That's the only answer."

Chapter 21

$\mathcal{B}$y September, 1939, the Pack Horse Librarian Program in Pike county grew by sixty families, and the library office authorized Florence to hire the maximum of four pack horse librarians. In October of that year she hired Thelma Whitaker, who also taught elementary school part time. The school district didn't have the money for a full-time teacher even though she had forty-two children in her class. Thelma grew up in Pikeville and attended the University of Pikeville, earning her bachelor degree in elementary education three years earlier. She was three years older than Rowan and still lived at home.

Florence tried to serve all the families with three pack horse librarians but the recent change made it too great of a challenge. The demand from adults to learn how to read grew, and the pack horse librarians volunteered to take on the job. Rowan was eager to teach people to read. "This is how I change lives," Rowan often said. By December Florence agreed with the staff to hire a fourth librarian. She posted an ad in the Pikeville newspaper, and Lucas was kind enough not to charge a fee for it.

Three women applied for the job, which Florence had not expected. The major requirement for the job was to ride well, supply your own horse or mule, and be familiar with the hills around Pikeville. Of the three job seekers, one lived just a mile and a half out of town on a small tobacco farm with her husband and two children. Hazel Chambers lived in Pike County all her life and could even navigate the hills on horse in the dark. Her children were old enough to stay at home by themselves and because of the tobacco farm, they kept two horses. Florence hired Hazel the day she interviewed.

With four employees who never usually saw each other, Florence had staff meetings once a month on Thursday mornings. Each meeting was limited to one hour. Florence created an agenda and allowed fifteen minutes at the end of the meeting to bring up any topic they wanted to discuss. The January agenda, Hazel's first meeting, read as follows:

Pikeville Pack Horse Librarians
Weekly Meeting
January 4, 1940

I. *Review library duties*
    a.   *Sort magazines*
    b.   *Create cards for card catalog*
    c.   *Inspect books donated*
    d.   *Shelf books*
    e.   *Create scrap books*
    f.   *Sweep floor*

II. *Report on routes from each librarian*
III. *Report on Tru-Vue circulation*
IV. *Report on reading instruction*

Florence arrived at the library at eight-thirty with a cup of coffee in hand. "Good morning, ladies. Are we ready to begin?"

"Yes, Miss Pruett," Hazel said.

"We are informal here, Hazel, and we use first names – so Florence, please. Hazel you've been with us for almost four weeks. How is it going?"

Hazel took a moment before answering. Biting her lower lip, she looked at Rowan, Emma and Thelma but avoided Florence's eyes. She hunched her shoulders. "Um, fine."

Hazel gave the impression that she had worked on a farm her whole life. She always wore a tan shirt, brown Levi trousers and boots. Her cropped haircut looked like it was cut with shears at home. She looked years older than thirty-five from a lifetime spent outdoors working.

"Well, let's get to the first item on our agenda: the jobs to get done on your days working in the library. With four of you I would like to have one person Monday through Thursday in the library and all of you on a route on Fridays. Do any of you have a preference which day you work in the library?"

Rowan raised her chin and licked her lips. "I want to work in the library on Thursdays after our meeting. Mondays and Fridays I have the most families. I like to collect some books on Monday after delivering them on Friday. Most children fly through the comic books and small books during the weekend. For those families who get a

Tru-Vue on Friday, I should expect them to return it on Monday."

"Your thoughts, Emma?" Florence asked.

"I agree with Rowan on the Tru-Vue. I don't care which day I work in the library. I have about an equal number of families on each route."

"Since I'm the newest, I'll work on whatever day you want me to," Hazel said.

Thelma looked at Florence, then said, "I need to learn more about the jobs in the library, but it doesn't matter to me what day I'm here. My job at the school is very uncertain. I haven't been scheduled to teach for weeks. When I ask the principal, he behaves like he didn't hear me."

"Fine. Let's try this. Hazel – Monday, Emma – Tuesday, Thelma – Wednesday and Rowan – Thursday. Now, report on routes."

Hazel raised her hand and spoke before being recognized. "I may have three more families. The word is getting around. How does that work? I mean who decides if we add a family to the route?"

Florence stiffened. "Well, I do. However, I rely on each librarian to tell me if the location of the family fits best in their route or another librarian's route. Talk to me about it when you come in this afternoon, Hazel. Any other reports?" The women shook their heads.

Thelma wrinkled her nose and moved to the edge of her chair. "I'm glad we're going to talk about the Tru-Vue use. I've noticed several of the films are in bad, bad shape. Do we have money to replace them?"

Emma laughed out loud. "Teachers are always wanting new material. But I agree with you. Those films are over two years old. The Tru-Vue is the most popular item we have. Do we have any money for replacement, Florence?"

Florence dropped her head and closed her eyes. "We have fifteen dollars for the year to replace books. Should we allocate part of that money to replace films? I think that's my decision. Rowan, what is your view?"

Rowan leaned in. "Most of our books are donated, and we don't spend to purchase them. We need money to repair books. What do each of you think?"

"We agree," Emma, Thelma and Hazel chimed in.

"Fine, I will order three new films this week," Florence said.

Rowan raised her hand before Florence finished her sentence.

"Yes, Rowan"

"I have an idea about the reading instruction. I have eleven families on my routes with both adults and children needing reading instruction. Teaching reading takes a lot of time. On the days I teach reading, I struggle to finish my route. That's why sometimes I don't get back until six o'clock and depend on Mrs. Perkins to save a warm plate for me for dinner. So, I thought we should have one of us do all the reading lessons and divide the delivery routes up among the others. I would like to teach reading. By accident I've discovered a new method to teach words. Instead of memorizing words, I have them sound out the word, and they learn the meaning of the word in the story's context. Thelma, you have a college degree. Maybe you should teach reading."

Florence had a tentative smile. "You never fail to surprise me, Rowan. How did you discover this way to teach reading?"

Rowan's chest puffed up and she sat straight up in her chair. "Accident. The adults got frustrated memorizing words so I pretended to have a spelling bee. So I started dividing words into parts, even simple words like "harvest or blan-ket.""

"My Lord, that is brilliant," Thelma said. "I teach history, geography and basic mathematics, not reading. I think your idea is amazing."

Florence shuffled her feet and squeezed her hands together. "At the risk of being skeptical, I think we should go slow."

"I only have one family I help read and I hate it. You can start today if I had my way, Rowan," Emma said.

"Well, each of you give me the list of families you are teaching to read. Tomorrow I will try to put together a route. Thelma, you can help me with the route and determine the time needed to ride the route. Oh, besides family names, write how much time you spend with lessons. Rowan, before we undertake this change, I would like to see how you teach," Florence said.

Rowan sat at the edge of her chair. "Tomorrow I visit the Teel family. Leland Teel has been working diligently because he feels it will help him get a job. I have said nothing about that to him, no false hope, but in my heart I feel he's right. Can you ride with me tomorrow?"

"I will make time," Florence said.

"Excuse me," Emma said with enthusiasm. "I have an announcement. My Rodney proposed and I said YES."

Florence flopped into her chair. "Well, this is unexpected."

"Not to me," Emma said.

"Do you plan on quitting?" Florence asked.

"Yes. This is my week notice," Emma beamed.

"A week," Florence repeated.

"Congratulations," the other women chimed in.

$

The next morning the sun revealed a clear blue sky, like a crystal. There was a fresh scent in the air that reminded Rowan of the magnolias blossoming in the spring. Rowan and Florence gobbled down breakfast and took their plates to the kitchen without saying goodbye to Mrs. Perkins. The women changed into riding clothes and bolted down the stairs. They found two brown sacks on the dining room table. Rowan peeked in to find a pimento sandwich, sweet pickles and an apple. She handed one sack to Florence. "Mrs. Perkins is absolutely the sweetest."

They stepped out onto the porch and paused. The boardinghouse faced east and the sun greeted the women with a soft warmth. They both took deep breaths to savor the freshness of the morning, and they turned and smiled at each other before a brisk walk to the livery.

"Gus will be surprised to see me this morning," Florence said. "I'll give him an extra quarter today for surprising him. He'll have a horse for me, won't he?"

Rowan chuckled. "Well, if not a horse, there's always the mule."

$

"Well, Miss Pruett, are you riding today?" Gus said.

"Yes, I am – if you have an animal for me."

"Absolutely. Old Sadie hasn't been out for two weeks.

Sadie was the first Tennessee Walker I ever owned. It will do her good to be on the trail again."

Rowen walked into the barn to get Ash.

"Is this a long route today, Rowan?" Gus asked.

Rowan had gone to the barn and was walking Ash toward Gus and Florence. "I'm sorry, I didn't hear you Gus. I was greeting Ash."

"Is this a long route today? I want to make sure Sadie is the right horse for Miss Pruett."

Rowan swung her leg up and mounted Ash. "No, we should be back by mid-afternoon. We only have ten families to visit and none of them are high in the hills."

Gus brought Sadie out and gave her two cubes of sugar and a few carrots to Ash. "Have a pleasant day, ladies." Florence handed Gus two quarters. "Oh no ma'am, it's only a quarter a day. Take this back now." Gus handed a quarter back to Florence.

"I deeply appreciate having a ride today, Gus. A person should plan but this opportunity just came up yesterday. You deserve a little extra. Now, give me a boost."

$

The women rode in silence until they were several miles from town. "I want to tell you something, Florence. I've decided to stop seeing Lucas. I'm sure he wants a romantic relationship and it's still too soon for me. The best thing for both of us would be to stop seeing each other."

Florence kept riding without making a comment. In her heart she felt Rowan was making a mistake but felt it was better to keep her view to herself. "Is the Teel family your first stop?"

Rowan understood the cue; Lucas was not a topic they would discuss. "Yes, I set the route up that way because we study reading. I spend a lot more time with them than when I just drop off materials. This is the family that I stayed overnight with when I was caught in the downpour several years ago. They are the sweetest."

"How did the reading study begin?"

"One day the children wanted to show me how well they read. There are three children: Ella – fourteen, Maddie – twelve and Wyatt – ten. Mr. Teel is ill from some unknown misery – he spends most his day in bed. During one child's reading demonstrations, Wyatt asked his father to read from a comic book. He held the book with both hands and studied the drawing. Using the drawing, he made up a story. After that I asked if he would like help with the story. He accepted and never admitted he couldn't read." Rowan reined in Ash. "That's their cabin nestled into the hill."

The children heard the hoofs of the approaching horses and ran out of the house, screaming and jumping up and down. "Miss Rowan, Miss Rowan!" Seeing Florence, they quit jumping and stared at her. "Who's that, Miss Rowan?"

Rowan and Florence dismounted. "This is the head librarian, Miss Pruett. She's my boss. Now, introduce yourselves properly."

"I'm Wyatt – the only boy – except daddy."

"Ella – the oldest."

"Maddie."

Wyatt grabbed Rowan's hand and dragged her up the wooden steps into the house. Florence motioned for the children to follow Rowan and was the last to go inside. The room was smoky from burning soft pine wood in the fire-place, but the smell of pine was pleasant. Florence looked around the room. They stacked the sleeping mats in one corner, and the dirt floor looked as if they had swept it this morning. They stacked clean dishes on one side of the washtub. A teapot sat on the wood table surrounded by enough cups for everyone. Not a single cup matched. Leland sat up in bed when Florence walked into the room. He wore a filthy t-shirt and covered himself up when he saw Florence.

"For God's sake, Sadie, get me my brown shirt – we got company. Rowan, who is this?"

Florence looked about the room for a chair to sit down but didn't see one and was reluctant to ask. "I'm Miss Florence Pruett, the Pikeville Librarian. I wanted to meet the families of our pack horse librarians."

Sadie grabbed Florence's hand with a two-handed shake. "We are honored to have you visit. We just love Rowan. Why, she's like a member of the family. It's a downright miracle how she's helping Leland with his reading. That Rowan has a gift – you mark my words, Miss Pruett."

A tear dropped from the corner of Florence's eye. She wiped it away with a quick sweep of her hand, hoping no one had noticed.

Sadie stared at Florence. "What in the world, Miss Pruett. What are you crying about?"

Florence stiffened. "I must have dust in my eyes from the trail, that's all. I have allergies too, maybe there's pollen in the air. Never mind."

Wyatt tugged at Rowan's sleeve. "What's in your bag for me, Miss Rowan?" Rowan opened her bag to search for a comic and pulled out a *True Detective* and a *American Detective* magazine. "I packed these especially for you, Wyatt." She dug into the bag again and found *Of Mice and Men* for Ella and a *True Story* magazine for Maddie. She handed Sadie several *Life* magazines. "How are you feeling about your words today, Leland?" Rowan asked.

Leland was struggling to button his shirt and wasn't paying any attention.

"Leland! Miss Rowan asked you a question."

"Huh?"

Rowan sat on the bed next to Leland. "Did you practice the sounds I left with you last week?"

"Oh yes. Mother, where's those sheets. I can't remember. But I practiced; I'll show you."

Sadie handed Leland three sheets of paper with neat printing. He took them from her and held them with both hands. "Ok, now I'll prove it to you.

"Long "ee" sound.

 "Feet. Sheep. Wheel. Need."

Leland shuffled the papers.

"'Ea' sound.

"Eagle. Pea. Leaf. Teacher. Seat.

"This is the last one.

"'O'.

"Snow. Elbow. Hollow."

"May I see those sheets please, Mr. Teel?" Florence asked.

Leland gathered them together and passed them to Florence. "My name be Leland."

Florence raised her eyebrows and studied the three sheets. *The distinctive perfect printing is familiar.* It looked like the cards for the card catalog Rowan had made.

"Just tryin' to remember words is way too hard for me. Now I sound them out and figure out how they make sense in the story. I have to read out loud, and sometimes it bothers mother."

"Is that a *Master Detective Magazine* by your pillow?" Florence asked.

"It sure is. I can read it too." Leland read several pages and took the time to sound out the words he didn't know.

Rowan had a broad smile when he finished.

"Leland, that was remarkable. You should be proud." Florence checked her watch. "This was delightful. I've enjoyed meeting all of you but Rowan and I must go."

Part III

Chapter 22

"Florence, Florence." Mrs. Perkins ran upstairs to the end of the hall to the last room, facing the street. She pounded on Florence's door. "Open the door, Florence, open the door, it's important."

Florence opened the door just enough to see Mrs. Perkins panting and waving a piece of paper. "Why are you so flustered?"

"You have a Western Union Telegram. A Western Union Telegram always means something important and rarely good news. I was sent a telegram when my husband had his accident on the railroad – the first telegram didn't even tell me it was a fatal accident. I hope nobody died; I surely hope not."

"Thank you, Mrs. Perkins." Florence reached out a hand, took the telegram and shut the door.

The room Florence rented in the boardinghouse was the largest one facing the street. It had a large bay window with Irish lace curtains. On one side of the window sat a royal blue swan chaise and on the other side a fauteuil-style chair with brown upholstery and light pine wood arms and legs. There was also a matching footstool. Florence sat in the chair and often read in the evenings until dusk. Hers was the only room with striped wall paper; all the others were painted. A large chandelier hung from the ceiling near the foot of her full-size bed. All the other rooms had single beds. She also had both a mahogany dresser with a full-size mirror attached and a matching wardrobe. Opposite the bed next to the wall sat a cherry-wood writing desk and matching chair. There were times Florence wished the room had a private bath. When this house was built, private baths were not considered. The entire family was expected to share a single bath. The home was unique because it had a bath on the first floor next to the laundry.

Florence went to the chair next to the window, put her feet up on the stool and placed the telegram in her lap. The telegram operator had written her name in pencil on the outside of the envelope. She agreed with Mrs. Perkins' sentiment that telegrams rarely brought good news. Mailing a letter with a penny stamp was much less expensive even though it might take a week or more to be delivered. A ten-word telegram would cost two dollars and seventy cents. There was no way to learn who had sent the telegram or where it came from by anything written on the envelope.

She kept her hands on her lap covering up the telegram. Florence rubbed her hands together until they turned red. She took a deep breath and tore the envelope open to pull out the telegram.

Dear Miss Florence Pruett,
    Opportunity at Frost Library. Arrive by May 31. No reply needed.
                           Dr. Norman Parsons

Florence closed her eyes and recalled the image of her college mentor, Dr. Norman Parsons. To describe Parsons as fastidious would be kind. He parted his black hair down the middle, combed it straight back and always used hair pomade, which made his hair glisten in sunlight. He was clean shaven except for a mustache he curled at the ends with mustache wax. His eyes were like a red tail hawk and his students swore he never blinked. Dr. Parsons had been the director of the Library Science program at Berea College since anyone could remember. He was often given credit for developing the program, but the actual history was lost.

During her years at Berea, Florence became fond of Dr. Parsons in the way that twenty-year-old college girls become attracted to their father-figure teachers. Dr. Parsons had a reputation of being stern but fair and an outstanding academic. He had a unique straightforward lecturing style. In part, he passed along knowledge, and in part, he required his students to engage in critical thinking.

Florence read the telegram again. Terse and to the point, as she would expect from Dr. Parsons, yet it took eleven words. She wondered how much the extra word cost Dr. Parsons or was the telegram operator willing to make a small allowance. She sat in the chair and looked at the oak tree in the front yard sway back and forth in the late afternoon breeze. Her mind wandered, recalling her college days, when life was so different. Florence reveled in the challenges of college. More than once she considered an advanced degree to teach college herself someday. That would have meant leaving Berea after graduation, and she needed a job not another degree. The timing of the job opening in Pikeville was perfect. Dr. Parsons wrote a glowing recommendation to the search committee. They offered Florence the job immediately following her interview.

When she attended Berea, Dr. Parsons had a staff of four librarians and three student assistants. Her freshman year Florence volunteered to work in the library to satisfy her work requirement. Dr. Parsons hired her as a paid employee in her sophomore year. Working as a librarian became Florence's dream in her second year of college.

Florence folded the telegram and returned it to the envelope. She leaned her head back in the chair to let the late afternoon sun kiss her cheek. She drifted off into a light sleep.

"Florence! Dinner!" Rowan shouted outside her door.

She jumped up, letting the telegram fall to the floor and knocking over the footstool. "I'll be down. I need to wash my face first."

$

Once a week the pack horse librarians shared dinner at the boardinghouse. Florence was quieter at dinner than usual. Thelma and Hazel bantered back and forth. The rest of the women were uncertain if their back and forth was in fun or had a serious, harmful undertone, but it occurred at each shared evening meal.

At breakfast during the week everyone was too intent

on finishing the meal and going to work. The weekend breakfast meal was relaxed and conversational.

Rowan felt Florence was staring at her during the meal, which made her uncomfortable because it was so out of character. Finally, Rowan couldn't contain herself.

"Florence – what? You've been staring at me the whole meal. Is there lettuce caught in my teeth or something?"

Florence cringed. "Oh, I am so sorry, dear. I am preoccupied."

"She received a telegram this afternoon. Everyone knows telegrams are bad news," Mrs. Perkins blurted out.

Florence folded her napkin and placed it on top of her plate. "Do you have plans this evening, Rowan?"

"Well, yes and no. I want to write up more of those word sound sheets but it can wait."

"Let's take a walk in the woods," Florence said.

§

It was warm for an eastern Kentucky spring day. Both Rowan and Florence wore sandals. Rowan even wore a square cut sleeveless blouse and shorts. Florence pulled her hair back into a pony tail to be cool but wore a long sleeve blouse like she wore working in the library. When the two women were at the edge of the forest, Florence rolled up her sleeves. The warm weather brought out the creamy white magnolia blossoms each with a delicate lemon-vanilla scent. Both women stopped and breathed in the intoxicating fragrance.

"I received a telegraph today, Rowan."

"Everyone knows. You would think Mrs. Perkins had never received a telegram."

"She has. When her husband died in the railroad accident."

"How horrible."

"My telegram was from Dr. Norman Parsons, the director of Frost Library at Berea College. He wants me to pay him a visit by the end of the month."

"Why?"

"I really don't have any idea, but it triggered an idea. I want you to join me on the road trip to Berea." Florence took a few steps. "Let's sit under that magnolia tree."

"Why do you want me to come?"

"I would like you to see the campus, meet some people. You are the perfect candidate for Berea College."

Rowan put her hands behind her head and leaned against the tree. She watched the sunlight dance through the leaves and giant blossoms.

"Rowan?"

Rowan sat up and turned toward Florence. "You think I'm college material – me?"

"Berea would be perfect for you. There is no tuition, but you will be required to work on campus about fifteen to twenty hours a week. If you live in the residence halls, it will not cost you, and they provide meals six days a week. You should be able to earn enough working on campus for books, entertainment and the necessities of living on a college campus. I could help you get a job in the library. Your experience as a pack horse librarian would make you a shoe-in."

Rowan leaned back against the tree once more and let the thought of attending college swirl around her mind. She would never have thought about attending college. It was never a desire, and even now with Florence's offer, it wasn't a goal of hers. She just couldn't picture it – a plain girl from Marion County. Working in the Pikeville library was satisfying for Rowen. She often imagined herself working at the library until she retired. The Pack Horse Librarian Project was so popular Rowan thought it would carry on for years.

Florence gave Rowan space to ponder the idea. "Well, let's walk back. Tomorrow morning I'll let the other ladies know I will be gone a few days next week. I'm leaving bright and early Monday morning. Let me know by Sunday evening if you'll make the road trip with me. It will be fun. Really. Give yourself a chance, Rowan."

Rowan spent the week deciding whether to make the trip. Her self-confidence was not high, and she feared making another radical change in her life from the comfort of Pikeville. In the past few years she had made a home in Pikeville, felt safe and lost her fear of abandonment. She felt going to college would be like tossing her fate to the wind. She took several walks around town and to the edge of the forest. She tried very hard to imagine a picture of herself attending college, she would be older than the other students and because of finances would need to live in the residence halls. She wondered what would it be like to live with eighteen-year-old women?

Rowan lost her appetite and avoided going to meals for several days. By Friday Florence knew she had to try and help Rowan; she seemed incapable of making a decision. After dinner Florence tapped on Rowan's door.

"Rowan, Rowan we need to talk. I'm going to come in now."

Florence walked into the room and shut the door

softly behind her. She found Rowan curled up in a fetal position on the bed with her back to the door.

"Young lady, we need to talk. I certainly didn't intend to turn your world upside down by inviting you to visit Berea College with me." Florence sat behind Rowan and rubbed her back in long, soothing strokes. "I invited you so that you could experience for yourself the wonder of attending college. You are an intelligent, resourceful young woman with all the skills needed to be successful in college. You're not making the big decision to leave Pikeville now. By visiting campus with me you can find out for yourself, that's all." Florence sat on the edge of the bed for a few minutes then left Rowan alone.

Chapter 23

After breakfast Saturday morning, Rowan secluded herself in her room to be alone and think through the offer to visit Berea. She sat on the side of her bed and stared at her reflection in the dresser mirror. She thought she was plain. Her brown hair parted on one side and cut just below her ear. Sometimes she would wear a red or blue barrette in her hair just to add a bit of color. Her eyebrows were light. She had a fair complexion from her Irish heritage. Rowan thought makeup was an unnecessary expense, even lipstick, which she never wore. Her shirt was plain green with a small collar and buttoned to the top. *Do I look like a college woman? I don't have any idea how a college woman looks. When people met Florence for the first time, they knew she was a college woman after a brief conversation. Florence didn't have any accent like the Pikeville town folk.* Without Florence in her life, Rowan would never have moved to Pikeville. Those months after Eli's death were a blank in Rowan's life. The only thing she could remember was staying in Union Hall, cleaning and cooking. Florence rescued Rowan. Rowan remembered Florence didn't give her a choice about moving to Pikeville and becoming a pack horse librarian. At least Rowan didn't feel like she had a choice; she was following directions. Looking back on her life, Rowen knew the risk Florence took was unbelievable. Rowan couldn't ride a horse, not well, anyway, didn't know the hill country and had never even visited Pikeville before moving there. Reflecting on the move, Rowan realized it was blind faith – she had put her entire life into Florence's hands.

Florence had more faith in Rowan than she had in herself. *College?* She knew she would be older than all the other students. She graduated from high school five years ago. She enjoyed school but she wasn't a scholar – a good B average was her mark. *What would I study?* Rowan was sure that Florence would want her to study library science. *Not a terrible choice,* Rowan thought. If she went, Rowan thought it would be best to explore other areas of study. She loved working with the adults and teaching them to read. *Maybe I could study to become a teacher.*

Rowan worried it would be lonely at Berea. She would live in a residence hall, eat meals with strangers, have a schedule every day that couldn't change and that she would have no control over. There would be classes she loved and some she had to take because it was a requirement. She would have to learn a new job. Her thoughts twirled into a storm in her head. She shuddered to imagine how her life would be turned inside out. The face in the mirror was in panic. Rowan gripped herself and rocked back and forth on the edge of the bed. Her stomach felt queasy and tightened into a knot. Rowen knew she would have to abandon everything she knew in Pikeville. *Stop!* she said to herself.

She jumped off the bed and shouted out loud. "Lucas!" Rowan covered her mouth and hoped none of the other girls were in their rooms and heard her. She grabbed the hair brush off the dresser and brushed her hair until it shone. While her green blouse and tan trousers were simple, she was satisfied with her appearance. She walked in short, quick steps as fast as she could to Lucas's office. Since they stopped dating, Lucas worked at the paper every Saturday to guarantee a first edition would be out on the streets Monday morning.

Rowan found Lucas hunched over his desk. He didn't notice Rowan standing a few feet from him.

"Lucas!"

Lucas scratched his head and looked up. "What are you doing here? Can't you see I'm busy?"

"I owe you an explanation," Rowan offered.

"Oh, I figured it out already. I was a stupid good-time-Charlie."

"Lucas, I'm married."

"Married? So where the hell is your husband? Since when do married women take dance lessons with a single fella? Where is this husband of yours?"

"In a cemetery in New Hope. He died in the New Hope mining accident two and a half years ago."

Lucas sat silent at his desk drumming his pencil on the pile of papers. "Well, I'm sorry. Why didn't you say you were married?"

Rowan looked around the office and pulled a chair up to the front of Lucas' desk. "I don't know, it's the best way I can say it. I still love Eli – my husband – with all my heart. The truth is my heart just isn't big enough for another man – another relationship. I honestly don't know if my heart will ever be that big. God knows I don't want to hurt you, Lucas. You are the most kind, decent, hardworking man in the world and you deserve to be loved. I'm just not the person to love you. Can you forgive me? I didn't intend to mislead you."

Lucas shook his head back and forth then jumped out of his chair. "Do you want a soda pop? I've got ice cold soda pop. Don't ask me to forgive you. You've given me a lot to take in. Anyway, have you heard? Senator Burke has introduced a bill in the Senate to make men from age eighteen to forty-five register for the selective service. The draft, Rowan, the draft. We've never had a draft – not even during the civil war. I thought we were neutral. Oh sure, we're sending tons of stuff to the British and the allies, but we're not fighting. Why do we need a draft if we're not getting into the war? Roosevelt's not been on the up and up with the American people – I just know it."

"Well, that is news. That's not why I'm here. I have news too. It's not as important as the draft but in my life it is overwhelming. I really need a friend I can trust right now."

"Oh God, Rowan, I had no idea. Sorry for spouting off like that. I can be a friend, I can."

Rowan's mouth was dry, she gulped the soda, then had to resist burping from drinking too fast. "Well, Florence received a telegram last Wednesday, and it was from this professor she knew at Berea College, and he wants her to come visit him by the end of the month. Florence showed me the telegram and it was very brief – very brief." She ran her hands through her hair several times.

"Anyway, she can't even guess why this professor wants to talk with her but it must be very important for her to drive all the way to Berea. She told me it's about a four-hour drive – a very long way – so she doesn't want to wait, and she's leaving bright and early Monday morning. Florence invited me to take a walk in the woods with her, and when Florence invites you to take a walk, a person must go because it will be important. So we walked in the woods, and I was given the surprise of my life – Florence wants me to go to college. She wants me to go to Berea College because she graduated from Berea College seven years ago and it is free – students attending Berea College don't pay tuition.

"I graduated from high school – almost everyone does – except in Pike County, but I never thought about going to college. I'm not sure I'm smart enough for college. But Florence thinks I'll do fine because she wants me to study to be a librarian, like her. I so love working at the library and riding my route; I could do it the rest of my life. Going to college scares me to death. I would have to live in a residence hall and maybe share a room with a stranger. I've never lived with anyone else – except Eli – but that was different. I've never been to Berea. I don't have any idea what the people are like there. Have you been to Berea? Where did you go to college, Lucas? Did you like college? I guess you probably studied journalism. I've been thinking, I like it here in Pikeville, all right, but I don't want to get stuck here. For my age I think I've been too content.

"I'm so happy you've been my friend and understood why I couldn't date you – you are a real gentleman, Lucas. I tell all the girls you are a real gentleman. I am so proud that Florence wants me to attend college. It would be a real challenge for me and that's good for a person my age to have a challenge. I suppose I should at least check it out; there's no harm in that. I don't have to make a decision right away. But if Florence thinks this is the right thing to do, then I need to check it out – a road trip with Florence could be fun. Whew. Thanks, Lucas. It's settled – I'm going with Florence on Monday. You are so kind. I won't take more of your time. Oh, thanks for the soda. Goodbye."

Rowan jumped up and rushed through the door.

"Goodbye, Rowan. Have a pleasant trip."

Lucas directed his attention back to editing the column on the draft since the deadline was approaching.

Chapter 24

"We should stretch our legs, shouldn't we? We've driven over four hours and my back is stiff from driving for so long."

In the early afternoon the campus was quiet, the students were all in classes. It was the perfect temperature for a short sleeveless blouse. As they walked, birds were chirping and calling in the trees. Rowan stopped to listen but couldn't identify any of the birds from their calls. Florence didn't pay any attention to Rowan and walked on ahead. She wanted to unravel the mystery of Dr. Parson's request for her to visit him as soon as she could.

"Florence! Wait up; I'll get lost."

Florence stopped, jerked her head back to watch Rowan run toward her with panic in her eyes. "Oh, Rowan. Calm down. You won't get lost. If you find you don't know where you are, just ask anyone you see. These are friendly people at Berea. Frost Library is a few blocks on our right. Trust me, you can't miss it."

Rowan caught up with Florence and concentrated

on walking right next to her and keeping pace. "Are you nervous, Florence?"

No. Not nervous. It's hard to explain. This is so unlike Dr. Parsons. What could be so important to summon me from Pikeville? Why don't you browse around the library while I meet with Dr. Parsons. I have no idea how long the meeting will be. Are you comfortable being on your own?"

Rowan gave Florence a gentle push on the shoulder. "In a library? I'll be fine. Don't waste a single thought on me."

As they walked up to the huge Classical Revival building, Rowan gasped and stared at the enormous columns.

"Mr. Carnegie donated the money for this library, and they built it in 1905. Mr. Carnegie liked classic Greek architecture limestone buildings. It looks like the Parthenon. It has almost 30,000 square feet. For years it was the largest college library in Kentucky."

Rowan couldn't take her eyes off the Greek columns. She had never seen such an extensive library in her life. "What's the brick building in the back, somehow it doesn't fit."

Florence broke out into a soft laugh. "I remember reading in the alumni magazine they built an addition in 1936. I understand it is a very large reading room. I don't understand the brick addition any more than you do. Now, when we walk in, you're likely to be surprised by what you see. Just take your time exploring the library, and don't be afraid to talk to the librarians. Dr. Parsons office is in the front, and I'm going directly there. Ok?"

Rowan hooked Florence's arm and walked with determination into Frost Library. Once inside she stopped. Florence broke away to walk to Dr. Parson's office. Rowan looked up to gaze at the huge skylight. The afternoon sun created an immense circle of light on the floor. Rowan felt warmth on her cheeks. Particles of dust danced in the light and reflected off the marble floor. *Florence was right.* Rowan blinked; she had never seen a skylight in her life. She thought it was a beautiful way to shower the inside of the cavernous entrance with light. Rowan stood in the center of the light and twirled in a circle. She spread her arms out as she turned and made an audible sigh.

Rowan was feeling dizzy when she heard a voice. "It is amazing, isn't it? First time in the library?"

Rowan stopped. A woman about her height but younger with horn-rimmed glasses was standing in front of her, smiling. She wore a white, sleeveless blouse, tan, creased trousers with saddle shoes. "Vivian. I'm a sophomore and have been assigned to the library. I want to be an elementary teacher, so I guess working at the library fits, doesn't it?"

Rowan shuffled back several steps, not accustomed to boldness. *Or was it openness*, she thought. "I'm Rowan Daly. I'm visiting with my friend Florence Pruett. Florence has a meeting with Dr. Parsons. They're meeting right now, as a matter of fact. This is such an enormous library."

"Oh yes, we were told to be ready for Miss Pruett. Problem is no one told us what she looks like, so it's impossible to be on the lookout for someone you can't recognize. Oh well. Would you like a tour? I have time."

Rowan broke out into a broad grin. "Perfect, Vivian, thank you."

§

Florence stood outside Dr. Parsons office and paused before reaching for the shiny brass handle. He always kept his office door closed, no one knew why. She could smell his fragrant pipe smoke even in the hall. His office was likely to be filled with thick, oily smoke. Florence worried she may choke and that would be embarrassing. She took a breath, held it and knocked on the door hard enough to make sure he would hear it.

"Come in! Please! Come in, come in."

Florence pushed against the solid oak door, walked in and closed the door behind her. She remembered that Dr. Parsons expected all his visitors to close the door. The afternoon sun streamed through the smoke-filled office. The smoke particles danced in the air around Dr. Parsons.

Dr. Parsons' office was famous on Berea campus. He sat straight up behind his pecan desk with a glass, green shaded lamp to his left and a brown desk pad filling the center of the desk. There was a pen holder with an inkwell on the side of the desk. Dr. Parsons preferred a pen with an inkwell rather than a fountain pen. Florence felt he had not aged a day since she graduated seven years ago. His coal black hair was still parted in the middle and combed straight back. A walrus mustache curled around the corners of his mouth and hid his upper lip. Most of the time a curved briar pipe rested in his mouth. He boasted that he had his own blend of tobacco made in a shop in Louisville, which was shipped to him monthly.

Dr. Parsons looked up, not surprised to see Florence. "Florence Pruett, most excellent. Good to see you, young lady. Prompt. I remember that about you. You were always prompt. Please, have a seat." He pointed to the two arm chairs in front of the desk.

"It's good to see you again, Dr. Parsons, but I am perplexed."

"I understand. I just could not write the reason I wanted you to visit in a telegram that might be seen by a...a...others."

Florence's fingers and toes tingled as she waited to hear Dr. Parsons' explanation.

"Now, see here, Miss Pruett. This country is going to war. I don't know when but surely we cannot avoid aiding our allies in Europe. I have been called by the Department of the Army to Washington D.C. to create an information collecting organization."

Florence covered her mouth with her hands. "Oh my. What does that have to do with me, Dr. Parsons?"

"Simple. I have selected you to take my position here as the director of Frost library. You won't have any academic responsibilities as I have had. However, you will be fully responsible for the operation of the library. You should be aware, Miss Pruett, that you have quite a reputation from your leadership of the Pack Horse Librarian Project in Pike County. Oh yes, I've spoken with Dr. Hutchins, our new President of the College, and she fully supports this appointment."

Florence froze in her chair; she couldn't breathe. She stared straight ahead but couldn't focus or see Dr. Parsons' face. She felt a tightness in her chest. Dr. Parsons sat still with his hands folded on the desk. He packed his pipe with tobacco and lit it, waiting for Florence's response.

After a few minutes passed, Florence looked down at her hands. "Maybe you should repeat what you said." Doctor Parsons repeated what he said word for word, he had a reputation for being a precise individual.

Florence covered her mouth with her hands and mumbled, "Why me?"

"Florence, there have been rumblings in Washington D.C. that the Pack Horse Librarian Program is going to be shut down when war comes, and it surely will come. Women will need to work here at home. Anyone who wants a job, will have one. Dr. Hutchins is determined that Berea College remain open during the conflict, and Frost Library is a critical institution in the college. You know Berea College; you have organizational skills and can adapt to what we need in the community. Berea College needs Florence Pruett; it's just that simple. I will leave in November for Washington D.C., before I formally begin my duties in January. I would like you to begin on August 15th, that way we can have a few weeks together before classes begin in September. I will be available to consult with you in September and October, but it is critical that you are working as director on the first day of class. Dr. Hutchins was insistent."

Florence's mouth was dry; she found it difficult to find words. Professionally this was the opportunity of a lifetime. *Rowan? What about Rowan,* she thought. *This would be a perfect time for her to begin her first year of studies at Berea. We could move together; that would save a little money.* It wouldn't be appropriate for a staff member and a student to live together but Rowan could be assigned to the library for her work assignment. Florence felt herself take a deep breath and find the words she needed.

"I am honored, Dr. Parsons. I accept the job. However, I do have one favor for you to consider."

"Hmm, a favor?"

"Yes, I am encouraging one of our pack horse librarians, Rowan Daly, to apply to Berea college for the fall semester. She's here with me today. I will give her a tour of campus. She's dazzling, creative and capable of so much more than a librarian on a horse. She developed scrapbooks for women in the county based on their interests. She also designed a new way to teach reading that doesn't require word memorization. She is a true innovator. Would you help her with the application? Maybe even a recommendation would guarantee her acceptance."

Dr. Parsons set his pipe, then his hands on the desk and twiddled his thumbs. "Perhaps I should meet Miss Daly. You say she's here? Find her and bring her in. I'll have an informal interview. She'll never know it's an interview."

Florence's smile couldn't be contained, and her cheeks flushed pink. "I'll be right back, Dr. Parsons. Today my life takes a new path. I am blessed."

Chapter 25

*F*lorence and Rowan parked in front of Mrs. Perkins' boardinghouse just before supper time on Friday. They both looked at the stately boardinghouse, their home for over three years.

"Will you miss it?" Florence asked.

Rowan sat still, unable to move a muscle. A tear ran down her cheek. "Oh yes, I have so many memories here." Rowan sat up straight and forced a smile when she looked at Florence. "This book is finished. It's time for me to start a new book."

"How do you want to tell them?" Florence asked.

"They will have a million questions. Let's try to wait until dessert in the parlor later."

"Yes, I agree."

Thelma and Hazel saw Florence's car parked at the curb and came rushing out.

"Welcome back. You were gone a long time; we expected you back by Wednesday," Thelma said.

"Do you need help with your luggage?" Hazel asked.

"Well, they do. Florence, pop the trunk open," Thelma instructed. "Hazel and I will take your luggage upstairs."

"You know supper will be in about thirty minutes. You'll have time to freshen up then we have to hear about your trip. I'll let Mrs. Perkins know you're back so she sets places for you," Hazel gushed.

Mrs. Perkins walked into the dining room with a tray of carrots and celery. She dropped the dish on the table when Rowan and Florence walked into the room. "Well, if it isn't the two vagabonds. I'm so happy to see you. When you didn't return on Wednesday, we all worried so. Please don't do that again. Now, dinner will be in thirty minutes. We're having Friday night fish fry. You two scurry upstairs and scrub off your travel."

Rowan and Florence found it difficult to eat because the three women pommeled them with questions – How long does it take to drive to Berea? Is Berea a sizeable town? What did Dr. Parsons want, Florence? Did you visit with old friends? Rowan, what did you do there for so many days? How many students are at Berea College? Rowan, did you see any cute men there? Isn't Berea the college that doesn't have any tuition? What took you so long?

Florence folded her napkin and placed it on top of her plate. "Well, I saved room for Mrs. Perkins' cobbler. I need to write a few letters. Let's all meet in the parlor about seven. Rowan and I need to talk with you. We have a...a... well, I guess you could say we have an announcement to share with you."

Mrs. Perkins hands trembled. "Oh dear, that sounds so serious. An announcement. Hazel, Thelma, help me clear the table. I'll wash up the dishes and make sure the cobbler is ready by seven."

Rowan and Florence took a deep breath and went to their rooms to prepare to tell their friends they would leave in several months. Rowan removed her savings box from its hiding place in the wardrobe. She spread the bills out on her bed. As she laid the last bill on the bed, she said, "Two hundred and twenty dollars – I'm wealthy!"

From the first month she started her job as a pack horse librarian in September 1936 Rowan had saved five dollars every week. Sometimes it had been rough, but now she was proud of herself. She had enough in savings to make the move to Berea. She thought her savings might even last the whole four years of college. Rowan plopped backward on her bed and stared at the ceiling. Her thoughts drifted back to Berea; she tried to imagine what her new life would be like.

"Rowan, come down here. Mrs. Perkins has a bowl of cobbler in the parlor for you, and we can't wait any longer. Florence is already here," Thelma shouted up the stairs.

Rowan and Florence sat next to each other on the sofa. Mrs. Perkins handed them each a bowl of warm peach cobbler. "Well, ladies, we have been patient. Tell us, what is the announcement you have?"

Florence could no longer hide her excitement – her eyes gleamed. "Dr. Parsons, the director of Frost Library at Berea College will leave in the fall, and I have been offered the job as the director of the library. It is truly a once in a lifetime opportunity. I've accepted."

She looked around the room at each of the women to gauge their response. They sat motionless, staring at her. "I will leave mid-August. I will have the opportunity to work with Dr. Parsons for several months before he leaves Kentucky. I need to share with you ladies what Dr. Parsons told me. He's convinced me we are going to war in Europe to help our allies. He's been recruited by the Department of the Army and is moving to Washington D.C. He expects there will be a draft this fall and it will require all men over eighteen to register."

The women were speechless a few minutes. Mrs. Perkins set her bowl on the floor, unable to finish. "God help us," she said.

"What about you, Rowan; you have an announcement too?" Thelma asked.

Rowan flushed and grabbed Florence's hand. "Florence has convinced me I have what it takes to attend college. They have accepted me at Berea College. This will be the biggest challenge of my life. Florence believes in me, so I need to believe in myself. I'm going to study to be a librarian. Every student is assigned a job to help pay for lodging and meals. I'm going to work at the library for Florence."

Hazel and Thelma jumped up to hug Rowan. "Oh my God, I can't believe it. I just can't believe it," Hazel shouted.

Tears streamed down Thelma's face. "Oh, I'm going to miss you both so much. What's going to happen to the Pack Horse Librarian Project."

Florence brushed her hair back with her hand. "I must be honest with you ladies. Dr. Parsons said a lot of the programs will end once we get into the war. He guessed the war might go on for a year. But don't worry, there will be plenty of jobs. I am writing a letter to Mayor Woolridge and will meet with him tomorrow to let him know my last day will be July 31st."

Thelma fell back into her chair. "July 31st – six weeks. What about you, Rowan?"

"The fall semester starts September 8th so I will be here until August 31st."

Mrs. Perkins sighed. She stiffened and wasn't able to talk. Mrs. Perkins looked around the room at each face and tried to memorize how they looked. Her world was being shattered and there was nothing she could do about it. "It's wonderful news. I am honestly happy for both of you. Excuse me, I need to be alone."

Thelma put her bowl down. "I have a lot of questions, now let's just get right down to it. First,..."

Chapter 26

Rowan pulled her calendar from the dresser drawer and put an X through Saturday. In just six days she would be on a bus to Berea College. She had already purchased her ticket. The bus would leave Pikeville at seven thirty-five a.m. and arrive in Berea at five-fifteen at in the evening. The route went through Lexington so the bus took twice as long as a car trip.

The day Florence left was a terrible day for everyone at the library and the boardinghouse. The day before she left the library, staff hosted a picnic in Pikeville City Park and invited the community. Mrs. Perkins helped prepare all the picnic favorites: fried chicken, potato salad, three bean salad, homemade pimento cheese sandwiches, sweet pickles, sweet tea and apple pie. Rowan guessed at least one hundred people spent most of the afternoon in the park. Mayor Woolridge presented Florence with a key to the city and impressed on her she was welcome back any time. Florence helped recruit Amelia Harman, who graduated from Berea College in June, to take over her duties as library director. She was handpicked by Dr. Parsons for the job. Mayor Woolridge was impressed with her maturity and manner during the interview and hired her on the spot. Florence and Amelia worked together for six weeks. Amelia insisted on accompanying Thelma and Hazel several times on their route to meet the families and learn how they depended on the pack horse librarians.

Rowan hoped no one was planning a sendoff like that for her. Florence was a fixture in Pikeville. Rowan was out on her route and not as well known in the community. Rowan begged Thelma and Hazel to not throw any kind of going away party. They had promised to heed her wishes, but Rowan was not sure she could trust them. She stared at her calendar and decided she needed a list of things that must be done before she left.

Today would be a day of rest because it was already so hot and muggy that even with her windows wide open, Rowan was sweating. Her list read:

> *Sunday – rest – go for ice cream sundae*
> *Monday – ride route 1 for the last time*
> *Tuesday – ride route 2 for the last time*
> *Wednesday – work in library*
> *Thursday – visit Gus at the livery and pay for apples for*
> *Ash for a month*
> *Friday – pack*
> *Saturday – 7:35 a.m. take bus to Berea*

She fell back on her bed and let her thoughts drift where they pleased. Sometimes she felt uneasy about attending college and other days she was excited about the change and looking forward to the challenge she was giving herself. She was never ambivalent about her decision to attend the school. Florence had talked with her about what to expect at Berea. One of the major changes would be living in Fairchild Residence Hall with ninety-five other women. *It would be like living in a crowded hotel,* Rowen thought. Florence told her the rooms were small, and there would be a line to use the bathroom. The meals were cafeteria style so there were lines for each meal. The admission packet she received noted that meals would cost five dollars and sixty cents a week. *Not bad for twenty-one meals,* Rowen thought. Rowan planned to pay for the meals from her savings.

Rowan sat up in bed and looked around her room, which she guessed was much larger than her room at Fairchild Hall. She had lived in Mrs. Perkins' boardinghouse almost four years. She wanted to burn the image of her room into her memory.

$

Friday arrived sooner than Rowan expected. The morning sun shone through the window. Rowan raised all the windows to breathe in the humid Pikeville air on her last day. She took her clothes from the wardrobe and laid them out on the bed, then pulled her suitcase from underneath the bed. She took her time to fold each item to place it in the suitcase. The suitcase was full. Several items were left on the bed, and she still had to empty the dresser drawers. Rowan couldn't fathom how she had gained so many clothes. Her riding boots were standing in the corner. She scratched her head, wondering if she should take the boots to college. *A pack horse librarian had to have quality boots to do the job but would a college student need riding boots?* The question puzzled her, and she collapsed into the chair by the window to consider her conundrum. The morning breeze made the curtains dance in her room. She stared at the boots and remembered how difficult it had been to choose the right boots four years ago. To Rowen, the boots were perfect. Rowan's mind drifted with the curtains. When she looked again at her riding boots, she thought they were soon to be a part of her past, not her future. She decided her boots needed to be donated to the Salvation Army. *Maybe I could exchange the boots for another suitcase.*

§

Rowan returned from her trip to the Salvation Army and finished packing by lunch time. Thelma and Hazel were at work, so Rowan and Mrs. Perkins ate together. The dining room table was too large for just two people.

"Rowan, I'd like to cook a special going away meal for you this evening. You can have anything you would like."

Rowan bit her lip and thought for a long time. "Oh, Mrs. Perkins, that is so sweet, but you really don't need to. I love everything you cook. I'm sure the quality of meals at Fairchild Hall won't come close to your wonderful meals."

Mrs. Perkins stiffened. "I insist."

Rowan wrung her hands and tried to decide on a favorite meal. "Ok, meatloaf with mashed potatoes and gravy, fresh corn on the cob and apple pie for dessert. It's such a beautiful afternoon, I'm going to walk to the livery stable and if Gus hasn't rented Ash for the day, I'll take her for my last ride. Let me take the dishes to the kitchen. Do you need help washing up?"

"No dear, I can manage. You enjoy your last afternoon in Pikeville."

Tears welled up in Mrs. Perkins' eyes, she turned away so Rowan wouldn't see her.

§

Rowan tossed and turned all night. She couldn't get comfortable in bed. Her night dress clung to her skin even though she kept the windows wide open. Memories of her four years in Pikeville flashed through her mind like watching a movie at the cinema. When the sun beamed through her windows, she decided it was safe to get up. She checked her alarm clock – six a.m. It was early enough to use the bathroom before Rowan got up. She snapped her two suitcases up and walked downstairs. She tried to be quiet but Mrs. Perkins met her at the bottom of the stairs.

"I thought I would serve breakfast about quarter to seven today. It shouldn't be more than a ten-minute walk to the bus station, is it?"

Rowan's voice wavered. "Yes, about ten minutes. I want to leave by seven fifteen. I don't want breakfast. My stomach is in knots."

Mrs. Perkins smiled and touched Rowan's hand. "I understand dear. A cup of tea, maybe?"

"Yes, please."

While Mrs. Perkins made tea, Rowan went upstairs to fetch her suitcases. She looked around the room one last time. *So many memories.* Rowan plopped down on the chair, hid her face in her hands and let the tears roll down her cheeks. In an instant she sat up straight, wiped the tears away and made her way downstairs with a suitcase in each hand.

"There's our college girl." Thelma greeted Rowan with a brave smile. "I'll carry one of those suitcases to the bus station whenever you want to leave."

"Thank you, Thelma, that's kind."

Mrs. Perkins came out of the kitchen with a steaming cup of tea. "I'll be walking with you too, but you can carry your own suitcase, dear. Now, you have time for this tea."

The three women arrived at the bus station ten minutes before the bus was scheduled to depart. The bus was at the curb, door open but no driver. "I suppose I should wait for the driver," Rowan said, setting her suitcase on the sidewalk next to the bus.

"Absolutely, he'll put your suitcases in the hold for you. You must be the only person leaving Pikeville today. Oh look, here comes Hazel. I knew she wouldn't miss the great farewell," Thelma said.

"Those children of mine. I was afraid I would miss you this morning, Rowan. Oh dear, I am so happy for you but so sad for us. You will write?" Hazel asked.

"I will write. I won't promise how often but I will promise to write."

A tall, thin man in a fresh pressed uniform and hat walked out of the bus stop and tipped his hat at the three women. "Well, looks like you're the only passenger today, ma'am. If you don't mind, I'll throw those suitcases in and we'll get underway."

"Yes, sir," Rowan said and cleared her throat. She

slung her arms out to embrace Mrs. Perkins, Thelma and Hazel in a group hug.

Mrs. Perkins handed her a paper sack. "Lunch, dear."

The bus driver took his seat, leaned over the wheel and shouted out the door, "Ready, miss?"

The three women hugged for the last time, and Rowan entered the bus, taking a window seat near the rear. As the bus pulled away from the curb, she waved. Just as the bus entered the street, Lucas came running up waving. "Good bye, good luck, Rowan. Remember to write."

Rowan pulled down the window and shouted, "Thank you for coming, Lucas. I'll write soon. Bye."

The bus was out of town heading northwest to Lexington in a few minutes. Rowan calmed herself by taking in the countryside and imagining her new life as a college student.

Chapter 27

*T*he bus driver remembered that Rowan had two heavy suitcases so after stopping at the bus station in downtown Berea, he drove to Fairchild Hall on Chestnut street. "Here ya go, young lady."

The driver pulled her suitcases from the luggage area and set them on the sidewalk. Both of them turned to look at the hall. It was an imposing, three-story brick building with a balcony that stretched the full width of the second floor. It was larger than any hotel in Pikeville. Rowan's legs were weak and her stomach was queasy.

"I need to go. Best of luck to you, young lady." The bus driver tipped his hat and drove away.

Rowan felt like her feet were stuck in concrete. She took a deep breath, picked up her suitcases and walked into the hall.

A middle-aged lady, with her hair pulled back into a bun, greeted her from behind a mahogany desk similar to a library welcome desk. "Welcome, welcome, welcome.

You must be one of our freshman. What is your name, dear? I'll look up your room assignment."

"Daly. Rowan. Rowan Daly." Rowan hung onto her suitcases rather than setting them on the floor.

"Let's see." The woman turned several pages and ran her finger down the page searching for Rowan's name. "That would be spelled D-a-l-y, correct?"

"Yes."

"Here we are. Third floor, number 301 – the room on the end. Oh my, that's a fine room. You'll be able to look out on the green. Now, let me get your key, and I will help carry one of your suitcases. It's a long trek up to the third floor but excellent exercise."

§

The matron opened the door and let Rowan go in first. The room was less than half the size of her room at Mrs. Perkins' boardinghouse. To the left was a vast window with a small pine desk and chair underneath. To the right was a single bed with linen folded in the center. A washstand with a washbowl and a pitcher were tucked in a corner. Rowan would need to make up her own bed, just like at the boardinghouse. In the back was a single closet. This would be Rowan's home for the next four years. Rowan rubbed her hands together, not sure what she should do next.

The matron cleared her throat and began her memorized speech. "There are forty-eight rooms on both the second and third floor, which means ninety-six ladies live in Fairchild Hall. All the rooms are the same. The bathroom is in the center of the floor near the staircase. The first floor has the dining room, a reading room and parlor with a piano. This year the dining will be cafeteria style. As a freshman you will be assigned one week of washing dishes every month. Now, why don't I let you get settled. Dinner is at six. You have a few minutes to unpack and freshen up. After dinner there will be an orientation in the parlor. I will have a packet of information for you which includes the rules for residing here and the schedule for dish washing. Do you have questions before I leave you?"

Rowan turned to look at the matron and realized she didn't know her name. "What is your name, matron?"

"Arizona Miller.

"Forgive me for saying anything, dear, but you appear older than most of our freshmen women."

"I'm twenty-three. The last four years I have worked as a pack horse librarian in Pike County."

Arizona slapped her hands on her cheeks. "Oh, that is so wonderful. I have read about that program. Sometime you just must share some of your stories with me. Maybe you'll even consider making a presentation one evening. I am sure the other ladies would be interested. Well, I should go. I am sure you are exhausted from your long bus trip."

Miss Miller left Rowan alone in her room. She made up the bed and lay down. She drifted off to sleep in a few minutes.

§

Rowan woke to loud voices in the hall and doors slamming up and down the hallway. She grabbed the pitcher and walked down the hall to find the bathroom. When she returned to her room, she noticed the door across the hall from her room was ajar. She couldn't resist; she leaned forward and peeked in. She saw a young woman with curly blonde hair and two older people she guessed were the young woman's parents.

The woman saw Rowan in the hall and greeted her with a broad smile. "Hello, my name is Martha Payne. What's your name?"

"Rowan Daly."

Martha waved Rowan into her room. "Come on in. These are my parents, Mr. and Mrs. Payne. They're helping me move in. I'm trying to convince them to stay for dinner downstairs before driving back to Louisville. Are your parents gone already?"

Rowan bowed her head and stared at her shoes. "I don't have parents any more. I lost them seven years ago."

Mrs. Payne reached out to touch Rowan's arm. "Oh, that is just tragic, dear. Well now, you just join us for dinner downstairs. Are you an upper-class student?"

Martha jumped into the conversation. "I'm a freshman and I'm going to study to be a teacher. I'm not sure what grade yet, but for sure I'm going to be a teacher. What are you going to study, Rowan? Oh, that's such a pretty name – Rowan."

Rowan stepped backward overwhelmed by Martha's enthusiasm. "I've been working as a pack horse librarian in Pike County the last four years. I'm going to study to be a professional librarian. I've already been assigned to work at Frost Library. A friend of mine, Florence Pruett, just got the job as director of the library. She was my boss in Pike County. If you don't mind, I still need to unpack. Knock on my door and I'll go down to dinner with you."

Rowan turned on her heel and left before Martha could object to her leaving.

§

Martha and Rowan took the time to explore campus in the week before classes started. They compared registration cards and both had five classes a week plus twenty hours of work a week. Their schedules were similar in having classes in the morning with study time and work time in the afternoon and evenings. Rowan's work schedule included one evening a week in the library. They assigned Martha cleaning in Draper Hall, one of the academic buildings built just two years ago. There were ten departments in the building, including her own Education Department. Most of the work was light cleaning such washing chalkboards, dusting, sweeping and taking out the trash.

Rowan wasn't sure when she should visit Florence. She waited until the first day to be assigned work at the library. Rowan thought it would be ill advised to be too familiar with the director of Frost Library even though they worked together for four years. They scheduled Rowan to report to Florence at three p.m. the first day of class.

Rowan walked to the welcome desk and asked the location of Florence's office. She knocked on the door. "Come in and close the door behind you."

Florence leapt out of her chair and gave Rowan a big hug. "We don't want the other students to see us embrace but I just can't help myself. I am thrilled we are back working together again. To be honest, I will need your help. Oh, please sit down."

Rowan sat in the chair, trembling. "My help?"

"I have learned in the six weeks I've been here that most of my responsibilities are administrative – not librarian work. There are three other students assigned to the library and none of them have library experience. There are three other local women who work here, but not as librarians. They put numbers on books and shelve them, do a bit of cleaning and try to answer student questions when asked. I want to assign you to circulation right away. We need to find out what books and other resources students need. Dr. Parsons was trying to do it all himself, along with the administrative duties."

Rowan flushed and wiggled in her chair. "You have a lot of faith in me."

"I've seen you work, remember. I must be honest; it may take over ten hours a week."

"This is an opportunity for me. I don't care how many hours a week it takes."

Chapter 28

Most mornings Rowan and Martha had breakfast to-gether, and they walked to Draper Hall for their first morning class. The rest of the day they had classes in different buildings but met for lunch. After lunch Rowan spent the afternoons at the library. Her first job was to research the books and other materials checked out to determine the most popular materials. She developed a short one-page survey and asked each student when they walked in if there were materials they needed for their studies that were not available at the library. Rowan spent the evenings studying in her room. She tried studying at the library but found it too tempting to work on library projects and not her classwork.

As with most freshman, Rowan's classes were basic the first semester: English, mathematics, geography, life sciences and music. The courses reminded Rowan of high school classes, but she still needed at least three hours every evening to study. Her goal was to maintain an A average.

Rowan was so absorbed the first month that she didn't take time to write her friends in Pikeville. She didn't even realize it until one day a letter arrived from Lucas.

Dear Rowan,

I hope my letter finds you well and enjoying your classes. I already miss our talks. You are so easy to talk with.

Since you left, the world has changed a lot. The Selective Service bill passed Congress in mid-September and the draft will start this week. I have decided that I don't want to be drafted to serve my country. I am going to volunteer after I mail this letter.

I have talked with the recruiting sergeant and he explained journalists will tell the story of America going to war. I want to do my part. Sarge said I'd make a lousy soldier, but I will attend basic training for ten weeks to learn how to fire the new M1 rifle. I hear it has a heck of a kick. It can't be worse than grandpa's twelve gauge.

After basic training, I will be assigned to one of the Army training camps to cover the story of turning citizens into soldiers.

I wish you all the success at college. It must be so different for you. I know you will be an immense success.

When I have a post office address, I will send it to you. I would appreciate it if you write me once in a while. No one knows, or will say, when we are going to war or how long it will last. The one thing I know for sure is our world will be topsy turvy.

> *Your friend,*
> *Lucas*

Rowan folded the letter and slid it back into the envelope. It was postmarked five days ago. She guessed Lucas might already be in training. Rowan had been so busy that she hadn't taken the time to read a newspaper so everything Lucas explained was news. In that moment she promised herself to devote time every day to reading a newspaper. *Being in college doesn't mean being cut off from the world.* Rowan scolded herself for not writing to Thelma and Hazel and Mrs. Perkins in Pikeville. Rowan worried she might have given them the wrong message by not writing.

She took paper from her desk and wrote each of them a letter. She shared her experiences in college and asked each to write her back with an update on their lives. As she licked the envelopes, Rowan had a pang of guilt and hoped Thelma and Hazel didn't have to cover her route for too long.

Chapter 29

*T*he morning temperature was near freezing in early December. After breakfast Rowan took a walk around campus. Most of the leaves had fallen and were shifting like sea waves with the slightest wind. It didn't snow often in Berea but today it felt like there was a lot of moisture in the air and the clouds blanketed campus. On Sundays Frost Library didn't open until one o'clock, and Rowan wanted to begin the new assignment Florence had given her to review the cataloging in the library archive. Rowan would have volunteered for this project if Florence had not had the insight to assign it to her. Rowan felt safe in the second basement of the building and the musty spell of hundreds of old volumes was appealing to Rowan.

The envelope with mid-term grades was under Rowan's pillow for two weeks. She stuffed it there the day they delivered it. Working in the library was fun but classes were much more difficult than Rowan expected. Soon after classes began she had a strict routine of studying by herself in her room for three hours after dinner. At nine o'clock she cleaned up, got her clothes out for the next day, then read for thirty minutes before going to bed at ten. The girls on her floor thought she was a bore for having such a strict routine. Rowan knew the only way she could survive this academic world was to work as hard as she could because she felt she wasn't gifted with natural intelligence.

Every morning she fought off a panic attack. She was always the first person at breakfast so she could gobble down as much food as her stomach would allow and then be out of the residence hall before most girls came to the dining hall. Rowan packed up her books for her morning classes and wouldn't return to the residence hall until lunch. To calm herself she took a brisk walk through campus and arrived at her first class at least fifteen minutes early to be sure to get a front row seat. As students trickled into the classroom, she strained to be pleasant, smile and say "Morning."

One evening after dinner Rowan marched up to her room, saying nothing to the women at her table. She promised herself after dinner she would grab the envelope under her pillow to learn her mid-term grades. She was panting by the time she reached the third floor. She went straight to her bed and threw the pillow on the floor. She grabbed the envelope, tore it open and read: Mathematics C+, English A, Geography B+, Life Science C, Music C.

Rowan screamed out loud "No, No, No, No!" She tore the paper up into little bits and threw them on the floor. Tears streamed down her face and she threw herself on her pillow. The tear-soaked pillow muffled her sobs.

Her worst fears were true – *I'm not smart enough for college.* She wanted to earn an A in every course but she just couldn't. *College was a mistake – a monumental blunder*. She felt Florence had pushed her to come to Berea and now she was a failure.

She barricaded herself in her room for two days, not going to the dining room for meals. The women on her floor didn't seem to miss her because no one came to her door to ask about her, even Martha. By Monday at lunchtime her hunger overcame her dread of being around other students. She went to lunch late and found a seat by herself.

From the end of the dining room the matron stood up and rang the farm bell she used to get everyone's attention. "Ladies, ladies, your attention please." In a flash you could hear a pin drop in the huge dining hall. "I have just learned that at twelve-thirty today President Roosevelt will address the nation with an announcement. We will have the radio on in the parlor. Attendance is not required. I believe this will be an important announcement and suggest you make time in your day to listen. Now, we only have about thirty minutes. Everyone, please help clear the tables. We can finish dishes this afternoon. Thank you."

Rowan took her dishes to the kitchen and was the first to slip out of the dining hall and walk to the parlor to sit down next to the radio. This event was the distraction she needed to not obsess about her grades.

The women looked at each other unable to imagine what the President would talk about on a Monday afternoon. The fireside chats were always in the evening about seven-thirty. A Monday speech was very unusual.

The matron had the radio on loud so even the students leaning against the back wall heard. The announcer sounded grim. "Ladies and Gentlemen, we have been given a script of the President's remarks this afternoon and I must tell you to prepare yourselves. Our world is about to change forever. Here's the President:

"Mr. Vice-President, Mr. Speaker, Members of the Senate, and of the House of Representatives:

Yesterday, December 7, 1941, – a date which will live in infamy. The United States of American was attacked by naval and air forces of the Empire of Japan....

The attack yesterday on the Hawaiian Islands has caused severe damage to American naval and military forces. Yesterday, the Japanese government also launched an attack on Malaya. Last night Japanese forces attacked Hong Kong. Last night, Japanese forces attacked Guam. Last night, Japanese forces attacked the Philippine Islands and Wake Island. And this morning, Japanese attacked Midway Island...

With confidence in our armed forces, with the unbounding determination of our people, we will gain the inevitable triumph. So help us God.

I ask that the Congress declare that since the unprovoked and dastardly attack by Japan on Sunday, December 7, 1941, a state of war has existed between the United States and the Japanese empire."

The matron rushed to the radio and clicked it off with a snap. She looked at the women crowded into the parlor. Some were crying, some were holding their stomachs, some buried their face in their hands, some stared out into nothingness.

"Ladies, I think this is a good time for silent prayer. Please bow your heads." Everyone followed her instructions. After what felt like at least fifteen minutes, the matron spoke again. "Please join me in the prayer of our Lord and Savior, Jesus Christ."

"Our Father, who art in heaven, hallowed be Thy name, Thy kingdom come, Thy will be donw on earth, as it is in heaven. Give us this day our daily bread, and forgive us our trespasses, as we forgive those who trespass against us, and lead us not into temptation. But deliver us from evil. For Thine is the kingdom, and power, and the glory, for ever and ever. Amen."

One by one the women stood and returned to their rooms. Rowan threw on her jacket, scarf and hat. Martha caught her in the hallway. "Where are you going?"

"The library, I'm scheduled there this afternoon anyway. I need to see Florence. What are you going to do?"

"I'm going to call home. I'm sure my little brother, Joe, will volunteer. He graduates from high school in May, but he's already eighteen. He was held up a grade – you know what I mean. I hope my Dad can knock some sense into him about volunteering."

"I'll talk to you later." Rowan walked as fast as she could to the library. Listening to the President's message made her late for work but she wasn't aware of it.

§

Rowan found Florence in her office staring out the window, watching students crisscross the campus. She ran up behind her, wrapped her arms around her tightly and buried her head in the nape of her neck. "Oh my God, Florence, oh my God." Tears streamed down her face like a waterfall and stained her blouse collar.

Florence stood stiff and unmoving.

"What's the matter, Florence? You're as stiff as a wood fence post."

Florence turned around and embraced Rowan. "Our motto, Rowan, our motto," she whispered.

"Our motto?"

"Yes, dear: 'God hath made of one blood all nations.' We are at war, and I'm sure they will declare war against Germany and Italy. The entire world will be at war less than twenty-five years after the War to End All Wars. It will be impossible to live our motto."

Rowan pulled away from Florence and wiped her face dry with a handkerchief she kept in her sleeve. She sat in the chair across from Florence's desk to absorb what her mentor said. "I never thought about the Berea College motto before. I guess I should have."

Rowan took a deep breath and sat straight in the chair. "I need to talk to you, now."

"That sounds like a demand. I have time now. What do you want to talk about?"

"I'm leaving."

"Leaving?"

"I'm going back to Pikeville this week. College isn't for me. I don't have what it takes and I have the proof."

Florence fell into her chair not eager to listen to Rowan's lament. "What proof?"

"Mid-term grades."

"I don't understand, Rowan, mid-term grades are just to let you know where you stand and where you could use a little more effort. Only final semester grades are used for your GPA."

"I know that."

"Will you share your grades with me?"

Rowan looked down at her hands folded in her lap. "I'm ashamed."

"Now Rowan, knowing you as I do, my guess is you are being much too hard on yourself. Do you have your grades with you? I'll look at them."

"I tore them up and scattered them on the floor."

"Oh."

Rowan wiggled in her seat and avoided eye contact with Florence. "OK one A, one B+, one C+ and two Cs."

A smile spread across Florence's face and she relaxed in her chair. "Why those are fine grades, Rowan. What's the problem?"

"I have a strict routine. I study three hours straight every night – even on the weekends. I want to be in the top of my class. I want all A's but I could live with a few B's in tough courses like math. I can't do it. I'm not smart enough for college. You pushed me into college, and I resent you for it. You meddled in my life and now look what's happened."

Florence got up, walked to Rowan's chair and gave her a hug. Rowan stiffened and turned away. Florence pulled her chair next to Rowan. "Rowan Daly, look at me. I have two things to say. First, what do you want? In the past you've told me you want to work as librarian. Well, you need a college degree. Period. If you don't want to be a librarian, fine. Leave. Second, you must believe in yourself. You don't need to earn all A's and B's. Besides college subjects, you're learning about yourself, you're learning about life. Now, what do you want, Rowan Daly?"

Rowan slumped in her chair and hid her face in her

hands. Florence didn't move. She decided she would stay seated next to Rowan until she had an answer.

Rowan wasn't able to look at Florence. It took her a few minutes to whisper from behind her hands "My dream is to work in a library."

"Fine. And do you *believe it is* your life calling?"

"I'm a little shaky, but yes."

"Let me share a secret with you – call it a life lesson. The key to getting what you want in life is believing. If you believe in yourself; if you see yourself serving others as a librarian, well, then it will happen."

"Really?"

"Really."

"Do you think I graduated with all A's? I didn't. The truth is chemistry did me in, I struggled to earn a C-. I'm just not a science person. So what? I think I'm a good librarian."

Rowan's head popped up and her eyes widened. "You got a C- in chemistry?"

"Yes."

"Didn't you want to quit?"

"No. I worked hard. I worked to the best of my ability. It's all I could do. I was determined to graduate and work as a librarian so I stuck it out."

The two women sat in silence for quite some time.

Florence crossed her arms. "Well, there's still work to do. Start your work in the archive this afternoon – it will be a great distraction. This evening maybe you can write letters to Thelma and Hazel. I don't know what will happen to the pack horse librarian program now. Maybe you need time to yourself this evening to decide your direction. Actually, that is exactly what you should do – forget about coming to my house like we planned unless you want company or need to talk further.”

Rowan pushed herself out of the chair, gave Florence a bear hug and left for the archive. As she walked through the door, she wiped tears from her face and turned toward Florence. “I want to be a librarian. I can do this. I will do this.” Knowing Florence earned a C- in Chemistry helped Rowan judge herself less harshly. Abandoning college after half a semester was rash, Rowan decided. Rowan promised herself to never abandon her dream.

§

The phone rang. “Yes, Dr. Hutchins, I’m available. Two o’clock in your office. I expected you to take the initiative. I look forward to meeting with the deans and department heads. Goodbye.” Florence felt the faculty would learn Berea’s fate this afternoon.

Rowan walked back upstairs to let Florence know she was making progress on her project but needed a break.

“Come in, Rowan, Dr. Hutchins is calling an emergency staff meeting.”

“What’s going to happen to Berea? Will we close?” Rowan asked.

“I doubt it. Students still need an education to contribute to society and the war effort. Dr. Hutchins is a very practical woman. She will want to determine how Berea can support the effort to win this war. Now, you head back downstairs, young lady. I need time to prepare for the meeting. I am sure there are ways for Frost Library to take a lead role. Be sure to go to classes tomorrow like normal.

I am certain classes will continue through the end of the fall semester."

Rowan found the archive level of the library quiet, peaceful and offered a special sense of security. The world above her could be in a rage but she was safe with her volumes of books. She searched in a closet to find a fan. The air in the archive room was dank and sometimes difficult to breath, she felt light headed. *How do I organize this mess?* She couldn't begin by date of book, subject, or some other criteria. Her thoughts wandered off and she couldn't help but think about Lucas. *Where was he stationed? He would want to be in the thick of it, letting the folks in Pike County know the story of the war.*

§

Berea College decided to hold a special graduation for those who completed their major and had sufficient number of credits to graduate. Dr. Hutchins wanted to provide as many college graduates as she could to the war effort. As the months progressed, the number of men on campus dwindled. By the December 31 graduation, the only men remaining were those earning their bachelor degree – only ten men. While Rowan couldn't say she had male friends, there were several men who were acquaintances. The library science program didn't have any men. Rowan couldn't imagine why but it was just a fact everyone accepted.

A dark cloud hung over the ceremony. The men and several women were off to the war effort. They were not going home to great jobs in teaching, engineering and other professions. All of the parents arrived with a mix of joy and sadness. The clapping during the ceremony was very reserved. Dr. Hutchins gave the commencement message. She admonished the graduates to keep Berea's values and lessons in their hearts and in their daily lives.

The decision was made to keep Berea open even though the student population was expected to decrease by a third or more, and the incoming freshman class would be only twenty students. The staff felt the mission for Berea College was even more critical now, during the war. Rowan was relieved when Florence explained the decision before it was officially announced to the student body.

Thelma and Hazel wrote to her that their jobs with the Pack Horse Librarian Project were not threatened for now, but no one dreamed those jobs could last very long. There was extreme pressure in Pike County to step up to take jobs men had before the war. Hazel and her husband were safe because farmers were exempt from military service.

Chapter 30

In the spring semester of 1942 there wasn't a single man attending Berea college. Kentucky men have a reputation for patriotism. All the Berea men volunteered; no one was drafted. At Florence's insistence Rowan continued with her project in the archive, although, as each day passed, Rowan felt the project was less relevant. One unanticipated consequence of the men leaving campus was that there was no longer competition to register for classes. Most of the courses Rowan needed were to fulfill basic requirements to graduate. They allowed her to take only one course each semester in her designated major until she was a junior, which was more than a year away. Rowan found she had no stomach for courses like chemistry and physics so she took courses in the physical sciences like anthropology and geology.

Before the war started meals at Fairchild Hall cafeteria were like eating at home, but after the war started meals changed. Most mornings breakfast was cold cereal with milk and toast with jam or peanut butter. Lunches were peanut butter and jelly sandwiches with cut up vegetables and ice tea or milk. On a good night dinner was meatloaf and mashed potatoes and cookies for dessert. As supplies dwindled in the pantry; hot meals were fewer and fewer. Oatmeal with cream vanished from the breakfast table. They often served soup for lunch with a slice of white bread and butter. Many nights soup was served again for dinner. Not a single student complained. Almost everyone had at least one relative in the armed services, and those still at home understood sacrifice was their contribution to victory.

In March of 1942 President Hutchins announced summer school would be suspended. She felt students needed to be home with their families for the summer and to devote their time and talent to the war effort. This announcement turned Rowan's world upside down and inside out. She was certain she would be the only student on campus without a family. Rowan walked the perimeter of campus several times to try and be calm and think through her problem. No one knew she didn't have family, not even Martha. Rowan had developed a unique skill of diverting conversation when it turned to family. As she walked, a knot grew in her stomach she couldn't control. Rowan turned and walked to Florence's house.

Florence opened the door just to see who was knocking. A smile glided across her face when she saw Rowan. "What a surprise, Rowan. Come in, come in."

"Oh my God, oh my God, what am I going to do? Where am I going to go? I'm sunk!" Rowan raised her voice at Florence, who sat unmoving, allowing her friend to rant at will. "I like to think I'm a rational person who can adapt. Not now. I feel as lost and abandoned as I did when Eli died six years ago. Six years ago? How my life has changed in the past six years."

Florence let Rowan have her panic time and stayed quiet. She poured both of them a cup of tea. Rowan was just twenty-five and needed space to find her place in the world. Florence understood that without a summer program, Rowan's world disappeared. Florence patted Rowan's shoulder and nodded in understanding.

"Well, I have news for you. I've talked with Dr. Hutchins about your situation, which is unique among all the students. She has agreed that you can remain on campus for the summer, if you agree to move in with me. There are a lot of plans to make for students to return next fall, and you can help us with those plans – you're capable."

Rowan jumped out of her seat and grabbed Florence's arm. "For the second time in my life, you've saved me. I'll move in with you. I won't be any bother. I'll cook all the meals and do the cleaning too."

Florence smiled, expecting Rowan's response. "A student living with a staff member is highly irregular. We will wait at least a week after all the students have left campus to move your things to my house. I will have cereal and milk or oatmeal for breakfast and you can make your own sandwich for lunch and plan to join me for dinner. Whatever you can contribute for food will be appreciated."

$

During the summer of 1942 they assigned Rowan the project of planning how student life would change when everyone returned to school in the fall. She was assigned to Dr. Hutchins' office and was given a small office just two doors away from the President's. The room was spartan, with a desk, lamp, chair, bookcase, typewriter and wastebasket. The desk had a drawer on each side, one filled with typing paper and the other filled with pencils, paperclips, stapler and miscellaneous office supplies. She would start by working with the Fairchild Hall Head Cook, Mrs. Davis. Rowan met her in her office in the back of the kitchen.

Rowan found Mrs. Davis bent over a piece of brown paper cut from a grocery bag. She held a pencil between her first and second fingers and printed each letter she wrote with precision.

"Mrs. Davis?"

"Yes, girl. What do you want?"

Rowan stood a few feet away from Mrs. Davis' desk. She glanced around the room for a chair or stool but there wasn't one. "I am working during the summer, and Dr. Hutchins sent me over to get your thoughts on how we can supply most of our own food in the fall when the students return."

"I must know how many students to expect."

"Dr. Hutchins expected you would ask. I went to the registrar's office on my way here. Every student was required to fill out a form before leaving campus to ask if they planned to return this September. I must tell you, I was shocked. Only eighty-six students – all women – will be back in the fall. This campus is going to be empty."

The expression on Mrs. Davis' face didn't change. She put her pencil on the table. "Eighty-six. I suppose they will all be required to live in Fairchild Hall. That would make sense, wouldn't it?"

Rowan thought a moment and scratched her head. "I don't know. I didn't ask. That would make sense."

Mrs. Davis got up and poured herself a cup of coffee without offering one to Rowan. "Some professors will be laid off if there aren't enough students to take their classes, like Latin, for example. Why teach a language no one speaks? A waste of money." Mrs. Davis chuckled like someone told a humorous story.

Rowan froze in place and summoned all the courage she had to speak. "I took Latin for two semesters."

"Why?"

"Because Florence, I mean Miss Pruett, suggested it would be good for a liberal arts education."

Mrs. Davis wiped the smile off her face. "Well, we have work to do. I've been thinking about this. I knew Dr. Hutchins would want us to take care of ourselves and not be a burden to the community. She is one smart lady. I knew Mr. Hutchins too – God rest his soul. First, we need protein and the cheapest is chickens, both to eat and for eggs. Next, I think we can raise hogs. Beef we will need to buy from local farmers – only hamburger, no expensive beef."

Mrs. Davis paused and looked off caught in a web of her own thoughts. "We're going to need a garden too, for vegetables and herbs. I was thinking potatoes, tomatoes, peppers, cabbage, thyme, basil, oregano. I don't know where Dr. Hutchins wants to put a chicken pen and a hog pen and a garden. Why don't you find out? I want to use heritage chickens and hogs because they are reliable. You can talk to the animal science department to find out which ones would thrive here. Those are big jobs. Can you handle it?

"Are you ok, girl? Did you hear me? Can you handle this?"

Rowan's eyes bulged out and her hands were sweating. "Who should I talk to?"

Mrs. Davis scratched her head with the pencil. "I don't know. Ask Matilda, she knows everything."

Rowan went straight back to the administration building to ask Dr. Hutchins' administrative assistant, Matilda, for guidance.

Chapter 31

Overnight, Rowan's education changed from liberal arts to agriculture and animal sciences. Professor Sapper in animal sciences suggested Delaware chickens because they could get to be eight and a half pounds, and the hens laid about a dozen large brown eggs a day. Professor Sapper looked like a farmer in from the fields rather than a man who taught college for a living. His blond hair was cut short and his cheeks were red from the Kentucky sun. From the middle of his forehead up, it was white as snow from wearing a John Deere tractor cap all the time. Rowan noticed his hands were large and brown.

He contacted the hatchery in Berea and ordered seventy-five chicks. He calculated the size of pen needed and drew a diagram and called the hardware store to order the supplies to build a chicken coop and yard.

"I'll volunteer to build the chicken area and recruit several of the other faculty to help. We can have it up in a week. We'll have eggs and chickens to harvest by September. This going to be fun. You need to find out where Dr.

Hutchins wants us to build it. We need Hampshire hogs for our pork. Did you know the Hampshire hog was developed right here in Kentucky back in 1893? No, of course you didn't know. I wouldn't expect you to know. How many students did you say are coming back?"

"Eighty-six."

"Oh, such a tragedy. I don't know what we're going to feed the hogs before the students return. You need to find out from Dr. Hutchins how much she's willing to spend on feed and where she would want a hog pen. You can tell her eight piglets should be enough to start. It's late in the season but I'll start asking around the farm community to see who has a few to sell to us."

§

Rowan was so busy the first week after the students left campus for the summer she didn't have time to organize herself to move to Florence's home in town. As each day passed, the move seemed less necessary. Mrs. Davis was kind enough to prepare meals as part of Rowan's compensation, and Dr. Hutchins decided she would waive room rent for the summer. Rowan's wages were reduced by 75 percent, which was enough for the few extra things she needed, like toiletries, and she treated herself to a hot fudge sundae at Whitaker's Ice Cream shop downtown on Sunday afternoons.

The weather turned warm and humid early in the summer of 1942. Rowan was working in her office with the fan on the desk and the window cranked as wide open as possible. Rowan was making lists of the number of chickens, hogs and feed needed for Dr. Sapper and the amount Dr Hutchins approved to spend for each. Dr. Sapper wanted the list first thing Monday morning. Rowan's office door was also open, hoping to get a breeze to pass through the tiny office. She was the only person in the building on Saturday.

Knock! Knock!

Rowan jumped in her chair and dropped her pencil on the floor. She turned to look and Florence stood in the door frame wearing a sleeveless blouse, shorts, sandals and her hair pulled back into a pony tail.

"Florence, you scared the wits out of me."

"You're working on Saturday?" Florence asked.

"I have to. Dr. Sapper needs these lists bright and early Monday morning."

"I haven't seen you all week, young lady. You're taking your responsibilities seriously. I was just wondering when you plan to move into my home."

Rowan rubbed the back of her neck and avoided eye contact with Florence. "I've been meaning to talk to you about that. You are so kind and have always taken care of me. I worried people would find out and feel I was singled out for special treatment."

"That is absurd."

"Well, that's how I feel."

"You should have come and talked with me, Rowan dear."

"Dr. Hutchins wanted to reduce my salary so she waived rent for the summer in exchange for my help. Mrs. Davis is giving me meals every day, so...I really don't need to move. You understand, don't you, Florence? Oh please, tell me you understand."

Florence leaned against the door frame, wiped her

face with a handkerchief and broke into her maternal smile. "Yes, Rowan, I understand. Will you have time to work on a few library projects? You know I always have projects lined up for you."

Rowan jumped up and hugged Florence. "Oh yes, oh yes. I've volunteered to take care of the laying hens, and I can do that in the morning and still have afternoons for the library. Let's go downtown for a hot fudge sundae. I can finish this tomorrow."

Chapter 32

$\mathcal{R}$owan was excited to have student move-in day set for Monday, September 7th. Dr. Sapper created a formula for his own chicken feed to help the chickens lay earlier. It would be close but Rowan noticed a few eggs in the nesting boxes last Wednesday. By the second week of classes the hens should lay on a regular basis. From her research on Delaware hens, Rowan expected an egg a day, which would give Mrs. Davis forty-five to fifty eggs a day. She wanted them for everything from scrambled eggs for breakfast to vanilla custard for dessert. The hen boxes Dr. Sapper and his friend Mr. Jensen made were perfect. The laying hens were just west of Fairchild Hall, no more than a five-minute walk for Rowan to feed and water them every morning. After the students returned, she planned to ask for volunteers to help collect eggs every day.

South of Fairchild Hall Dr. Sapper constructed a hog pen for eight animals. He wanted to wait and breed them next June because he said the litter could be as big as fifteen piglets, which would be enough to sell to local farmers. A few local farmers agreed to hunt rabbits, ducks, and geese to supply Mrs. Davis with a variety of meat. They also would supply venison. Because of the value of deer and the seasonal hunt, they demanded pay, which Mrs. Davis accepted without an argument.

Rowan and Dr. Sapper laid out the vegetable garden to the north of Fairchild Hall, just a short walk for Mrs. Davis. The student population dwindled so much that Mrs. Davis laid off her three workers. Rowan had her fill of planting tomatoes, cucumbers, corn, peppers, cabbage, potatoes and herbs like basil, thyme, mint and a few others she couldn't remember. Between her kitchen chores and library projects, she worked at least fifty hours a week. Most evenings she tried to have just an hour to read for pleasure before drifting off to sleep, just to repeat it all over again the next day.

Rowan found she did a lot of research to do her job right. While she helped her grandma raise the chickens as a child, she just followed instructions. She did not understand what type of feed to use, how to feed and how often to give the chicks fresh water. Her natural inclination was to scour books in the library. She felt guilty about relying on Dr. Sapper for such basic information. He was very busy with building chicken coops, a hog pen and putting in the vast garden. Rowan found her lack of knowledge of gardening embarrassing. She couldn't tell a basil plant from a tomato plant. Through life experience she understood the adage that necessity is the mother of invention. Over the weeks a pile of books grew on the reading room table. Rowan walked in the reading room to locate a book on fertilizing a vegetable garden. She went through the pile and created stacks based on topics. She paused, stepped back and looked at the stack of books. An idea flashed through her mind. Rowan planned on sharing her eureka moment with Florence.

§

Rowan was the only student using the library during the summer, and most days she and Florence had lunch together out on the lawn, if the weather permitted. For central Kentucky it was a normal summer with temperatures in the high seventies or low eighties and humid every day. It rained at least once a week; perfect for the garden. Rowan and Florence liked to sit under the oak trees in the center of campus. The trees formed a canopy that shielded them from the midday sun.

"Would you like ice tea, Florence? Mrs. Davis just made it this morning. We should drink it before the ice melts and dilutes the tea. I brought an extra glass."

Rowan poured the glass to the rim and handed it to Florence. "You're very animated today, Rowan. Why?"

Rowan leaned forward, putting her hands on her knees. "You know I've been putting all the books I've found on raising chickens, gardening and other topics on a desk in the reading room."

"Yes, I noticed. You have plenty of time to shelve them before the fall semester begins."

"I have an idea. I don't want to shelve them where I found them, scattered throughout the library. I spent hours searching for books. I want to create a new category of books called Self Help books. If you want to know how to knit or grow a garden or sew a dress, many practical things, you go to one place. It's like the scrapbook idea we had for families in the Pack Horse Librarian Project.

"Well, what do you think?"

Florence sipped her ice tea and let the idea rattle around in her mind for a bit. She broke out into a wide grin. "I like it. I like it a lot. You could create a collection and have it ready for the students in September. I give you credit, Rowan, you are an innovative librarian. Anything that makes the library easier to use, I am in favor of. Would you like some help?"

Rowan leaned over to give Florence a big hug. "Oh no, I can do it. You're busy with all your administrative jobs. Besides, the pile I have now is a brilliant start. It would help if you check in now and again and suggest other types of books or topics to add to the collection. I'll find a central location and make a big sign for it."

§

On Monday and Tuesday the next week Rowan didn't have time to stop in her own office. Wednesday morning she arrived by seven a.m. and found a battered letter on the center of her desk. Someone wanted to be sure she saw the letter, which was postmarked London, England, April 3rd, 1942. It had taken almost four months to arrive. She ripped open the letter and read:

Dear Rowan,

    I wanted to write to share my circumstances with you. I am in hospital in a little no-name town north of London. After training and a few weeks in Washington D.C., I was given the opportunity to cover the battle in the Western Front and was dispatched to London. The Germans have demolished most of London. Mr. Churchill holes up in a tiny bunker near Number 10 Downing Street. It is a miracle he conducts the war effort from there.

In March they gave me the chance to join British commandos on the St. Nazaire Raid in France. I went on shore with 611 of Britain's finest soldiers. The damn Nazi's found the boats we were to return to our ship in and blasted them to smithereens. I have never been so frightened in my life. There's a shortage of rifles so anyone in the press corps is only given a revolver, which isn't much use. I ran as fast as I could with the commandos. I was out of breath and fell several times in the mud. It was brutal. There were nearly 600 soldiers and only 228 of us made it back, and the rumor is they took over 200 prisoner – an accurate count will take days. A Nazi machinegun ripped my right leg to shreds. Two of the commandos carried me back to camp and saved my life. I will never forget them. I lost so much blood, I passed out and woke up in hospital.

I hope I will walk again but when I ask the doctor he turns away and puts my chart back on the end of the bed. I will be honest with you, I take morphine for the pain and to help me sleep. No one has said if I will stay in the hospital here or be shipped back home. I confess I have seen enough of this damn war and am very homesick. Please write when you can. Use the post office box on the outside of the letter.

Your friend,

Lucas Tate

Rowan folded the letter and put it back in the envelope. She was so busy she hadn't thought of Lucas over the summer and now felt ashamed and self-centered. In her mind she formed a picture of Lucas lying in bed alone. *I pray he doesn't feel I have abandoned him. That would be terrible. I will write Lucas a long letter this evening and mail it after feeding the hens tomorrow morning.* Rowan recalled the day she and Lucas first met when he gave her the first riding lesson on Ash. He sat so tall in the saddle. She chuckled to herself recalling he didn't say ten words to her. One mistake was the summer they took dancing lessons together and went to the movie show. Rowan learned she sent the wrong signals to Lucas who wanted more than just a fun time. The day Rowan told Lucas she didn't want to see him again was a disaster. He sat resolute in his office and changed the subject rather than admit his disappointment. While they didn't see each other often, when they did, it was cordial. Rowan was not good at having friends either female or male. She knew she was fortunate Lucas accepted her as a friend.

Chapter 33

$\mathcal{F}$or the next two years Rowan only left the safety of Berea College campus several times to run errands for Mrs. Davis. She set up the "How To" book collection in the reading room, and it became the most popular collection in the library. Students needed to learn how to pluck a chicken, how to fertilize vegetables, slop the hogs and many other jobs. Everyone volunteered to be part of the Berea College Victory Team.

Mrs. Davis asked Rowan to help with the chicken harvest. Rowan wasn't prepared to kill chickens. Some of the farm girls would pick up a chicken by the neck and twirl it around over their head several times to break its neck. Some took a hatchet and lopped off the head in one blow, then stuffed the body into a funnel with a bucket underneath to collect the blood. Rowan learned to grab the chicken by the legs, take it out of the funnel and swish it around in a steaming bucket of water. The chicken was then hung by its legs on a rope and the feathers plucked. The feathers were spread out on a blanket to dry and used for pillows and bedding. Once plucked, they were gutted and the livers and gizzards separated out. They fed the rest of the innards to the pigs. Mrs. Davis kept the blood, boiled it and made blood pudding that she fried in butter for Sunday morning breakfast. Rowan tried the pudding but couldn't stomach it. Sunday lunch was often fried chicken livers and gizzards. After a year Rowan learned to eat the livers, but the gizzards were a tough, tasteless lump of meat.

Dr. Sapper demonstrated how to harvest a pig. Rowan thought she should be a witness even if an unwilling one. Dr. Sapper shot the pig in the head with a twenty-two rifle. The pig dropped dead without a sound. It took him over four hours to butcher the pig. Rowan decided she had limits to what she would eat, even for the war effort. The most disgusting pig dish was boiled snout. Dr. Sapper swore it was the finest cut of meat, but few believed him.

With everyone chipping in on the work, the college remained tuition free during the war. By April, 1944, Rowan was excited for May graduation. The last two years her life were so focused she lost all sense of time. Florence allowed her to devote herself to developing the archive, and she was the resident expert in the collection hidden in a vault-like room two levels below the main floor.

On a Friday in April, Rowan was working in the library basement when she heard the clop, clop, clop of someone coming downstairs.

"Rowan. Rowan are you here?" Florence Pruett asked.

"Where else would I be?"

"Don't be sassy, Rowan. I have a note from Dr. Hutchins. She wants to see you this afternoon."

"Why?"

"Trust me, Dr. Hutchins is not in the habit of consulting with me when she wants to see a student. I suggest you delay whatever you're working on and be off to her office."

Rowan huffed, stacked a few papers, returned a few books to the shelves and left for Dr. Hutchins office.

Working in the archive, Rowan didn't realize what a beautiful April afternoon she was missing. All the trees in the central quad were leafed out and the magnolias were blossoming. She promised herself a walk around campus after dinner.

Rowan knocked on Dr. Hutchins' door.

"Come in."

Dr. Hutchins had her windows full open, which invited in a refreshing breeze. She put down her pen and looked up. "Oh, Rowan, how good to see you. I don't believe I've seen you for months. You keep busy, don't you?"

"Yes, Dr. Hutchins, I like to be busy."

"Well, sit down. Let's get right to it. I understand you are writing a biography on John W. Bate for your senior project."

"That's right. He's a fascinating man. Did you know he was born a slave? Of course you did. Silly of me to ask."

Dr. Hutchins got up to look out her window. "When will your paper be finished?"

"I'm turning it in next Monday."

Dr. Hutchins turned with a broad smile across her face. "Well, that's just perfect. Perfect."

Rowan sat back in her chair her eyebrows furrowing. "Why do you ask?

Dr. Hutchins moved to the side of her enormous desk, sat and leaned toward Rowan. "Well, each commencement we honor a Berea graduate. This year Mr. Bate turns ninety and we are overdue to recognize his educational accomplishments. I have invited him to attend commencement on May 7th to be given the Citation of Honor. I would like you to give a presentation on his accomplishments and escort him for the day."

Rowan jumped out of her chair and gave Dr. Hutchins a hug. Tears fell down her cheeks. "I am so honored, Dr. Hutchins. Oh, excuse me, I shouldn't have hugged you like that. Oh my, this is a thrill."

Dr. Hutchins guided Rowan back into her chair. "I'm pleased with your enthusiasm. Now, your presentation shouldn't be over fifteen minutes. You will speak just before we confer the degrees. I understand you are graduating with honors and will wear the gold tassel. What is your standing in your class?"

"Overall number three, and in the Library Science department number one."

"Excellent. I expect you to share your remarks with me no later than the Wednesday before commencement.

"You're excused now, Rowan."

§

Rowan brushed her hair fifty-five strokes and looked in the mirror. She used a bobbypin to balance her cap on her head. She put on the robe, zipped it up and broke into a broad grin at her reflection. Bending her head down she placed the blue stole with the Berea College emblem on the right side on her shoulders. She adjusted the stole several times before it was perfect. The final touch was her gold cord with tassels on the end that landed just above her waist. She had placed her speech on the dresser to practice before the ten-a.m. ceremony. Rowan looked into the mirror, took a breath and recited her presentation on John W. Bate from memory. The clock on the dresser ticked off twelve minutes. It was perfect. Florence had been kind enough to practice the speech with her at least twenty times during the week. As instructed, she gave the speech to Dr. Hutchins to review on Wednesday. Friday Rowan was called in to meet with Dr. Hutchins.

"Well, young lady, you should be proud. I've not changed a word your speech. I think this speech is the cap to your career at Berea College. You came to us as an innocent eager young woman and you leave us a mature accomplished woman, ready to take on the world. You have done such an excellent job you have earned the privilege of presenting the Citation of Honor to Mr. Bate yourself."

Rowan sat speechless a moment. "I...I really think you should present the award – as our college President."

"I know Mr. Bate well. It would mean more to him coming from a graduate. Now, that's settled."

Rowan left Fairchild Hall at nine-fifteen to meet John W. Bate at Phelps Stokes Chapel by nine-thirty. May 7th was hot, and the cap and gown were uncomfortable, like being stuffed into a potato sack. Rowan was sweating by the time she reached the chapel door and worried her hair would frizz out in the humidity. She was greeted at the door by an usher who told her the balcony would not be open today. There were only thirty-two students graduating. The usher took Rowan to the side office where John W. Bate waited.

Mr. Bate looked up. He stood out of his chair when Rowan walked into the room. A glass of water was on the table, and he mopped his forehead with a handkerchief. "You must be Miss Daly. I'm happy to meet you." He looked her in the eyes, which meant he was only five feet two inches. He offered a handshake.

Rowan reached for his hand and shook it with vigor. "Oh, Mr. Bate, the honor is all mine."

"Dr. Hutchins told me your senior project was to write my biography. Now isn't that something, to write a biography about an old slave. Oh my, oh my." He sat back down and took a long sip of water. "I wish my wife could have been here today. I lost her three years ago." A forlorn look crossed his face. He slapped his knees and looked deeply into Rowan's eyes. "I want to tell you something, Miss Daly. I'm tired. I'm eighty-nine now, you know." He chuckled and wiped his cheeks. "Of course you know, don't you?"

"I hope I can contribute like you have after graduating from Berea. You give me hope, Mr. Bate."

Mr. Bate leaned back in his chair. "I graduated from Berea in May 1888. That's sixty-three years ago. Berea College gave me a gift I wanted to repay. Education saved me, Miss Daly. On that graduation day I dedicated my life to education. After graduation I was the only teacher in a one room school house in Danville. Oh, I'm sure that must be in your biography. But did you know that the Black folk in the community didn't support my school. They wanted to send their children to private religious schools. Now, I'm telling you, religion and education should have nothing to do with each other. In my experience religion tries to dictate what is taught – evolution for example."

"What kept you going, Mr. Bate?"

"I am a stubborn man, very stubborn. I started with

just ten students until I hired the daughter of a local Black minister. God put hope in my heart, Miss Daly. Hope." He pointed to his heart. "Keep hope right here and everything will be ok, I promise."

"Did you really have 600 students when you retired?"

"Yes, 611 to be exact."

There was a knock on the door. The usher peeked in. "We're ready for you to take your places on stage."

Rowan and Mr. Bate sat next to each other in the center of the stage. All the windows were wide open and a soft breeze offered some relief to the chapel, which felt like Mrs. Davis' oven when she was baking bread. A string quartet from the Music Department played while guests filed in and members of the administration took their places on the stage. Rowan was pleased Dr. Sapper was on stage. He would present the achievement award in agricultural studies. Florence followed Dr. Hutchins on stage.

An usher came on stage and handed everyone a program. On the front page it listed: "Miss Rowan Daly presenting the Citation of Honor." There were only thirty-eight graduates – all women – receiving the Baccalaureate degree. No advanced degrees would be awarded this year. It listed the students under the departments that were giving their degrees. Rowan placed the program on her lap and looked out across the crowd. The chapel was only half filled with parents, grandparents, aunts, uncles, cousins and friends. Rowan caught her breath. There was no one in the audience for her. She was alone in the world and on graduation day it was a cruel reminder. Just as the quartet stopped playing, an usher escorted two women to the back pew. They rushed to sit down and not be noticed. Rowan recognized the ladies at once. Thelma and Hazel came all the way from Pikeville to attend her graduation. She couldn't stop a tear from rolling down her cheek.

Florence asked Dr. Hutchins' permission to give Rowan her diploma. When her name was called, Rowan stood and Florence stood at the same time. Rowan felt faint and swayed on her feet. Florence stepped toward her, taking her arm and offering her a hug and a kiss on both cheeks. Rowan's eyes blurred as they filled with tears. Florence kept Rowan steady.

"Rowan Daly, first in her class in Library Science. Congratulations, Miss Daly." Florence handed Rowan her diploma. Rowan stood still without moving. "You may sit down now, dear."

They provided a luncheon for the families, guests and graduates following the ceremony. This was Mrs. Davis' shining moment. Plates of fried chicken, mashed potatoes and gravy, greens and sweet tea and regular tea were served family style. Rowan found Thelma and Hazel after the ceremony to make sure they joined her at the table with Mr. Bate and Florence.

"Well, Rowan, you are the only pack horse librarian to graduate from college." Thelma announced to everyone at the table.

Mr. Bate put his silverware on the plate and looked at Rowan with kind, understanding eyes. "So, you were a pack horse librarian. I heard about a librarian in Pike County who developed a novel way to teach reading. That couldn't have been you, could it?"

Florence leaned toward Mr. Bate. "One and the same, Mr. Bate."

"Rowan, if you have time this afternoon, I would like

to learn more about how you came up with your teaching method. You should know I adopted that method in my school. It ended the fear students had of memorizing."

"Of course, Mr. Bate."

"Florence, Rowan gave a wonderful speech about Mr. Bate. I always thought she was too shy to get up in front of people and give a talk," Hazel said.

Florence smiled broadly. "Rowan has become more confident. Attending Berea was the right thing for her. How were you able to get off to attend today?"

"We left early Friday morning so we are only missing one day of delivering books. We'll double up on Monday to make sure all the families get books and magazines. We just couldn't miss Rowan's graduation," Thelma explained.

"Hazel, Thelma, it is very special that you took the bus from Pikeville to share in Rowan's graduation. The pack horse librarians are her family. Bless you, ladies. Now, I insist that you stay at my home tonight. Are you taking the bus back tomorrow?"

"Yes, ma'am."

Chapter 34

Rowan's duties to feed and water the laying hens had been assigned to one of Mrs. Davis' kitchen helpers so she had the luxury of sleeping in. When she woke, the sun was well up in the sky. She jumped up to check the time on her alarm clock – just seven-thirty. There was still time to rush down to the bus station to thank Thelma and Hazel again and send them back to Pikeville.

Rowan slipped on a pair of shorts, a sleeveless blouse and a pair of sandals. She brushed her hair just long enough to look presentable. She walked as fast as she could to the bus station because she couldn't remember what time Hazel said the bus left. As she rushed into the station, Florence, Thelma and Hazel were having a cup of coffee and a cake donut.

"So the graduate arrives!" Hazel blurted out.

"You know I wouldn't miss this, Hazel," Rowan said as she pulled out a chair and sat down.

"We were wondering..." Thelma said.

Rowan sniffed and wiped her nose. "Why the sad face, Rowan?" Florence asked.

"It has been a wonderful four years at Berea but I confess I miss Pikeville and all the wonderful hill families. How are the Teel's?"

"They're on my route," Thelma said. "Mr. Teel finally got well, and he's working in a boot factory. Mrs. Teel is making quilts and giving them away. She also teaches quilting once a week at the library. The oldest daughter graduated from high school and is now a teachers' assistant. They still ask about you."

Rowan looked off into space, remembering the first time she met the Teel family during a summer downpour. They took her in without question. The days of serving as a pack horse librarian were a thousand years ago. "I can't thank you enough for making the trip. You both are the best."

"Now that you have your diploma, what are you going to do?" Thelma asked.

Rowan grabbed Thelma's arm, her eyes bulged. "I don't know. That's terrible. I haven't thought about it at all."

Florence put her arm around Rowan's shoulder. "Don't worry, dear. We'll talk. Why don't you stop by this afternoon for tea."

All four women broke out in gigantic smiles and laughed. They walked the short distance to the bus station arm in arm. The bus drove up. Thelma and Hazel grabbed their suitcases and climbed aboard. They each took a window seat and waved until they could no longer see Florence and Rowan at the curb.

"Rowan, I'm guessing you haven't had breakfast. Let's

stop for a big bowl of grits, smothered in butter – just the way you like it."

§

Mid-afternoon Rowan went to Florence's office and found the door wide open. She was humped over her desk reading from a thick file. There were two stacks of books one on either side of the desk. She looked up when she saw Rowan standing in front of her desk without saying a word. "You are so quiet, Rowan. Are you rested now, dear?"

"Yes, thank you. Thelma's question has haunted me. I hate to admit it but I don't know what I'm going to do now. Dr. Hutchins said I could stay at Fairchild until the end of the month. Mrs. Davis offered to continue meals if I continue to pay her – I suppose that's fair. I will need to find an apartment, I guess. I should probably stop and buy a newspaper on the way back to the residence hall. I don't have any idea how to search for a library job somewhere. I really didn't think this out at all. Sometimes I am my own worst enemy."

Florence got up, offered Rowan a cup of tea and pointed toward the couch behind the visitor chairs. "Let's sit over hear. Now, you really haven't considered where you would like to live?"

Rowan hesitated a few minutes before answering. "Well, I can't imagine living anywhere except Berea. I would like to work in a library but I don't think the local library has any positions open, though I haven't inquired."

Florence scooted closer to Rowan. "Well, Dr. Hutchins and I have talked. I am desperate for help here at Frost

Library. I struggle to balance my administrative duties and librarian duties. While our helpers work very hard, they are not librarians. I have a proposal for you. I would like you to work full time. I have three assignments for you. First, you will be responsible for circulation. You have a keen sense of how the library can support Berea students, and you are good at collecting and reviewing collection data. Second, I want you to continue to develop the heritage collection. Think of ways to display part of the collection rather can hiding it in the basement. Finally, we need someone to curate displays in the library. You have a gift for curating, and it is a regular feature we need at Frost. I know that sounds like a lot – it is – but you are capable. Dr. Hutchins has approved a salary of one hundred and fifty-six dollars a month, beginning in June. We are always paid on the 15th of the month so you will need to fend for yourself for about six weeks. I assume you still have a little savings left."

Rowan swayed back and forth almost falling off the couch. She grabbed her tea cup with both hands. She stared at Florence and gasped for breath. "I...I...I..."

"You will say yes?"

"Yes. Yes. – Yes!"

Florence opened her arms and pulled Rowan toward her for a long hug. "You have earned the opportunity, Rowan, dear. We will work together again– now as librarians. My heart is full."

§

In the next six weeks Rowan was very busy. She found a furnished one-bedroom apartment just two blocks from

Frost Library and would be able to move out of Fairchild Hall by May 20th. She didn't want to take advantage of living in the residence hall until the end of May. She was eager to establish her independence. Without paying rent she still had the savings she brought with her from Pikeville and had even added a few dollars. She wanted to look like a professional librarian and splurged to buy herself a few dresses she could wear at the library every day. She had to visit several shoe stores to find shoes comfortable enough to wear standing most of the day.

She took time to visit with Mrs. Davis and Dr. Hutchins to thank them for their belief in her and giving her the opportunity to serve Berea College students. Rowan arrived for work at Frost Library at eight on June 1st. Florence greeted her under the skylight. "Follow me. I have a surprise for you." They walked toward the reading room. On the right of the reading room entrance was a door marked: "Miss Daly – Librarian."

"This is your office, Rowan." Florence opened the door to make sure she was the first person to enter.

Part IV

Chapter 35

*R*owan clicked the dial of her new Victrola radio and lay out her clothes for the first day of the fall semester while she listened. She felt like a little comedy would lighten her anxiety so she tuned into one of her favorites.

"Good evening, ladies and gentlemen. It's Sunday September 3rd, 1950. At the top of the hour we will broadcast the Burns and Allen Show starring George Burns and Gracie Allen. We bring this program to you this evening by Twenty Mule Team Borax...."

Rowan pulled up a chair to sit close to the radio so she could turn the volume down and not disturb the other lodgers on the floor. Living by herself in an apartment was too isolating and five years ago she moved into Murphy's Boarding House, just two blocks from the Frost Library. There were only two other boarders on the second floor, Gloria Hill and Alice Williams.

Gloria moved from her family's farm to work at the

soda fountain counter of the local pharmacy. She made soup, sandwiches and fountain drinks six days a week. Gloria had just graduated from high school in May and was desperate to be on her own and prove to her family she could make it She had the gift of quiet confidence in herself. When Rowan visited the store for her hot fudge sundae, Gloria would sneak an extra squirt of fudge for her.

Alice was a junior at Berea College who didn't enjoy living in the campus residence halls. She was studying for medical school and found the residence hall too noisy and distracting. Alice maintained a straight A average and didn't want to jeopardize her grades. Rowan saw Alice only in the library or at the one meal Mrs. Murphy served. She was reserved, not shy, and didn't bother to speak unless spoken to. Alice also limited her conversation to her studies. No one at the boardinghouse knew where she grew up, if she had siblings or any other personal information.

It was hot for early September in central Kentucky, and Rowan wanted to dress for comfort on the first day of the semester. She laid out a striped sleeveless blouse, broad leg trousers and sandals. She hadn't changed her hairstyle since moving to Berea ten years ago – a part on one side, cut just below her ear. Rowan never spent money for makeup. She learned to be comfortable without it, except maybe a little lipstick once in a while. She brushed her hair one hundred times while listening to Burns and Allen in another hilarious situation. Gracie was innocent and George wise. Tonight Rowan laughed so hard she cried.

When the program was over, she clicked off the radio and took her bath so she wouldn't compete with Alice and Gloria.

§

Mrs. Murphy caught Rowan in the hallway wrapped in her blue cotton bathrobe after her bath. "Are you excited about the semester starting tomorrow, Rowan?" Mrs. Murphy asked.

"I'm so excited, I doubt if I will sleep very much tonight – but that's ok."

"I will be right back. I have a special treat for you."

In a few minutes there was a soft knock on the door. Mrs. Murphy backed into her room with a wood tray. "Now, here's a slice of my barmbrack. My recipe is straight from Ireland, and I brought a glass of warm milk."

"You are the kindest person, Mrs. Murphy."

"Oh please, after living here five years you really should call me Fiona."

While listening to Fiona's story, Rowan finished two slices of barmbrack and the glass of warm milk. "That was delicious. You are such a talented baker, Mrs.... Oh, I mean Fiona. When did Mr. Murphy start work at Berea?"

"Well, for years we eked out a living renting rooms and Mr. Murphy doing odd jobs around town. It wasn't until the draft in 1940 and young men began leaving the county when Berea College advertised for a janitor. Mr. Murphy was hired the same day he interviewed. He had a reputation in town for being handy and soon his job became more handyman than janitor, which suited him just fine."

Rowan put the empty glass of milk, plate and fork back on the tray. "I was lonely. In Pikeville I lived in a boardinghouse owned by Mrs. Perkins – she is a widow. At my apartment near the library, I hated eating all my meals alone. I'm not a skilled cook so I made a lot of sandwiches and simple salads. Mostly it was the loneliness. I'll never forget the day I met Mr. Murphy and he told me about your boardinghouse. I love to hear him talk with that special lyricism in his voice."

"Thank you, we've had a pleasant talk this evening, Rowan. I should let you go to bed. I hope the barmbrack and warm milk help you sleep."

Rowan took Fiona's hand in hers. "Thank you. Thank you so much."

$

The next morning Rowan was the first one down to breakfast. Fiona was just setting the table. "Would you like some help?" Rowan asked.

"I never turn down an offer to help. Here, you can pour orange juice in the glasses and put a glass at each place."

"Fresh orange juice is such a treat, thank you, Fiona. You really don't need to splurge on us."

Fiona smiled and backed her way into the kitchen. "My pleasure."

In a few minutes both Alice and Gloria took their places at the table. As usual Alice didn't say a word while Gloria talked about all the students returning to class and how the lunch business would overwhelm today at the pharmacy. Mrs. Murphy set a piping hot bowl of cheesy scrambled eggs, a plate of toast and an enormous bowl of cream of wheat with a pond of butter on top on the table. This was Rowan's favorite meal.

Rowan thought maybe she and Alice could walk together to campus but Alice excused herself from the table and left a few minutes later without speaking to anyone. "Will Mr. Murphy be walking to campus soon?" Rowan asked.

"Oh dear, he had an early breakfast and left an hour ago. There's always so much to do on opening day. Thank you for asking, Rowan."

Rowan helped clear the table and walked part way to campus with Gloria, who was so excited she skipped all the way. Florence's door was cracked open, and Rowan stuck her head in to say good morning.

Rowan walked to her office and found Buck hammering something on her door. Buck was assigned to the library and admitted he didn't know how to read and wasn't interested in learning. This morning he wore blue bib overalls without a shirt underneath. Pounding on the door he didn't hear Rowan behind him. "Buck – Buck! What are you doing?"

Buck backed away from the door. "Puttin' up this sign. Miss Pruett, she told me to get the job done before you got to work. You must be early – huh. Ok, a couple more whacks with the hammer and I will be finished. You stand back now, Miss Rowan."

Rowan watched Buck from a distance. When he finished, Buck wiped the sign off with a cloth. It read: Miss Daly – Associate Director, Rowan screamed – "Associate Director!" She ran straight to Florence's office, not knocking on the door, just barging in. "The sign? Florence, the sign says 'Associate Director'."

Florence broke into a broad grin and opened her arms to give Rowan a hug. "I do so love a surprise. Yes, dear, you've been promoted to associate director. Dr. Hutchins has been impressed with your work the past six years. Trust me, you have earned the title."

"Oh, I have to sit down." Rowan fell into the nearest chair. She gasped for breath. "So a…"

"Yes, Rowan your new pay will be two thousand seventy-five dollars a year. I think that's fair because you haven't received an increase since you started in 1944; it's just an extra two hundred and three a year. Maybe you can take a little vacation during the summer." Rowan sat fanning herself and trying to catch her breath.

"I should explain that your duties will change a bit. You will get help managing the collection and one student will be assigned to set up the curated exhibits. This year I will teach you some of the administrative duties, and next year you will be on your own for a few administrative jobs. It's time for you to grow in your profession, Rowan. Why don't you go to your office and prepare for the day. Congratulations, dear." Florence took Rowan by the arm and led her back to her own office.

§

The next morning Florence couldn't find Rowan in her office. She walked through the first floor of the library and hoped Rowan wasn't distracting herself by shelving returned books. She had the habit of burying herself in menial tasks when she needed space to reflect on things. Rowan wasn't in the stacks. Unless she was late for work, which had never happened in the last six years, she was cloistered in the archive in the basement. Florence knew this meant Rowan needed to hide from the world. The promotion to associate director had surprised Rowan and caught her off guard. Florence had to admit this was the first time Frost Library had the position. This was also the first time there were two librarians with bachelor's degrees. This staffing reflected the growth in Berea academic programs and the more central role of the library.

Florence walked with care down the two flights of stairs to the archive room. She didn't want to startle Rowan. In a soft whisper Florence called, "Rowan, Rowan." There wasn't an answer. It meant Rowan was deep in the stacks. Florence sat at the table near the door and waited for Rowan to emerge from her place of safety. In a few minutes Rowan walked out of the stacks, carrying a variety of books that went up under her chin.

"Florence, I didn't hear you. I am so sorry. This must mean you were looking for me. You know the work in the archive is never done. However, I must admit the work is a solace to me."

Florence stood and gave Rowan a little hug. "I understand. I wanted to let you know that Dr. Hutchins has called a special all-staff meeting this afternoon. She's going to be announcing something that will significantly change Berea College forever."

"It sounds like you know what the announcement is."

"I don't pay attention to staff rumors. The truth is academics are terrible gossips. Anyway, in your new role you will be expected to attend all staff meetings. There may be times when I cannot attend so you will attend for both of us. The meeting is at three-thirty in the chapel."

"Can we walk over together?"

"Oh...Dr. Hutchins may also announce your new position. I'm not sure if it is widely known among faculty. I didn't want you to be surprised."

§

By three-fifteen most of the faculty and administrative staff had taken seats in the chapel. There was a noticeable air of electricity and anticipation in the air. Florence and Rowan sat at the end of a row near the front. There were no chairs set up on stage so it would be just Dr. Hutchins speaking.

The clock in the back of the chapel struck three-thirty and Dr. Hutchins walked to the podium and placed her hands behind her back.

"Distinguished Colleagues. I have news for you I can only describe as momentous. In 1904 the Kentucky Legislature created a law called Day Law, banning all interracial education and the governor signed the bill. In 1905 our administration was forced to comply with the law and asked all of our colored students to not enroll in the fall of 1905. By vote of the academic staff, Berea College sued, opposing this heinous law. The battle went all the way to the Supreme Court of the United States of America. We lost. Over the last 45 years Berea College has been forbidden from fulfilling our original mission of an integrated student body, no matter gender or race. Today, I announce that Day's Law has been amended. Interracial education, above the level of high school, is now permissible. We will once again be able to fulfill the mission of our founder the Reverend John G. Fee. We will continue to fight for integrated education for all grades. However, we must now turn our attention to recruiting students of color to our institution of higher learning. It is my goal to admit as many students as possible for the winter semester of 1951. We cannot wait an entire academic year to renew our mission.

"I would like the academic staff to work with our admissions staff to develop admission guidelines and to go throughout Kentucky to recruit eligible students. I have a list of people I will ask to take part: Dr. Sapper, Dr. Evans, Dr. Lambert, Dr. Fugate and one more that you may not be aware of. I have appointed Rowan Daly to the position of Associate Director of Frost Library, to serve on the recruitment committee. The Library will have a key role in welcoming our new students and integrating student life. Will you please stand, Miss Daly?"

Rowan flushed and wavered in her seat. Florence took her arm to help her stand. The assembly burst out clapping.

"That was an enthusiastic welcome, Miss Daly.

Assembly dismissed."

Everyone around Rowen grabbed her hand to congratulate her. Dr. Hutchins had to shout over the crowd. "Oh yes, the committee will report to me."

Rowan's legs were unsteady. She was perspiring and felt faint. She plopped down in her seat with a thump. It took several minutes for the room to empty. Rowan looked Florence in the eyes. "Did you know about this?"

"Well, I made a convincing argument to Dr. Hutchins about your participation. I know you live for challenges like this."

Rowan bowed her head. "It will be an honor."

§

The next week Dr. Hutchins called the Recruitment Committee to her office for a brainstorming session to develop a list of ideas on how to attract students of color back to Berea College. Dr. Sapper spoke first.

"I believe we should understand that many potential students have been raised on farms and a good agronomy education would be very useful to being successful in our new economy. It could also be a way for us to encourage a move away from growing tobacco to other crops that could be as profitable – hemp, for example."

Each person on the committee offered interesting suggestions. Dr. Hutchins looked at Rowan. "You have been quiet today, Rowan. That's not your style. What suggestions do you have for the library's role?"

Rowan sat up straight in her chair and squared her shoulders. "Well, Florence and I have had several spirited talks but we are in agreement. First, I want to create a special collection on the history of slavery and the emancipation of Negroes in America. It is important for a people to know their history. Second, I want to curate a permanent display on the contributions of Negro Americans to our society to include, at least: Fredrick Douglass, Sojourner Truth, Harriet Tubman, George Washington Carver, the Tuskegee Airmen and recently Jackie Robinson. I'm interested in developing a seminar on Negro -American accomplishments that could evolve. I want our students to be proud of their heritage and let them know a Berea College education will prepare them to make their own contributions.

"Rowan, I would like to suggest you work with Dr. Lambert in the history department. He has written scholarly works on the transition of Negroes from slavery to freedom after publication of the Emancipation Proclamation. I think you will make an excellent team."

"Thank you, Dr. Hutchins. What a great opportunity. It's a long way from being a farm girl without parents to working with a college professor."

Chapter 36

Recruiting Negroes to a small, little-known college in rural Kentucky, proved to be a daunting task. In January, 1951 four women enrolled, all in the Education Department. Rowan convinced all four women to live at Fairchild Hall and agreed with them their transition would be easier if they lived on the same floor. One of the women, Helena, selected Rowan's old room, 301.

§

On Sunday afternoon Rowan gave a presentation at the library on the accomplishments of Negro Americans. Her first presentation was close to a disaster. As she walked up to the podium, her mouth went dry and she wasn't able to speak a single word. Florence rushed to get her a glass of water while Rowan stood at the podium shuffling her feet and rearranging her notes.

She took a long drink of water, looked at the handful of students and faculty fidgeting in their chairs on a warm afternoon. Rowan took a deep breath, planted her feet and began talking about Frederick Douglass. She didn't follow Florence's advice to practice in front of a mirror so her presentation was choppy. And she read a great deal, she droned on for at least an hour, but when she started asking the audience for questions, she noticed on the clock only about fifteen minutes had passed. None of the students asked questions but several of the faculty asked simple questions they thought surely Rowan could answer. Rowan had spent hours researching for her presentation and she knew the facts well. Her problem was interpreting the facts and putting them in a larger historical context.

People stood and walked toward the door. Florence jumped up to make an announcement. "We have refreshments. There's tea and my famous Kentucky butter-cake cookies in my office. There's plenty for everyone. Please stay."

Rowan was glued to her position behind the podium. Florence grabbed her by the arm and escorted her to her office where the goodies were waiting. "Oh Florence, you really didn't have to do this."

"Oh yes, I did. Now, grab a cookie and a glass of tea and mingle. Introduce yourself. Ask people if they learned anything from your talk. Ask them what topics they would like to learn about. Not to be rude but you may want to ask Dr. Lambert for a few tips on making presentations. Now, this is a good program. I want you to plan on presenting a seminar once a month in the library. You may even consider a presentation with other faculty. You get along well with Dr. Sapper; he would be delighted to present with you, and as I've mentioned Dr. Lambert is known for his intriguing almost theatrical lectures. You'll learn, I know you will, dear."

§

Recruiting Negro men proved to be an overwhelming challenge. Good jobs were plentiful and taking time away from their lives to attend college wasn't valued. Dr. Sapper had an interesting idea to recruit men for agronomy classes, but it proved a hard sell to go to college to learn to be a farmer. Dr. Sapper knew there also wasn't any interest in giving up a lucrative cash crop like tobacco. Many soldiers learned to smoke in the service, and their habit continued when they came home. Doctors and athletes all made commercials for different brands of cigarettes that made smoking glamorous.

Dr. Fielding, from the Business Department, developed a recruiting program based on teaching basic management, accounting and banking skills. More Negro men were attracted to these programs. The key was to link a graduate with a job soon after graduation day. Dr. Fielding used the library to develop a list of companies that hired without regard to race. Rowan assigned one of her assistants to research companies with open recruiting, and Dr. Lambert dug into corporate history and the history of Negroes working in each company.

While Rowan was busy with recruiting students and other library duties, Florence gave herself the task to develop a manual on library policies and operations. Unlike other college libraries, Berea College didn't have a separate library board or even academic oversight. This level of independence was unique and one that Florence cherished.

Several times a week Rowan would check on Florence, and each time she found her buried in books and typing on her Smith Corona typewriter. Rowan noticed several baskets at the corner of her desk overflowed with discarded pages.

"Florence, would you like to take a break and walk downtown for a little lunch?" Florence jumped when she heard Rowan's voice. "I didn't hear you come in."

"Lunch?"

"No, not today. I bought a peanut butter sandwich and a banana for lunch from home. With that new salary of yours, I guess you can afford lunch out."

"Florence Pruett, that was cruel. I just thought it would be nice to chat and have a little lunch. You seem demonic with your effort to write the policy manual and operation guidelines. I hope to have time to read it someday. So, never mind, I'll walk downtown by myself,"

Rowan noticed that Florence hadn't given her any administrative duties as she had promised. Though Rowan was busy enough with the recruitment program that she didn't want to remind her.

During the summer of 1951 the two women worked at the library and rarely saw each other for weeks. Rowan teamed up with Dr. Lambert to refine her seminars and went to visit churches, schools, social clubs, anywhere she could to talk with Negroes about attending Berea College. She found extreme doubt and suspicion that there was no tuition at Berea. It just made little sense to many prospective students and was beyond their life experience. Rowan would tell her own story of working as a pack horse librarian and with Florence's help entering Berea College as an "older" student. She gave herself as living proof that Berea offered everyone an equal opportunity.

The 1951 fall semester Berea enrolled twelve Negro students, eight women and four men. All of the men signed up for business programs. Dr. Sapper was discouraged not to have a single student in the agronomy program but pleased to have male students in the student body. Rowan felt an increase in Negro students from four to twelve was a monumental accomplishment. She was ready to return to her librarian duties and leave recruiting to others. She missed Florence and had only seen her several times during the summer recess and once at the church summer picnic. Florence was distracted and not conversational. Rowan flip-flopped between being offended and worried that something just wasn't right about Florence.

On the first day of the fall semester, Rowan stopped in the Amish bakery and bought two huge glazed donuts. At work she brewed a pot of coffee and took a tray of donuts and coffee to Florence's office. For Kentucky, early September was cool, and Rowan felt coffee and donuts was the perfect treat to begin the day.

Rowan walked into Florence's office without knocking. "Good morning Florence. How about a yummy Amish donut?"

Florence's chair was turned to face the window. She said nothing when Rowan entered. Rowan set the tray on the desk and walked around to greet Florence again. Florence appeared to be sleeping, her eyes were closed and her breathing shallow.

Rowan gasped. Sleeping at nine in the morning wasn't normal. Rowan whispered, "Florence?" No response.

Louder. "Florence?" Again, no response. *Could Florence be that exhausted?* Rowan asked herself. Rowan touched Florence's shoulder. No response. Rowan spoke and shook Florence's shoulder.

Florence shook her head and wiped her eyes with her hands. "Oh, Rowan, what are you doing here?"

"Coffee and donuts!"

Florence breathed in and stretched, then sat straight up in her chair. "Those donuts smell like they just came out of the oven. I could use a little pick me up. You are always so thoughtful." Florence sipped her coffee and took a big bite out of the donut.

Rowan pulled a chair up to Florence's desk and watched her enjoy the baked goods. She had known Florence for fifteen years and she didn't appear to have aged a day. Rowan's faced had filled out and while not overweight she wasn't as slender as her college days. She leaned in close to Florence to look for any sign of weariness.

"Rowan, why are you staring at me?"

"I don't mean to stare, it's just that, well, you know, sleeping at nine a.m. isn't...well, it just isn't normal – especially for you. We've known each other for fifteen years and you've always been a morning person – full of vim and vigor. Are you feeling well?"

Florence popped the rest of the donut in her mouth and washed it down with a bit of coffee all the time staring at Rowan. "Well, I have to admit I have put a lot of work into the policy manual and operating procedures. By next week I hope to sit down with you and review both of the documents. They're just a draft at this stage. My problem is I don't know any other college library directors. I suppose I should get out more – travel to other campuses in Kentucky."

Rowan scratched her head. "What did Dr. Parsons do after the war? Could you write to him? Maybe send him the drafts?"

"You have such wonderful ideas, Rowan. Funny you should mention Dr. Parsons. I don't know what he did after the war. One day about a year and a half ago I received a very long letter. He is working at the Library of Congress now. I'm not sure what his position is, but he loves living in Washington D.C. He has an apartment near the Smithsonian. I never thought of him as an urban person, but I really knew him as a student, not a colleague."

"Library of Congress. That's impressive. Well, then you have his address. You could write to him and ask him to review what you've written. I don't need to read them now. It would be better to get Dr. Parsons' perspective. I'm surprised he never composed these documents while he was director here."

"Rowan, remember that besides serving as the library director, he had teaching and researching responsibilities. After having this job for...oh my, this semester starts my eleventh year – can that be? Well, it is, isn't it? Thank you for the morning treat and the talk. I'll write Dr. Parsons today. I can walk to the post office at lunch. Feel like lunch today?"

Rowan returned to her office to plan a new display on Negro American accomplishments. She had been researching the record of the amazing Tuskegee Airmen. She felt they deserved their own unique display.

Chapter 37

*T*hat year Rowan's reputation on campus grew. When she walked on campus, at least a dozen students would greet her with "Miss Daly – the library lady." She polished her seminars and was invited by local church groups and civic groups to speak. She developed an easy, conversational style. Her lectures expanded to an hour, and questions often took another thirty minutes.

At the beginning of the fall semester, two Negro women volunteered to work with Rowan in the library to fulfill their work requirement. Elisha Russell and Lily Alexander grew up in Lexington and had known each other since first grade. Their fathers were partners in a dry-goods store in Lexington and were well respected in their community and the Baptist church. Elisha's mother, Annie, wanted her to attend a Baptist college. Her father, Ezra, had other ideas. He wanted his daughter to have a liberal arts education. Lily didn't know what she wanted to do after high school and didn't have any notion of attending college. She was content to work with her father in the dry-goods store. When Elisha announced at Christmas dinner the two families had together that she would attend college, Lily chimed in that she would too.

§

Rowan heard shuffling feet and looked up to see two students standing just outside her office door. "May I help you? Are you looking for something in the stacks?"

"Elisha Russell and Lily Alexander from Lexington," Elisha said. "We're freshmen. Our high school counselor told us all about you and this library. We want to work at the library. We were told you needed two students so here we are."

"Oh." Rowan sat straight up in her chair and folded her hands on her desk. "Ok, which one of you is Elisha and which one Lily?"

Besides being shy, Lily was short. Rowan guessed she stood just under five foot tall. Elisha was as tall as Rowan. Both girls were dressed well and were polite, almost too polite. Rowan guessed they came from a traditional Baptist upbringing.

Lily stuck her arm up in the air. "I'm Lily."

"That's a good start. Now, why don't you take a seat and tell me about yourselves. I expect I will have others to interview at the library." Rowan's mind raced, she never imagined that Negro students would work at the library. Of course, she met Negro recruits but none had ever shown any interest in the library. Rowan tried to hide her discomfort.

Elisha sat toward the edge of her chair and gave a detailed recitation from the first day they met in first grade to this very moment. When she finished, she sat back in her chair and asked for a glass of water. Lily noticed a pitcher of water and several glasses on a tray on a table behind Rowan's chair. She jumped up and poured a glass of water for Elisha.

"That's very interesting, now, as I said, I expect other students to interview, and I don't know when I will have an answer for you. Perhaps I can describe the type of work we have at the library so that you can make sure you are interested. Don't be afraid to let me know if you would be interested in other things. Every year I curate a new exhibit on special accomplishments of Negro Americans. This year I want to create a display on the Tuskegee Airmen. Did you learn about the Tuskegee Airmen in your high school history class?"

Elisha couldn't contain herself and began sharing everything she knew about the Tuskegee Airman. "In fact, we know a Tuskegee Airman. His name is Edward Mitchell. He was a captain in the war and flew one of those red-tailed airplanes. He owns a Tuskegee Airmen school in Lexington, and he knows our fathers very well. He's even spoken at our church. Not a sermon; he tells war stories."

Rowan fell back into her chair and squeezed her eyes shut. "You are two amazing young ladies. Do you think Edward Mitchell would accept an invitation to speak at our Christmas convocation this year? You can help me draft a letter and provide an introduction.

"Take time to think over working at Frost Library and come back tomorrow afternoon at 2:30 p.m. I will share with you a few of your regular library duties such as re-shelving books, dusting and checking out materials. Initially, if you want to work here, I think you should spend half your time on the Tuskegee Airmen exhibit and half on regular duties. I would like to have the special exhibit on display by November first." Rowan gestured toward the door. "I look forward to seeing you tomorrow."

§

That evening Rowan reflected on her interview with Elisha and Lily. All the time she spent recruiting Negroes to Berea she never imagined she would work with Negro students. It was one thing to recruit for the college and another to work with Negroes every day. There were Negro share croppers in Marion County where she grew up, but they always kept separate. Looking back on her work in Pike County she didn't remember ever hearing of a Negro family living in the county. For some reason Negroes were not miners.

Rowan took a walk through campus as the sun set. She was uncertain about working with Elisha and Lily. She didn't have any reason to turn down their request to work at the library. *I'm not a racist, at least I don't think I am. I surprise myself in being uneasy about working with two Negro students. I need to live the Berea motto – 'God has made of one blood all the peoples of the earth' – not just recite the words.*

Chapter 38

*R*owan didn't listen to the weather report on the radio before walking to work, a mistake in December because the temperature could change from day to day. Rowan slipped on her green winter coat with a fold-over collar. She forgot to bring a hat and gloves. A sheer white blanket covered the grass. She walked faster than usual to campus and kept her hands in her coat pockets for the entire walk.

"Oh, Rowan, I thought I heard you come in. Put your coat away, dear, and come in. I received a package from Dr. Parsons. Oh my, you didn't wear a hat and gloves today? You didn't listen to the weather report on the radio again, did you? All right, why don't you make us both a cup of tea. I want to share several of Dr. Parsons comments with you."

Florence handed the document to Rowan and took her cup of tea. Florence slurped her tea and was distracted by this new habit, which sounded like the hogs at the slop trough. Rowan flipped through forty to fifty pages, and each page had red ink notes printed in the margins.

"I'm sorry, Florence, I just don't have the context for all of Dr. Parsons' comments. I haven't read it yet."

Florence ruffled her hair and sat up bolt upright. "Well, yes, I had no idea how long it would take him to respond. Never mind. Here, give it back to me. I sat up all night reading every comment, and I have a scathing headache this morning. What I wanted to show you was this separate note he sent with his comments."

Florence placed several type-written pages on her desk and shoved them toward Rowan. The note was very formal:

Miss Florence Pruett,

Overall, the draft college library policies and procedures is well thought out, clear, concise and professional. This is what I would expect from you. As noted, I have made minor comments in the margins for your consideration. Please accept these as suggestions and not direction. I would like to propose an experiment that I am certain you will consider radical. I propose that all late fees be eliminated. I have come to the opinion that late fees are punitive and antithetical to the notion of an open, accessible library. I understand late fees are designed to provide library patrons with an incentive to return books and materials when they are due. In fact, many libraries depend on the revenue from late fees to help fund operations and collection development. If you would undertake this experiment, I would recompense the library for any lost revenue. I only ask that you keep data on book returns to compare when fees are charged and when they are not charged. My hypothesis is that returns will improve when no fees are charged. One more factor. I believe charges for lost books should cover both the cost of the material and an appropriate administrative fee. I suggested that lost material fees be set at twice the replacement cost. This should, in part, off set revenue lost from late fees.

Please consider my proposal and write your response soon. I would like the experiment to start in January with the spring semester.

Yours,
Dr. Parsons
Library of Congress
Washington, D.C.
October 31, 1951

The pages slipped from Rowan's grasp and floated to the floor. Rowan gasped for breath. She gathered the pages together, placed them on top of Florence's desk and shoved them toward her. She reached for her cup of tea to calm herself. Florence watched Rowan's reaction with interest. She folded her hands on top of her desk and gave Rowan a few minutes to collect her thoughts.

Florence expected Rowan to be surprised but she had not foreseen the shock she displayed. "Well?" Florence asked.

"Well," Rowan whispered.

"What do you think of Dr. Parsons' experiment?"

"Unbelievable. Every librarian knows that patrons bring back materials to avoid the fee. Why, it's just common sense, isn't yet?"

"If I remember correctly, last year we collected about

fifty-eight dollars in late fees. I've thought about what Dr. Parsons said. Is that the only reason patrons return books on time?"

Rowan moved her chair closer to the desk. "You raise an excellent question. I just never thought about it at all. So, what do you think?"

Florence crossed her arms and leaned back in her chair. "Well, I am intrigued and curious. He'll cover any revenue we might lose, so there's no risk to the library. I think we should accept his challenge, that is if you will collect the data and draft the initial report."

Rowan squirmed in her seat. "Do you think we should talk with Dr. Hutchins first?"

Florence stiffened and stared at Rowan. "I do not need her approval. I am in charge of this library."

"Oh, I don't mean you need her approval. I just think it would be a good idea if she's aware of the experiment before we announce the change. I don't think Dr. Hutchins likes surprises."

Florence's face softened and she smiled. "Yes, you are right. I suppose I should speak with her before writing to Dr. Parsons."

"What kind of information should I collect for this project?" Rowan asked.

"Get a pad and pencil and let's write up a list."

§

Later that afternoon Florence rushed from Dr. Hutchin's office to share her news with Rowan. She took short, quick steps and was out of breath by the time she reached the front doors of the library. She used all of her weight to push open the door. Outside her office she leaned against the wall, looking from side to side and hoping no one saw her. Florence took a few minutes to compose herself and catch her breath.

Rowan's office door was closed, which meant she was working someplace in the library and it could take Florence thirty minutes or more to find her. On a whim Florence opened the door without knocking. Rowan jumped and dropped her pencil on the floor. "Oh, you're here." Florence said.

"Where would I be?"

"Don't give me attitude, young lady. Most of the time your office door is wide open. I just took a chance that you might be in your office."

"I need extra quiet. I'm collecting information on late returns. I'm learning it's tedious and boring."

Florence looked around the small office and pulled the only chair from the side of the room to sit in front of Rowan's desk. "I just came from Dr. Hutchins' office. I explained the no fee project to her and she was open to the experiment. She worried about losing revenue from fees but when I explained that Dr. Parsons was going to cover any loss, she relaxed. Dr. Hutchins suggested if we implement the policy, we have another source of revenue to replace fees. She is not keen on adding general revenue funds to our annual budget. Oh, I'm talking too much. Why are you doing the data collection yourself. Why don't you have those students...a...a oh, I can't remember their names."

Rowan leaned back in her chair and stared at Florence for a few minutes. "Are you feeling yourself? It's not like you to forget names."

"Yes, I'm fine. I was up late last night poring over Dr. Parsons' comments so I'm tired this morning. I'll be fine. A good night's sleep and I'll have vim and vigor tomorrow." Florence stood up and motioned toward the door. "You know you shouldn't be wasting your time collecting this data. You should concentrate on analyzing the data once it's all together. Let the students collect the data for you."

Rowan slapped her pencil on top of the desk. "Their names are Elisha and Lily. I plan to let them collect the data. Before assigning the job, I want to develop the format I need and determine how long it will take them so I started myself. I've been working with students for eight years. I know how to guide their work."

Tears ran down Florence's cheeks and she hid her face in her hands. "Oh, I am so sorry, Rowan. I'm just so tired. I should go home now. Tomorrow I want to share with you a new event Dr. Hutchins wants to begin in December. Excuse me, please." Florence stood and left Rowan's office without closing the door behind her.

Rowan stared into the hallway and pulled at her hair as she tried to understand how and why Florence was acting so odd.

§

The next morning Rowan found Florence in her office humming "Mona Lisa" by Nat King Cole to herself. "You're chipper this morning."

Florence set the papers down and smiled. "Yes, a good night's sleep can work miracles. Do you have time now to hear about Dr. Hutchins' idea?"

"I'll make us a cup of tea and be right back." Rowan turned on her heel and left the office.

"I'm sorry about what I said yesterday. I shouldn't have snapped at you like that." Florence apologized.

"Forgotten already," Rowan said over her shoulder.

Rowan returned in a few minutes with a pot of tea and two fresh peach scones she picked up at the bakery. "Oh, peach scones, my favorite. Thank you, Rowan, you are always so thoughtful. Now, Dr. Hutchins is worried the faculty is isolated. Outside of their department meetings, they don't talk with each other, learn what research is underway at Berea or aren't collegial."

Rowan nodded her head. "Mmmm. I agree."

"So, Dr. Hutchins wants to begin a social gathering once a month on the second Wednesday of every month. The event will begin in the late afternoon, say four or four-thirty, and each department will take turns sponsoring the event. The department will provide beverages and light appetizers. Staff could mingle and the hosting department will have a brief presentation for fifteen to twenty minutes on a current project or research they are undertaking. She wants the first event to be in December – a holiday kick-off, if you will."

Rowan's eyes widened. Her smile turned into a smirk. "You volunteered the library for December, didn't you?"

Florence couldn't control herself from giggling. "Yes."

"You want me to organize it, don't you?"

"Yes, yes I would."

Rowan leaned forward, moving closer to Florence. "It sounds like fun."

"That's the spirit. Thank you, Rowan."

Chapter 39

$\mathcal{F}$lorence finished the policy and operational manuals while Rowan took responsibility for planning the first Second Wednesday event on campus. Rowan assigned the information collection for the no-fee research project to Elisha and Lily. Sitting in her office sipping tea before doors opened, Rowan felt the division of work was fair and everyone was working in an area they could excel.

Rowan and Florence discussed what they should highlight at the Second Wednesday event. Florence insisted it was premature to mention the no-late-fee research project. She wanted to review the data from the past several years before proceeding so she would know the potential revenue loss, even if Dr. Parsons had agreed to make the library whole.

Rowen nodded in agreement. "What about the Tuskegee Airmen display? It would be perfect to highlight. First, it's current. Second, you could explain the students' role in curating the project and their contribution to invite

Tuskegee Airman Mitchell for our Christmas convocation. Finally, you could explain how you curated the display."

"Oh yes, that's a wonderful idea," Florence said.

Rowan took a deep breath to calm herself. "Well, that's the decision then. I suppose I should accept it as an honor – and a lot of work."

Florence peered over her reading glasses at Rowan. "That will be enough, young lady."

Rowan took a pad and pencil and placed them on top of Florence's desk, ready to take notes. "Do I have a budget for refreshments? What if Elisha and Lily need to work more than ten hours a week?"

"I can't estimate what to budget for refreshments. The key will be to have excellent food. I have a discretionary budget that I rarely use. We can tap into that. It will help if you use Mrs. Davis' kitchen rather than local businesses even though it might be nice to support the town. If Elisha and Lily need to increase their hours, that's fine. We can adjust next semester. I don't want to take advantage of them."

Rowan took careful, printed notes. "Do you want to approve the menu and review the presentations prior to the event?"

Florence took off her reading glass, looked at Rowan and broke out into a chuckle. "I have worked with you a very long time – my gosh it must be – oh my – sixteen years if you go back to the start of the Pack Horse Librarian Project. Does that seem possible, Rowan? Anyway, in all those years the one thing I have learned is that you love your independence and the more latitude you have the better the outcome. No, I don't need to review your progress."

Rowan tilted her head back, smiled and jumped out of her chair. "I am ready to take this on. Thank you, Florence. I apologize if I was brisque earlier."

§

Rowan met with Elisha and Lily that afternoon to explain the Second Wednesday event and asked them to prepare remarks explaining their work on the project. Elisha paid rapt attention to Rowan, nodding when she spoke. She jumped to the edge of her chair. "I have an idea, Miss Daly, why don't we invite Captain Mitchell to attend. He wouldn't have to speak, just be here to answer questions about the Tuskegee Airmen."

Rowan leaned forward, her eyes widened. "Oh Elisha, do you think he would come? That would mean two trips to Berea for him in December. I don't think I could even pay him for his gas. Well, wait, maybe we could."

"I will call my Dad tonight and ask him if he thinks it's a good idea and if Captain Mitchell would be willing. Maybe he could even mention the idea to Capt. Mitchell to get his reaction."

"What do you think, Lily?"

"I agree with Elisha, I always do."

"It would be a good idea to have Florence send him a written invitation. We'll only do that if your father gets a positive response. Thank you so much, ladies. You are so well connected. You will make this a very special event. I'm sure Florence and Dr. Hutchins will be thrilled."

Rowan worried about what to serve for refreshments in the middle of December. While it was a good idea to ask Mrs. Davis to cater the event, Rowan worried that Florence didn't realize the event coincided with when dinner was served in the residence hall. Rowan scheduled a meeting with Mrs. Davis at two the next day, when she took a break before beginning evening meal preparations.

§

With Elisha's father's help, Captain Mitchell agreed to attend both Second Wednesday and the Christmas convocation. Elisha's father offered to cover all of Captain Mitchell's traveling expenses.

The day of the event Florence didn't come to work. She left Rowan a message that she would be in by four. Rowan expected Florence would help set up. Florence was changing, becoming more aloof. Rowan didn't have time to reflect on Florence today. She put her emotions in a little box to open another day, but she promised herself to open it before the end of the week.

Mrs. Davis's staff arrived with the food by three thirty so they had enough time to serve dinner at the residence hall. Rowan called Elisha and Lily to ask if they could work the entire day at the library. Both had morning classes and agreed to be at the library no later than one thirty. When the students arrived, Rowan was immersed in finishing the Tuskegee Airmen exhibit. She still needed over six signs printed. Elisha and Lily rushed in, threw their coats in the cloak room and found Rowan talking to herself.

"Miss Daly, who are you talking to?" Lily asked. Rowan dropped the airman's hat she was placing in the display and let out a faint scream.

"Sorry, we didn't mean to interrupt you," Elisha explained.

"Oh, Elisha, Lily, I am so worried. I don't know what's wrong with Florence. The biggest day of the semester for the library and she's at home and I'm here by myself. Well, I won't worry about that now. You are both so sweet for coming in. Now, which one of you is the best printer? I need six signs printed in two-inch letters. The wording for each sign is on my desk."

Lily raised her hand. "I have a fine hand. Once I won a writing contest. I have beautiful cursive too."

"Well, these need to be printed, Lily, if you don't mind. Elisha, you can help me finish the display and set up tables for the food and maybe set up a few chairs around the library if people tire of standing. Oh yes, ladies, will you please serve during the event?"

Elisha and Lily stiffened, looking at each other in disbelief. Lily shuffled her feet. Elisha stepped away from Rowan, her eyes flared. "You want Negro students to serve food to the faculty?"

Rowan rubbed the back of her neck and stared at the floor, unable to look Elisha and Lily in the face. A thousand words flashed through her mind but standing in front of the women she was speechless. She hugged herself and raised her head. Lily and Elisha stood waiting for her answer. "I am so sorry. I am under such stress today. Please forgive me, I'm desperate. That doesn't excuse what I asked, but I hope you know me better and can overlook my request."

They reached out to Rowan for a three-way hug. "Moving on. Lily, if you would make incredible signs, and Elisha you and I will finish this display."

"What about serving the food?" Lily asked.

"It's going to be a buffet. They can help themselves," Rowan suggested.

§

Florence snuck into the library at four p.m. She was pale and exhausted. She went to her office without inspecting the Tuskegee Airmen display, the food display or looking for Rowan.

Making her last rounds, Rowan noticed Florence's office door was closed. She strode in without knocking to find Florence slumped in her chair, a thermos on the desk smelled like Earl Grey tea. "Florence, are you all right?" Rowan said in a shrill voice.

Florence looked up, took a sip of tea but couldn't focus. "Rowan?"

"Yes, Florence. You are ill and shouldn't be here. You could have called."

Florence held her face in her hands. "I'm sorry, dear. I just can't make any welcome comments today. I'm not sure I can stand. You can welcome the faculty, can't you?"

"I insist tomorrow you visit your doctor. You need to sort this out. I have never seen you this way and it frightens me. Can I ask the faculty to stop in your office if they want to speak with you?"

Florence closed her eyes and leaned back in her chair. "I suppose, if you must. It wasn't good judgment for me to come today. You're right, I should have called in. I've tried everything – eating prunes, drinking three glasses of orange juice a day, taking Geritol. I'm just so listless."

"I'm going to make an appointment with Dr. Edgerton tomorrow and ask him to make a home visit. It isn't safe for you to drive in your condition. After this event, I will find someone to drive you home."

A faint smile crossed Florence's face. "Thank you, dear. Now, go welcome the faculty to our library."

$

Rowan tapped a glass with a spoon to get the attention of the people milling around the library lobby.

"Good Afternoon. My name is Rowan Daly, I am the Associate Director of Frost Library. Our director, Florence Pruett is not well and is staying in her office, if you would like to speak with her."

Florence forced herself out of her chair and stood in the doorway to listen to Rowan.

"The Frost Library is honored to host the first Second Wednesday event. We will share with you a curated exhibit on the Tuskegee Airmen. It is my pleasure to introduce Capt. Edward Mitchell from the 332nd Fighter Group of the Army Air Corp. We relied on Captain Mitchell to ensure our display is accurate and represents the airmen. He donated several of the items in the display. He has agreed to answer questions you may have about the famous Tuskegee Airmen. I would like to point out that Capt. Mitchell owns a civilian flight school in Lexington and is a member of Negro Airmen International.

"I am indebted to our students, Elisha Russell and Lily Alexander, for hours of work they devoted to helping me curate the exhibit. Elisha, Lily, please step forward."

Florence leaned against the door jam, unable to stand. She had a fever and felt faint. Rowan heard a thud, like a brick hitting the floor behind her. She swung around and saw that Florence had collapsed. She rushed to Florence's side. "Florence! Florence." Rowan noticed she was sweating and felt her forehead. Others gathered around, staring. "She has a horrible fever. Someone get her some water."

Dr. Hutchins leaned over Rowan. "Look, she's bleeding from her nose. That isn't good. I'm calling an ambulance."

The ambulance arrived and whisked Florence to St. Joseph's Hospital. Dr. Hutchins pulled Rowan into Florence's office. "That was frightening, wasn't it, Rowan? I hope you can continue with our Second Wednesday event. There's nothing we can do for Florence now, of course. I'll go to the hospital this evening. If this event is too much, I can dismiss everyone. It's your decision; I will support you either way."

Rowan paced in front of Florence's desk and breathed to regain her composure. She looked at Dr. Hutchins several times, trying to read her face for direction. She took a deep breath, stood straight and faced Dr. Hutchins. "Florence would want us to carry on. Of that I am sure. Yes, let's continue. Let's invite the faculty to try our appetizers. Elisha and Lily can explain their role in creating the exhibit. Finally, we can ask Capt. Mitchell to take questions."

Dr. Hutchins gave Rowan a big hug. "You are an amazing young lady."

§

Elisha and Lily helped Rowan clean up after the event so the evening janitors weren't overwhelmed with the job. Rowan insisted that both Elisha and Lily take food back to the residence halls to share with their friends. Rowan took a plate of food even though she had no appetite. As she put things away, her thoughts drifted off to Florence, hoping they were taking good care of her at St. Joseph's.

"Thank you, ladies. You made the first ever Second Wednesday a complete success. I wish I could convince you to study library science."

Lily and Elisha giggled. "You tease us, Miss Daly." Lily said.

"We're proud to tell the story of the Tuskegee Airmen. Capt. Mitchell was just wonderful," Elisha said.

"I will write a thank you note to your father tomorrow, Elisha, for paying Capt. Mitchell's travel expenses. He is a generous man. Will your parents be coming for the annual Christmas convocation this year?"

"They haven't missed one yet. It's the start of the holiday season for them, and we ride home with them afterward to start the semester break," Lily explained.

"Well, thank you again. I need to leave. I'm guessing it's at least half an hour walk to the hospital."

As Rowan walked she scolded herself for feeling Florence abandoned her for the Second Wednesday event. She was ashamed she was so sensitive and not empathetic to Florence. It was clear Florence was a sick woman and would need Rowan's unflinching support.

§

St. Joseph's was a square, three-story brick building with no other buildings around it. Rowan lived in Berea for twelve years and never visited the hospital. The entrance was small but inside, the lobby opened into a magnificent room, taking the entire first floor. An older woman with wire frame glasses sat behind an imposing desk. She shuffled through papers, placing them in three different stacks in front of her and didn't notice Rowan standing nearby. Rowan cleared her throat.

The woman looked up, narrowed her eyes, as if she had to work to see Rowan. "May I help you?"

"Yes, what room is Florence Pruett in?"

The woman turned in her chair to check the clock on the wall. "The patients are still having dinner. Visiting hours begin in fifteen minutes. You can have a seat over there. Today's newspaper is on the table, if you're interested."

Rowan looked around to where the receptionist pointed. "Thank you. What room did you say Miss Pruett is in?"

The receptionist shuffled through several stacks of paper and scratched her head. "When did you say she was admitted, dear?"

Rowan shuffled her feet. "Well, I don't know. I'm guessing about four thirty today. They brought her in by ambulance."

"Oh, by ambulance. Why didn't you say so, dear? Here it is, yes, Miss Florence Pruett – room 235. The elevator is behind me, and the stairs are to your right. You should check in at the nurse's station before going to the room. Do you understand?"

"Yes, ma'am."

Rowan picked up the newspaper, glanced and the headlines but couldn't focus on reading any of the articles. She checked the clock every few minutes and watched the clock hands move to six thirty. Rowan jumped out of the chair and climbed the stairs, two steps at a time.

The nurse's desk was in the center of the floor. Several nurses were working behind the desk and they all smiled at Rowan as she walked up.

"I would like to see Miss Pruett, if that's possible."

A thin middle-aged woman with a nurse's cap propped on top of her head, smiled. "Yes, she's in room 235. Please follow me. I believe we convinced her to finish at least part of her supper. Are you family or friend?"

"I'm a friend. We work together at the Frost Library on the Berea campus. She just collapsed this afternoon at a college event."

"She is just in for observation this evening. We have notified Dr. Edgerton. He has ordered several tests and will make rounds in the morning. Miss Pruett was exhausted and Dr. Edgerton has suggested a sleep aid. Please don't stay too long."

Florence was in a private room with the bed shoved up against the wall. On one side there was a small white table and a single chair. Florence lay in bed with closed eyes, the sheets tucked in tight around her. Rowan could still smell the tray from Florence's dinner, it must have been meatloaf and mashed potatoes. Rowan felt a growl in her stomach that she ignored. She walked to the side of the bed and took Florence's hand in hers.

Florence opened her eyes half-way and stared at Rowan's face, then opened her eyes wide. "Oh, Rowan, I hope I didn't ruin the Second Wednesday event."

Rowan couldn't resist laughing. "You are so selfless, Florence. Now, what happened to you?"

"Well, I don't know exactly. One minute I was listening to you and the next I was being put into this bed. Everything is a blank. The nurse told me Dr. Edgerton ordered a series of tests this evening. He will review the results with me tomorrow morning. Now, tell me, was the event a success?"

"More about that another time. The nurse won't let me stay long this evening, and I want you to finish all the tests the doctors ordered. When can I visit tomorrow?"

Florence took a few minutes to answer. "I think I would like to have you here when Dr. Edgerton reviews my test results. Yes, I would like that."

"How will I know when to come?"

"Oh, I don't know. Ask the nurse, dear. Thank you for coming. Please go home and take care of yourself."

Chapter 40

On her walk home Rowan had second thoughts about seeing the doctor with Florence in the morning. She agreed in a moment of weakness and extreme empathy. When she first walked into Florence's room, she looked as if she had passed. Rowan took her hand to see if it was warm. *Florence was too young to be facing death.* The memory of Eli lying in the cheap wooden coffin flooded through her mind. She shook her head back and forth as if she could shake the memory from her consciousness. *Do I have to watch Florence die?*

Rowan forgot her key and it was late enough the door to the boarding house would be locked for the evening. She knocked on the door just loud enough to be heard in the kitchen where Rowan guessed Mrs. Murphy would be baking something delicious for breakfast.

Mrs. Murphy brushed flour from her apron and went to answer the knock at the door. She thought it was unusual to have anyone visit this time of night. "Rowan?"

Mrs. Murphy opened the door with a quizzical expression on her face.

Rowan blushed. "I was so nervous this morning when I left, I just now discovered I forgot my key. I'm lucky you were in the kitchen. I'll look for the key in my room right away."

Mrs. Murphy returned to her baking, and Rowan searched for her key. She found the key where she left it every night, on top of her dresser. She looked into the mirror. She didn't like what she saw. Her hair was disheveled, her eyes were dull and gray, and her mouth turned down in a scowl. She cleaned up and slipped into her pajamas. The warm water on her face felt good, and the Ponds cold cream soothed her skin. Routine activities helped distract her from thinking about Florence in the hospital and the fear of what Dr. Edgerton would say tomorrow. Dr. Edgerton didn't see the need to visit the hospital when Florence was admitted so maybe that meant Florence's illness wasn't too serious. Rowen hoped so.

Rowan noticed the time and turned her radio dial to the Doris Day show, one of her favorites. Doris Day was so relaxed on stage and her voice natural and melodic. Rowan plopped on her bed, but once there her imagination flew out of control, she was certain they would diagnose Florence with some horrible disease. She turned up the volume of the radio to drown out her thoughts. The radio was so loud she didn't hear Mrs. Murphy knocking at the door. Lying on the bed, Rowan closed her eyes tight and followed along with Doris singing "Whatever Will Be Will Be" – it was the perfect song for the moment. Rowan was lost in the chorus when the radio snapped off. She jumped off the bed and had to catch herself from landing on the floor. Mrs. Murphy was standing next to the radio scowling. "Do you realize how loud your radio is? I like Doris Day too but I shouldn't be able to hear her singing in the kitchen. I'm surprised one of the other ladies didn't knock on your door before I did. This isn't like you, Rowan. Is something wrong, dear?"

Rowan sat on the edge of the bed. Tears cascaded down her cheeks in a steady stream. "I am so sorry, Mrs. Murphy, I am."

Mrs. Murphy sat next to Rowan and took her in her arms. "Now, when you're ready, tell me what this is about."

"Florence Pruett fainted at the library this afternoon. We called the ambulance to take her to St. Joseph. Her behavior has been radical; she falls asleep at her desk; she comes in to work late and leaves early; she complains about not sleeping at night. When I visited her in the hospital earlier this evening, she was so still lying in bed I thought she had passed. Her doctor ordered a lot of tests. Florence asked me to be with her tomorrow morning when Dr. Edgerton shares the test results with her. I don't know what I was thinking when I said yes. I don't like doctors because they always have bad news – always. Why did I ever agree to see the doctor? I can't back out now; Florence would be disappointed and frightened. Oh, I'm frightened, Mrs. Murphy."

"Well, you agreed to see the doctor because you are a good friend, and I'm sure you never gave it a second thought when Florence asked. It's what I would expect of you. Now, I'm going to make you a glass of warm milk. It will settle you down and help you get some sleep tonight."

While well intentioned, the warm milk didn't work. Rowan tossed and turned all night. Remembering Eli in the coffin haunted her and thinking of death made her nauseous. She counted backward from one hundred several times until she fell into a restless sleep.

$

Thursday morning the sun was bright and there was a faint white dust of frost on the lawn. It was cold for mid-December in Berea. Rowan took her time getting ready and missed breakfast. Mrs. Murphy saved a plate for her, but a nervous stomach prevented Rowan from eating.

Rowan could see her breath as she walked to the hospital. In the lobby the clock chimed nine-thirty. Rowan couldn't decide if she should go upstairs and sit with Florence before the doctor came at ten or wait in the lobby. Her stomach knotted up. Rowan winced in pain. She went upstairs at nine forty-five.

They had propped Florence up in bed with several pillows. Her color was normal and she was leafing through a National Geographic magazine. "Florence, you look terrific."

"That little pill helped me sleep through the night without waking up once. I can't remember the last time I've slept through the night. This morning I had a bowl of oatmeal with cinnamon sugar on it – yummy. Those testes were tiring last night. You don't look like you had as good a night as I did, Rowan."

"We don't need to talk about my evening. I'm relieved you look so well this morning. Maybe you just need a vacation. When was your last vacation? If I can't remember, it's been too long. Semester break is two weeks away – you don't need to come back to the library. You should think about taking a break."

Florence's look became stern the longer Rowan babbled on. "Give me your hand, Rowan. Thank you for being with me this morning. I couldn't stand the thought of learning the test results by myself. There are some things a person should never do alone. Talking with your doctor is one of them."

Dr. Edgerton was well respected in Berea. He walked into the hospital room without Florence and Rowan noticing.

"Good morning, ladies." Looking at Rowan he extended a hand. "I don't believe I know you, I'm Dr. Edgerton. Has Florence asked you to join us this morning?"

Rowan moved to the end of the bed and let Dr. Edgerton stand close to Florence. "Yes, doctor. I work with Florence at Frost Library. We also worked together on the Pack Horse Librarian Project in Pike County sixteen years ago."

"That was an outstanding program. I wish the federal government hadn't eliminated the program. The need is still there."

"Let's get to it, Dr. Edgerton. How were my test results?" Florence was impatient.

Dr. Edgerton read over the clipboard in his hands and cleared his throat before answering. "Florence, the blood test is conclusive. You have acute leukemia. It's cancer in your blood. We don't know the cause; it happens. With this leukemia you will need aggressive chemotherapy starting today."

Rowan felt her legs weaken. She grabbed the bed railing to stop herself from falling. Her breath was erratic, and she wasn't able to focus. Florence didn't react at all. Her face remained calm; she even smiled. "I'm not surprised, Dr. Edgerton. I am a librarian and I've researched my symptoms. How long will I need chemotherapy?"

"I don't know. We begin with an aggressive dose of medication, monitor you for side effects, then test your blood daily to determine the efficacy of the drug. I wish I could give you more guidance but I can't."

"This chemotherapy – does it cure my type of leukemia?"

"No, it retards the disease. Extends your life. There is no known cure."

Rowan bristled. "You are blunt."

Dr. Edgerton turned toward Rowan, crossed his arms and narrowed his eyes. "Florence deserves honesty."

Florence stretched out her hand toward Rowan. "Come here, dear. It's all right. Now, doctor, would I live months or weeks longer with chemotherapy?"

Dr. Edgerton's eyes softened and he spoke in a whisper. "No one knows. Each patient is unique. It wouldn't be fair to you to make a guess."

"I've read the side effects can be worse than the disease."

"Some side effects I've seen are loss of hair, stomach cramps, loss of appetite, numbness in the legs, headaches and difficulty sleeping."

Florence pulled Rowan close to her. "Well, I don't want to start chemotherapy today. I want to think about this. I have a choice, don't I?"

"Take all the time you want. You can notify the nurse when you've decided and we'll visit again." Dr. Edgerton left to continue making rounds.

"Rowan, I need some time alone to reflect and make a lot of decisions. Can you come back this evening after dinner?"

Rowan sat up wiping tears from her cheeks.

"On the way out can you stop at the nurse's station and ask one of the nurses to stop in when they have time?" Rowan gave Florence a hug so strong it made her ribs sore.

$

Florence drifted off to sleep until a knock on the door woke her. "Miss Pruett? You asked for a nurse? My name is Nuala Byrne, I work with Dr. Edgerton often. How can I help you?"

Florence couldn't help chuckling. Nurse Byrne spoke with a deep Irish brogue. "When did you immigrate from Ireland, Nurse Byrne?"

"Well, my secret is out isn't it? Every time I open my mouth the Irish just comes flowing out. Well now, I've been in the states for thirteen years. My husband was intent on finding his riches, but his abilities didn't match his dreams. Ten years ago he passed from pneumonia. We traveled a lot. We started in Boston because of family, then moved to Louisville for a job and finally to Berea. It was too much for Mr. Byrne. Two months after moving to Berea the pneumonia took him from me.

"Enough of my story. How can I help you?"

Florence grabbed nurse Byrne's arm. "Well, we all know we are going to die but it's different when you learn you're going to die soon. I have acute myeloid leukemia. How long do I have before...ah...ah expiring?"

Nurse Byrne took both of Florence's hands. "Four to

six months. There is no evidence chemotherapy makes any difference."

Florence sobbed and squeezed nurse Byrne's hands as hard as possible. "How will I die?"

Nurse Byrne drew close to Florence's face to capture her eyes. "Most likely a stroke. It will be fast. You will be very weak and not conscious, and then the Lord takes you away with a single stroke."

Florence pulled nurse Byrne closer and buried her face in her shoulder. She let herself exhaust her tears to this stranger, her new-found friend. After a few minutes, Florence released the nurse and fell back on her stack of pillows – exhausted.

"I'm guessing you don't want the chemotherapy, Miss Pruett?"

"Please – Florence. No, I've done my research. This is my fate and I want to let death come to my door – not fight it."

Nurse Byrne reached around Florence, puffed up her pillows, tucked in the sheets and offered her a glass of water with a straw. "There is another path, palliative care. Back in Dublin the Irish Sisters of Charity started a program to help people die. The concept is to alleviate pain and suffering to make sure the patient is comfortable. I worked at Our Lady's Hospice for eighteen months as part of my nurse's training in Dublin. I could provide hospice to you in your home but Dr. Edgerton would need to approve."

Florence relaxed and set the glass on the table. "Death with dignity, mmmm, I'm tired, Nurse Byrne. I will talk with Dr. Edgerton when he makes rounds."

§

Friday morning Rowan opened the library and let Elisha and Lily work with students so she could visit Florence. She arrived by ten a.m. and went straight to Florence's room without stopping at the nurse's station. Florence was standing at the side of the hospital bed stuffing things into a pillowcase type bag the hospital provided. Rowan stopped and stared at Florence, not believing she was out of bed.

"What are you doing?"

Florence turned to see the shock on Rowan's face. "Packing, sort of. I'm going home."

"Home? Dr. Edgerton is aware of this?"

"Dr. Edgerton discharged me thirty minutes ago."

Rowan walked to the bed and leaned against the edge facing Florence. "I don't understand, Florence."

Florence patted Rowan on the shoulder and drew her close for a quick hug. "Help me with these things and call a cab. Come home with me and I'll explain everything."

"I left Lily and Elisha at the library alone. I should go back."

"Of course, dear, how thoughtless of me. Why don't you come over for dinner tonight and we can have a wonderful talk. I have a few ideas I would like to share with you."

Rowan brushed her hair back. "I guess this means you've decided against chemotherapy."

Florence stuffed the last few items in her bag and walked toward the door. "That's right, Rowan. Can you call the cab, please?"

Chapter 41

$\mathcal{R}$owan couldn't wait to close the library at five o'clock. She sent Lily and Elisha home when she returned from the hospital. She spent the afternoon alone trying to find things to distract herself. It was clear if Florence decided against chemotherapy, her life expectancy was a big question mark. While Rowan respected Florence's decision, she didn't understand it. A few students straggled into the library in the afternoon to have a quiet place to study for finals. The click-clack of their heels echoed throughout the library. Without Florence there, the library felt hollow and lifeless.

Rowan pulled the library doors shut tight then walked to Murphy's Boardinghouse to change clothes and let Mrs. Murphy know she wouldn't be there for dinner. She noticed on her walk to the boardinghouse a bit of frost had spread across the sidewalk and it was slick. Rowan changed into wool slacks, a blouse and sweater and wore boots and her heaviest wool coat to walk to Florence's house.

Florence greeted her with a warm smile and a long

hug. The smell of fried chicken made Rowan's mouth water, and she realized she had not eaten all day. Florence took her coat and hung it up in the front hall closet. She turned on every light in the house, which gave it a cheerful appearance.

"Are you hungry, dear?"

"Well, I forgot to eat today."

"You forgot? What am I to do with you? Everything is ready. Help me set the table, will you?"

Rowan visited Florence enough to take the dinnerware from the sideboard, including cloth napkins. Florence insisted on using cloth napkins, which Rowan felt was formal but it helped to make a meal with Florence special. Rowan helped herself to a huge chicken breast, mashed potatoes with gravy and green beans with onions and tomatoes. Florence watched her relax and enjoy the only food she had all day. Florence took a few green beans and mashed potatoes but no chicken. She didn't tolerate fried food very well, and she didn't want to be sick this evening. She planned to have a serious talk with Rowan.

Rowan was so hungry she didn't notice Florence wasn't eating chicken. After finishing a chicken breast, she helped herself to a chicken leg and a second helping of mashed potatoes. She scooped the last bite of potatoes up and smacked her lips. Rowan looked at Florence, who was swirling the potatoes on her plate before taking a small bite and pushing the plate away. "You're not hungry, Florence?"

"No. I'm so pleased you enjoyed your meal. I'm sorry, I ran out of time and made nothing for dessert."

Rowan reached out to touch Florence's hand. "This was so delicious. I don't need dessert. Now, you go in the living room and rest, read a magazine or something. I'm going to clean up these dishes, then I'll join you."

This time of year it was dark by the time they finished dinner. A glass chandelier hung from the center of the ceiling, which drenched the small room in light. A settee sat against one wall, and there was a wing chair and over-stuffed chair on the opposite side of the room. A small table with a lamp sat next to the overstuffed chair and there was a stack of magazines on the floor. Florence searched through the magazines until she found her favorite, the December issue of National Geographic. With the help of the magazine, Florence traveled the world.

When Rowan walked into the living room, Florence was sitting in her favorite wing chair with her head back, asleep. Rowan sat on the sofa opposite her and picked up a magazine to leaf through it. After a few minutes, Florence blinked a few times and opened her eyes. "Oh, I'm so sorry. You should have said something, Rowan."

"I didn't want to disturb you."

"Well, I want to get straight to the point this evening. As you know, I've decided not to have chemotherapy. I'm afraid the medication will rob me of any quality of life I may have left and that's unacceptable. Dr. Edgerton believes I will have four to five months before I die. Nurse Byrne told me about a program called hospice, which started in Europe. Hospice gives a patient palliative care."

Rowan picked up a box of tissues and blotted tears from her eyes. She handed the box to Florence. Rowan took Florence's hands into hers. Having a good cry was what both women needed. Florence pulled away, sat up straight and took deep breaths to calm herself before speaking again.

"Palliative care?" Rowan's eyebrows squished together.

"Make the patient comfortable, control the pain. A guide to dying."

"How can pain be controlled?"

"Morphine. Injected by the nurse based on what a person says their pain level is. Nurse Byrne has agreed to provide hospice service when I need it, and Dr. Edgerton has approved. At first, I will likely need very little – maybe once a month. Toward the end, every day."

Florence got up and joined Rowan on the sofa. She put her arm around Rowan's shoulder and drew her close. Her face was only inches from Rowan's. "I will visit with Dr. Hutchins on Monday and resign from my position immediately. I'm too young to retire, but I believe I will be eligible for some small amount of severance pay. Money is not an issue. I own this house, my car, a savings account and I have invested in a few stocks over the years. I will also visit my lawyer on Monday. I'm giving you the house and car. I'll be donating my books to Frost Library to create a special collection. I'll also create an endowment. It was embarrassing not to have the resources to pay Captain Mitchell for his travel expenses and a small stipend. Rowan, you're taking our library in new direction to provide cultural, enrichment and historical programs. I believe strongly you are leading our library in a the direction it must go. I want to make sure Frost Library will always have resources to finance this type of programming and not rely on the vagaries of the annual college budget."

Rowan grabbed Florence's arm and shook her head back and forth. "Oh Florence, you are so generous but I can't accept this house and your car. I just can't."

"I've owned the 1936 Ford Tudor for sixteen years

now, and it doesn't have 10,000 miles on it yet. I've made sure it had a tune up and oil change every year and the tires are like new. Do you remember, that's the car we drove when we moved you from New Hope to Pikeville? Oh yes, that old car has memories. I want to ensure you never have financial worries and this is my solution. Please, please, Rowan, accept my gift. There's something much more important I will ask you. In the past few days I've realized there's been a wall between us preventing us from becoming real friends. I've always been your boss, and I felt it wasn't appropriate to befriend someone working for me. Well, that's no longer a problem. The one circumstance we share in life is that neither of us have any family – no parents, grandparents, cousins, aunts, uncles. We are orphans in the world, but we have each other. I want you to move in with me when the semester ends. We can share Christmas together." Florence sat still to let Rowan absorb everything she said. "You don't need to decide tonight, I mean about moving in."

Rowan sat with her hands folded in her lap. After a few minutes, she turned to look at Florence. "I have a question; you're going to be surprised, but I've always wondered, what is your middle name?"

Florence flushed. "What...what did you ask me?"

Rowan got up to leave. "Oh, never mind; it was just silly."

Florence grabbed Rowan's hand and led her to sit down next to her again. "I don't have a middle name. Don't know why. By the time I was old enough to be curious, there was no one in my family left to ask."

Rowan giggled then broke into a donkey-like laugh.

"Rowan, what is the matter with you?"

"Being orphans in the world isn't the only thing we have in common. I don't have a middle name either. My grandmother said my name came from her grandmother in Ireland. I guess my mom didn't feel a middle name was needed, so I'm Rowan Daly – period."

Rowan stopped laughing, then a pensive expression crossed her face. Florence was mother, sister, and friend all in one to her. Years ago Rowan decided she was alone but not lonely. Now, in the moment's depth she had to be honest with herself and concede she has been lonely. Rowan shook all over and let herself fall into Florence's welcoming embrace. She searched for the right words and in a few minutes gave up. Two words would suffice. "of course, I'll move in on the 20th."

On her walk back to the boardinghouse that evening Rowan was chilled and brisk wind blew her hair. The clouds were so thick she couldn't see a single star. What will my life be like without Florence? The world was such a frightening place to Rowen and she was overcome with the knowing sense of being abandoned again.

On Monday afternoon Rowan was summoned to Dr. Hutchins' office. She knocked on the door and found Dr. Hutchins staring out the window. Without turning around Dr. Hutchins spoke.

"Miss Pruett, Florence, visited me this morning. You know she has resigned. It's abrupt, but I understand. Now, I'm going to name you Interim Library Director, effective today. We need you to see us through the end of spring semester. I don't know what your ambitions are. I would hope you would stay here at Berea; you've accomplished so much. To fill the job for the fall I'll appoint a search and screen committee, it's required. However, I want you to know, privately, I support you for the permanent library director position. I simply cannot share my view with the search and screen committee."

Rowan was lost for words. She didn't anticipate being promoted when Florence resigned her position. She wrung her hands together.

"You accept, don't you?"

"I...I...I, well, yes, I wasn't expecting..."

"It's my job to ensure there's continuity in our institution and the library is key. It may appear unfeeling but believe me, it isn't. Thank you for being willing to carry on."

"You know I'll be moving in with Florence before Christmas?"

"Yes, she mentioned it."

"I'm going to take care of her. I'm going to share this journey with her in whatever way I can. I may need to be away from the library, I don't know, I don't know what will happen. Maybe by spring I won't be able to care for Florence and be at the library full time. Can you accept I may not be able to be at the library full time? I don't need to be the interim director; I could just keep my associate's position."

Dr. Hutchins turned away from the window and sat down in her chair. "I understand you have great faith in Elisha Russell and Lily Alexander. I will ask for volunteers from the faculty, and when you need to be with Florence, we will make sure the library remains open. We're a family at Berea and that's what families do in a crisis."

Dr. Hutchins walked around her desk and gave Rowan a long hug. "My door is always open to you. Whatever you need. Whatever Miss Pruett needs, let me know."

Chapter 42

$\mathcal{M}$r. Murphy didn't take the news well when Rowan announced at breakfast Saturday morning she would move out in a week's time.

Mr. Murphy threw his napkin on the plate, his eyes flared. "Next Saturday! We won't have time to advertise for a lodger. Who's going to move in during the holidays? What a selfish girl you are."

Mrs. Murphy patted her husband's hand. "Sean, calm yourself. Rowan's going to care for Miss Pruett. Haven't you heard? She quit her job. She has leukemia. Rowan is an angel."

Rowan looked down, unable to look Mr. Murphy in the eyes. "You've both been like parents to me. I am sorry but Florence has asked me to move in with her and I need to care for my friend. I want to be fair. I will continue to pay rent until you have another lodger. That's only fair."

Sean Murphy's chest caved and he slumped in his chair. "I'm embarrassed. I was the one being selfish. You must take care of Miss Pruett. Don't worry about the rent. We'll get by – won't we, Fiona?"

§

Rowan gave Fiona Murphy a check for the January rent before she left to buy a new suitcase and visit Berea Press about an idea she had for Florence's Christmas gift.

The next week Rowan visited Florence every day. She tried to convince Florence to attend the Christmas convocation, but Florence didn't want to go out in the cold weather. Rowan didn't realize Florence wanted to avoid the outpouring of sympathy she would receive from the Berea staff and her colleagues. Dr. Hutchins announced Rowan's interim position at the beginning of the convocation, which was greeted with a warm round of applause. Once again Rowan was at a loss for words. Lily and Elisha chastised her after the event for not sharing the news with them.

After the convocation Rowan walked to the library and inspected the building before winter break. Classes were scheduled to begin in mid-January, so the building would be empty for three weeks. *An empty library is one of the most desolate places in the world*, she thought. For her last stop she sat in Florence's office. It wasn't Florence's office any longer. During the week the maintenance man removed Florence's name plaque and put up Rowan's. Rowan knew she would make some changes to personalize the space but it was too soon. *Maybe waiting until after the spring semester would be better.* Rowan wasn't ready to fill Florence's shoes or her office.

The next morning everyone at the boardinghouse said

their goodbyes after breakfast. Rowan reminded everyone she wasn't moving to another state and would still be in Berea and able to visit. Mrs. Murphy nudged Mr. Murphy with her elbow. "Look here, Rowan, I'll drive you over to Miss Pruett's place."

"Thank you, Mr. Murphy, that's kind of you."

Florence was up before dawn, eager for Rowan to move in. She spent the last few days cleaning the spare room and moving her things out of the room into her bedroom. She brought up a box of Christmas decorations from the basement every day and stacked them in the living room. She thought decorating for Christmas would be an icebreaker for Rowan moving in – to give them a creative activity. Saturday morning Florence brought the last box upstairs and set it on the coffee table. She felt dizzy and let herself slide into her reading chair. She rested her head in her hands. Florence drifted off to sleep without realizing it. Pounding at the front door startled her awake.

"Miss Pruett, it's Sean Murphy. Are you in?" He shouted loud enough to raise the dead.

Mr. Murphy walked in carrying a suitcase and a box under one arm. "Where do you want these?"

"End of the hall – the room on the right. Where's Rowan?"

Sean Murphy answered as he walked down the hall. "Oh, she's still saying her goodbyes. I'll bring her in the next trip."

"Does she have much more to bring?"

"Just a few boxes of books and another suitcase."

Within a half hour Sean returned with Rowan and Mrs. Murphy. Mrs. Murphy was determined to inspect how Rowan would live and make sure it would be right for her. While Mrs. Murphy had never had her own children, she delighted in being a mother to all her boarders, and Rowan had lived with them the longest.

Florence sensed Mrs. Murphy's mission and offered to give her a tour of her house, which didn't take over five minutes to see every room in the bungalow, except the basement. "Rowan, I believe you will be very comfortable here." Mrs. Murphy couldn't bring herself to say more.

Rowan shut the door behind Mrs. and Mr. Murphy then turned to see Florence sitting in her reading chair with her eyes closed. "I'm sorry about that, Florence. They do care for me."

Florence sat for a few minutes before saying anything. A faint smile crossed her face, and there was a hint of a glimmer in her eyes. "They are such kind people. Would you like some lunch? I have vegetable soup on the stove. After lunch I'll take a brief nap, let you settle in a bit, and then I have a project for us this afternoon."

Rowan gave Florence a big hug and held her for a few minutes and noticed how shallow she breathed. "I love projects. What are we going to do?"

"Decorate for Christmas."

$

While Florence napped, Rowan explored the stack of boxes in the living room. There were three boxes full of snow globes; there must have been at least thirty of them. She didn't picture Florence as a collector but then here was the proof. When she thought about it, a librarian is a natural collector. There were at least four boxes full of tree ornaments and lights for the tree. Another box contained a beautiful wreath for the front door that Florence had shellacked for preservation. Rowan was so busy exploring boxes she didn't hear Florence come into the room.

"You've been busy. Did I sleep that long?"

"No. What a wonderful assortment of decorations you have."

Florence clasped her hands together. "Well, it has been years in the making. Now, there seems to be one very important box you haven't discovered. Let me see." Florence picked up the boxes one at a time and stacked them on top of the sofa. "Here it is!" she shrieked. She opened the box and took out what looked like parts of a pine tree.

Rowan gasped. "What is that?"

"It's my artificial tree. I've had it at least ten years. I ordered it from the Sears Roebuck store in Louisville. It's a lot cheaper than getting a fresh cut tree every year."

Rowan jumped up, shoved the branches back in the box and folded the lid shut. "Not this year, Florence Pruett. I'm going to buy us a real tree. The Baptist church is selling them in their parking lot. I'm going to walk down there and pick one out."

"Oh, you are insistent. Let me grab my purse and I'll give you some money."

Rowan shook her head back and forth. "No, I can afford it. This will be my treat for the holidays. Think of it as a Christmas gift, if you like."

§

The tree was delivered just as dusk was sliding into evening. The high school boy from the church helped them set the tree in a stand with water. "Be sure to water it every day and it will last through New Year's." As the boy turned to leave, Florence gave him a few coins for the delivery. "That's ok – no charge for the delivery."

"Please, I insist."

The boy looked down and blushed. "Well, ok, I'll give it to our food pantry collection. This time of year a lot of folks need help putting food on the table. Merry Christmas, ladies."

Rowan and Florence took their time decorating the tree, stepping back many times to see if the ornaments were in the perfect location. After an hour both were satisfied the tree was outstanding. Rowan opened a box of the snow globes and took one out with each hand. She shook them and watched the snow fly around inside and then settle back down. "So, tell me about all these snow globes?"

"Well, it started back in Pikeville. One of our families wanted to express their appreciation for the book delivery services and gave me a snow globe for Christmas. Their gesture was so endearing. Then word got around that I liked snow globes and every year one or two other families gave them to me. After we left Pikeville I bought myself a snow globe every Christmas season to honor those families and to remember our days in the Pack Horse Librarian Project."

"Well, do you want to set them out or would you like some help?"

"There are so many, dear, I could use some help." It took them an hour to put each of the snow globes in the right place. Florence stood in the center of the room and turned to view them. She broke out into a beaming smile. "Yes, that's perfect. Now, make us a cup of tea, Rowan."

Rowen made tea and brought it into the living room. Florence sat, looking self-satisfied at the Christmas decorations. "I do like having a fresh cut tree – it adds such a delicate fragrance to the room. It's like having a little bit of the outdoors, indoors. It's perfect for my last Christmas. Thank you for insisting, Rowan. Thank you for the tea."

§

December slid into January and every day Florence and Rowan's friendship grew. Rowan felt comfortable returning to the library when the spring semester began the second week of January. Florence took a nap every afternoon and was always in bed by eight. Otherwise, under Rowan's watchful eye, Florence didn't display other symptoms of leukemia.

The third week of January Nurse Byrne visited to check on Florence. She visited in the early evening so Rowan could take part in the visit. The three women drank their tea and had glib chitchat.

"Now, Florence – Rowan, this is not a social visit. One of the primary principles of hospice is for the patient to be aware of the dying process. I want to share with you what to expect."

Rowan got up and turned to walk back to her room. "Rowan, you need to hear this too – assuming it's all right with Florence.

"Florence?"

In a flat, monotone voice Florence responded, "Yes."

Rowan returned to her seat and folded her hands in her lap to prepare herself to learn the truth.

Nurse Byrne sat up straight with an air of confidence to demonstrate her authority and knowledge. "Florence, I understand you take a nap every afternoon and are in bed early in the evening. You must feel worn out – no pain yet."

"Yes."

"In the next few weeks you may need to take a nap in the morning and the afternoon. How is your food, Florence?"

"My food?"

"Yes, are you eating solids, a piece of fish or a bit of chicken?"

Florence stared at the floor before answering as if she couldn't remember for sure. "Yes, a few times a week, I guess. Rowan?"

"That's right, I guess maybe three times a week. Florence likes soup – vegetable soup. Florence has been a brilliant teacher. I've always lived in boardinghouses and didn't need to learn how to cook. Florence said I needed to learn to cook for one person. She's right, I guess."

Nurse Byrne smiled. "That's excellent. In the next few weeks you can expect Florence will want soup more often and soft foods like mashed potatoes. By March I expect she will only want clear soups and broth. If you can make ice chips that will help too. Also, by mid-March we can expect Florence will be confined to her bed. It would be helpful if you could read to her as often as she would like. By mid-March I will check in with you every day. Florence, if you feel any pain, please ask me for morphine. I will control the dosage so you can remain as alert as possible. By April you may struggle to be lucid. There will be what we call failure to thrive and you won't be eating at all. A bit of water or ice chips will be the best for you. I will then visit twice a day to make sure you are comfortable and have morphine when you want it."

Florence sat motionless in her chair as Nurse Byrne outlined how she would die in a cold, clinical tone. Florence turned white as she thought about dying. She was not afraid of death; she was afraid of not being a part of the world. *What will I miss?*

Rowan fell back into the chair and hugged herself. She doubted if she had the fortitude to remain strong for Florence. She was certain she wouldn't sleep tonight.

"Questions?"

Rowan and Florence looked at each other and flinched their shoulders. Rowan's eyes glazed over and Florence was listless.

"All right. You have my number; call anytime, day or night. Good night, ladies."

Rowan tossed and turned all night long. She just couldn't imagine a world without Florence. She also had no idea how to muster the strength to give Florence the care she needed.

Washing up in the morning, she saw bloodshot eyes in the mirror. She squeezed her cheeks for a bit of color and made herself busy making oatmeal for Florence's breakfast.

§

Living with another person always requires adapting and compromising. Rowan learned there were things Florence just would not compromise on. Every morning for breakfast she had steaming hot coffee with a bowl of oatmeal. She sprinkled a fifty/fifty mixture of sugar and cinnamon on the oatmeal then added fresh cream to cool it off. Lunch was a sandwich – her favorite: egg salad, with a piece of fruit or soup. Because it was winter she ate canned fruit, peaches with thick sugary syrup. Florence would not tolerate any fat on meat, refused to eat beef and ate a lot of chicken and fish. Every afternoon by three she had tea. Sometimes she would add toast with homemade jam with her tea. She never added milk or sugar to her tea. Also, every afternoon she read from the National Geographic magazine. Florence had a collection of National Geographics dating to 1930. She claimed to have traveled throughout the world without ever leaving the comfort of her reading chair.

§

As they had tea one afternoon, Rowan confessed she didn't have a driver's license.

"When I told you I was giving you my car, why didn't you mention you don't have a driving license?" Florence flushed with anger.

"I've just never needed one, and I've never owned a car before."

Florence sat her tea down and stared at Rowan. "A thirty-five-year-old woman in today's world without a driver's license. We need to remedy that soon, young lady, while I'm still well enough to teach you to drive. Go get a pad and pencil and we'll make a schedule for lessons."

Florence thought it prudent to teach Rowan how to drive in the evenings on the Berea campus when there wouldn't be any traffic and most students were inside studying. The idea was for Florence to drive to campus and then turn over the car to Rowan for lessons. Both women learned how weak Florence had become when she wasn't able to turn the steering wheel of her Ford sedan. While the car was parked, Rowan also found the steering wheel difficult to turn but once they were on the road it was easier. Rowan drove at a crawl from Florence's home to the Frost Library parking lot. She stopped with a jolt, put the car into neutral and turned off the key. The women looked at each other and broke out into laughter.

"This is going to be an adventure, Rowan." Florence laughed so hard, tears rolled down her cheeks.

By mid-February Rowan completed her driving lessons and passed her test on the first attempt. The women settled into a routine they both learned to tolerate. Rowan found it was much different to live with a woman than a man. When a man and a woman live together, they each have a role they understand and a basic notion of who does what. When two women live together, they need to invent roles and responsibilities. Rowan felt she was lucky she knew her role was to be a caretaker, and Nurse Byrne did a superb job of teaching her.

Winter stayed in Berea longer than usual, with no hope of spring until at least April, according to the weather forecast on the radio. The temperature never rose above forty, and the wind was blustery almost every day. Florence inspected how Rowan dressed before leaving the house every morning. Often, she asked Rowan to add a scarf or pair of gloves to stay warm. On those cool mornings Rowan walked almost at a trot, making the mile journey in less than fifteen minutes. By March Rowan found it difficult to concentrate at work. Elisha and Lily were remarkable in keeping the library open and helping students with their spring term papers.

One afternoon Dr. Sapper paid Rowan a visit to offer help. He sat in the chair opposite Rowan's desk without taking off his coat.

"Be honest with me, Rowan, how is Florence?"

Rowan shook her head back and forth. "For the first time yesterday she asked for morphine when Nurse Byrne visited after supper. She wanted to sleep."

"Well, then..."

"Nurse Byrne told me her request for morphine marked a turning point. Her body is fighting her. She has pain. She won't eat solid food any longer – just clear broth and a cup of tea once in a while."

Dr. Sapper slumped in his chair and crossed his arms. He toyed with a piece of paper in his hands. "Rowan, this is a list of staff who want to help you with the library. I've listed the name, phone number and the time during the day each person is available. Looking it over, we can keep the library open during normal hours until, until..."

Rowan raked her hand through her hair several times. She looked at Dr. Sapper and burst into tears. He let her sob a few minutes, then stood up. He placed the list on her desk in front of her. "I must go, Rowan."

Chapter 43

By the fourth week of March, Florence was confined to her bed and wasn't eating. Rowan made ice and chipped it into a cup she kept at Florence's bedside night and day. Nurse Byrne felt Florence was ready and could pass any day. On Wednesday evening Nurse Byrne asked Rowan for a cup of tea before leaving for the evening. They sat in the parlor with a wall of silence between them. Rowan knew there was something Nurse Byrne wanted to say but appeared reluctant.

Nurse Byrne finished her tea and looked at Rowan. "Has Florence given you instructions?"

Rowan winced. "Instructions?"

"Yes dear. Instructions for her funeral and burial."

Rowan wrung her hands together several times. "Well, I know she has a burial plot in the Berea Cemetery, and she has made arrangements with Dodd and Peters funeral home, but I don't know the details."

"She has a lawyer – a will?"

"Oh yes. Mr. Edwards. She gave me a copy of her will the first week I moved in but I haven't read it."

Nurse Byrne leaned over and took Rowan's hands into hers. "It's time to prepare, Rowan. Florence could pass any day. You must ask her what she wants for a service and type of casket."

Rowan had flashbacks of the priest asking her about Eli's service. "No!" she screamed. I'm not ready. Not yet. Not yet."

"Rowan, calm yourself. Listen. In the last days she will appear to be sleeping heavily and not be able to wake. I will take her vitals and decide on the dose of morphine she should have. In the last hours she will have a gurgling sound in her lungs, and she may shout out incoherent sounds. Don't be frightened. She will hear you so stay close and talk with her, reassure her and let her know she can let go – to move on."

As Nurse Byrne explained what would happen, Rowan lost self-control again and sobbed for several minutes. She dropped her tea cup on the floor, staining the carpet. "Oh no!" she shouted. Nurse Byrne let Rowan cry until she could take a few breaths to calm herself.

Rowan, tired of questions, shouted, "No, she hasn't told me anything. It just hasn't come up in conversation and I'm not ready to have that conversation. I don't want to know and you can't make me." Rowan turned away to let Nurse Byrne know it was time for her to leave. Nurse Byrne let herself out. As she closed the front door, she said, "You must have the conversation, out of respect for Florence. When she passes, call me. I will take care of the arrangements to move her body."

§

The next morning Rowan took Florence a glass of orange juice to brighten her day, even though it wasn't the normal morning routine. Florence held the glass with both hands, took a few sips through the straw then handed it back to Rowan. "Thank you, it was good."

Rowan took the glass to the kitchen. When she returned, she blurted out, "Do you believe in God?"

Florence leaned back against her pillow and asked Rowan for another pillow so she could sit up. She struggled to swallow. She took a sip of water from a straw from the glass that was always at her bedside table. "No, I don't believe in a personal God. You know, the old man in the sky who takes this remarkable interest in each of our personal lives. I have studied the religions of the world and I've found they all have one thing in common – controlling human behavior. In particular I've studied the history of the Bible, and I've concluded it is highly unlikely that Jesus rose from the dead. Other religions also claim resurrection so it isn't a unique story to Christianity. I believe Christianity offers wonderful instruction on how to live a good life. When Emperor Constantine made Christianity the state religion of Rome, everything changed. More questions?"

Rowan hugged herself. "Do you think you have a soul? What happens to you when you die?"

Florence opened her arms wide and drew Rowan close for a long hug. She whispered into Rowan's ear, "I don't know. I accepted death as a mystery a long time ago. I want you to know I'm tired. I'm ready. I'm ready."

Rowan got into bed with Florence and stayed until

Florence fell asleep. Remembering her talk with Nurse Byrne, Rowan couldn't avoid reading Florence's will another day. Florence left simple instructions for a memorial service, not a religious service in Danforth Chapel. She was very specific about not having a service at the grave site. She even listed the clothes she was to wear in the casket. She purchased a simple pine casket and refused to spend money for a vault. She also didn't want a traditional grave stone but a simple plaque with her name and dates of birth and death, to be embedded in the ground. The funeral home was in charge of all the details.

That evening Rowan couldn't eat and thought about Florence's view of Christianity and religion. Rowan wasn't churched when she grew up. There was too much work on the farm to waste a Sunday morning at church. Until this experience with Florence, Rowan ignored religion and church except the occasional church dance or ice cream social in the summertime. After reflecting on it for days, Rowan concluded not having strong religious beliefs or practice had not harmed her life.

Rowan checked on Florence one more time. She thought a hot bath would help her get to sleep. She decided there was no way to prepare for those final moments. It would just happen and Rowan had one desire – to be with her friend. Rowan mustered her courage and put her fear of abandonment in a box, tied it up and hid it deep in her subconscious.

Chapter 44

$\mathcal{T}$he morning of April 1, 1953, was so bright Rowan opened the curtains in Florence's room as wide as they could go. She made a cup of coffee for Florence and walked into her room with a light step. "Happy April 1st, Florence. Why, it's April Fool's Day, isn't it."

Florence was motionless and her color ashen. Rowan sat the coffee cup on the side table then sat on the bed next to Florence. She took her arm in her hand and checked for a pulse – nothing. She held the back of her hand up to Florence's face to check for her breath. Nothing. Rowan jumped off the bed and ran to the phone in the living room. *Where is that damn card?* She pulled out the drawer, it dropped to the floor, scattering the contents. Rowan threw papers across the floor searching for Nurse Byrne's card. The card wasn't there. *Where did Florence put that damn card? She knew it was important.* Trying to get the drawer back into its slot, she knocked the phone onto the floor. "Damn!" Rowan shouted. Nurse Byrne's card was underneath the phone. Rowan put the phone in her lap and dialed the number. "Nuala Byrne speaking."

"She's...it's... Oh my God..." Rowan slammed the phone down on the receiver.

§

Nurse Byrne arrived in less than fifteen minutes to find Rowan still sitting in the living room with the phone in her lap. The nurse knew her first duty was to the body. She had called the funeral parlor from home before leaving for Florence's. A death certificate would be needed to remove the body. Nurse Byrne checked over Florence's body. The dose of morphine the night before induced a deep slumber, allowing Florence to pass without pain or awareness. Nurse Byrne filled in the death certificate and guessed six a.m. for death. It didn't matter.

Two overweight men with a gurney pounded on the door so hard the glass rattled. Rowan ignored the racket. Nurse Byrne led the men to Florence's bedroom. Their faces were blank.

"I will bring instructions later this morning. Tell the embalmer not to do anything until I read her wishes. I will bring a copy with me. Please clean her body. I'll bring clothes too."

The men did their job in silence and shut the front door behind them. Nurse Byrne found Rowan still in the living room. She looked numb and was unmoving.

"Rowan, dear."

Rowan's eyes were bloodshot and swollen with tears. "It's not like I didn't know this was going to happen.

Things went along just like you told me they would. Oh God, it hurts to have her gone."

Nurse Byrne held Rowan for a long time, then gave her instructions for the day. "It's important to do normal things. Bathe, dress, have something to eat, even if it's only a piece of toast. I will register the death certificate. Visit her lawyer today. Visit Dr. Hutchins today and plan for her service. Let Dr. Hutchins notify the campus faculty and staff. Allow yourself time. You will heal – in time."

§

Danforth Chapel didn't have a seat left. As instructed, Florence's coffin stayed in the funeral home and only a picture of her draped in a black cloth sat on a table at the front of the chapel. Dr. Hutchins spoke first, reciting a list of Florence's accomplishments as director of Frost library. Dr. Parsons traveled from Washington D.C. to attend the memorial. He told stories of Florence as one of his students and recalled the day he invited her to take his position as director of the library. Finally, it was Rowan's turn. She stood up and grabbed the pew in front of her to steady herself. She swayed back and forth, then took a deep breath and walked to the table with Florence's picture. She looked out at all the faces. Her mouth was dry and words stuck in her throat. In a few moments she composed herself.

"She was my best friend." Rowan stood at the table a few minutes then sat down.

Only Rowan and Dr. Hutchins were at the grave site when Florence's pine coffin was lowered into the ground. Neither woman spoke.

Dr. Hutchins held Rowan by the shoulder. "I'll give you a lift home, Rowan."

Rowan sat in the car buried in her grief. She got out of the car without speaking. She was terrified of being in Florence's empty house alone. Rowan isolated herself in the house. She knew she had to bear her grief alone. Rowan felt like she had been lowered into the grave with Florence. No one in Berea saw Rowan Daly for the next seven days.

Chapter 45

$\mathcal{M}$onday morning was a bright, spring day, just like the day Florence died. Rowan took her time walking to the library and swooned in the fragrance of blooming magnolias. Elisha and Lily arrived at the library thirty minutes before Rowan because they didn't know if she would be back in the library or not. Seeing Rowan at the memorial service, Dr. Hutchins stepped in to organize faculty to oversee the library until Rowan returned. The morning Rowan returned, Lily ran to Dr. Hutchins office to let her know Rowan was back, as they instructed her.

Rowan called Elisha and Lily into her old office to thank them for keeping the library doors open during her absence. Rowan wasn't ready to move into Florence's previous office, even though it was empty of all of Florence's personal items and maintenance staff posted a sign reading – Interim Director Miss Daly. Elisha gave Rowan a list of the faculty members who worked in the library the past week. Rowan wrote each one a personal thank you note.

On Tuesday Rowan received a note from Dr. Hutchins to stop in her office when she was ready. Rowan worried her absence might not be excused and she may be asked to leave. It would be understandable. Rowan decided not to wait, folded the note, put it in her pocket and walked to Dr. Hutchins' office. As usual, Matilda was working in the outer office when Rowan arrived.

"Miss Daly, it is so good to see you. Dr. Hutchins told me when you arrived to go right in – so please do. Rowan knocked then entered Dr. Hutchins' office. The windows were wide open and the papers on Dr. Hutchins desk fluttered. Dr. Hutchins approached Rowan and without a greeting hugged her for several minutes.

"Elisha and Lily informed me you haven't moved into your new office."

"That's correct."

"Hmmmm."

"I called you in today to share with you our decision regarding filling the library director position."

Rowan stiffened to brace herself for disastrous news.

Dr. Hutchins sat at her desk with her hands folded. Her voice was calm and reassuring. "There will a five-member search and screen committee. Of the five there will be three faculty, one administrative person and one member of the Board of Trustees. The position will be advertised both throughout Kentucky and the nation for thirty days. The Board of Trustees insisted on a national search." Dr. Hutchins noticed Rowan was listening intently and leaning forward.

"The resumes will be reviewed for two weeks and three candidates selected for a personal interview. We hope a selection can be made after the initial interview. If not, there will be a second round of interviews. Questions?"

Rowan fidgeted with her hair. Her mind was a blank.

"Rowan?"

Rowan blinked. "No questions. It seems straightforward. Thank you for telling me."

Dr. Hutchins stood up to signal Rowan to their meeting was over. "This is the way it must be, Rowan. If you are selected, it will make your promotion unquestionable. I wish you the best."

Rowan stood and walked to the door. She held the door open, pausing to speak but deciding not to. She shut the door behind her and said good-bye to Matilda.

Chapter 46

Rowan took her time completing the items required to apply for the director position. She anticipated a job application and was surprised the process included submitting a resume and a five-hundred-word essay on the role of a library in a college education. An application would have been easy. Rowan didn't know the process for hiring a director or faculty member was so much different from other college positions. After her experience as a pack horse librarian, her entire career was at Berea, and she had never filled out an application or a resume for each of her positions. Rowan had no idea how unusual it was to work as an associate director without competing for the job. She was beginning to understand and appreciate how skillfully Florence pulled the bureaucratic strings behind the scene at Berea.

Rowan gave herself two weeks to complete her resume and write the essay. To be safe she decided to turn in all her materials directly to Matilda. She searched through the library for books on how to develop a resume.

She spent hours for several days leafing through at least a dozen books. Rowan pulled at her hair as she compared the various formats for her resume. At the end of the second day of research she slammed the last book shut and took a walk around campus to clear her head. The best fit for her was a resume that listed dates, positions and a one-line description of accomplishments. Using this format, her resume was three pages long but was succinct. Once she was satisfied with her resume, she asked Lily and Elisha to review it for her.

§

One morning they both burst into her office without knocking. "Oh Miss Daly, your resume is astonishing." Elisha gushed. "I had no idea you've done so many wonderful things. I especially like the technique you developed to teach hill people to read," Lily said.

Rowan leaned back in her chair; a broad smile spread across her face. "Do you think it will impress the search and screen committee?"

"Definitely," they said in unison.

"I need time to work on my five-hundred-word essay. Could you ladies cover the library for me for several days? I'll be in the office but don't disturb me unless absolutely necessary."

"We can do that," Lily said with a little salute.

Rowan chuckled. "I knew you would help. Thank you. Now, be gone!"

Rowan spent the rest of the morning staring out her window. She had no idea where to start her essay or even what she should write about. Her mind drifted off, and she recalled some of the last conversations she had with Florence while she was still lucid enough to talk. Florence always gave Rowan credit for bringing new programs to the library and finding new ways for students to use the library. Rowan picked up her resume and had to admit she was pleased that her work was well represented. Rowan took a yellow tablet and pencil and made a list of her accomplishments at Frost Library:

- Developing and maintaining a self-help library collection
- Curated display on accomplishments of Negroes in America
- Curated display on Tuskegee Airmen in World War II
- Organizing the archived book collection
- Working with Negro students in the library
- Organizing the Second Wednesday Program
- Developing public presentations on various topics
- Inviting Berea residents to participate in library programs

Rowan pondered her list for the rest of the morning, folded up the paper and slipped it into the drawer. She spent the rest of the day working with Elisha and Lily.

"It was fun to work together again," Rowan said.

Lily shelved the last book. "It doesn't happen very often any more. We miss it, don't we, Elisha?"

"We do."

Rowan glanced at her watch. "It's a few minutes before five. I think we need to be spoiled. Let's go downtown for a chocolate phosphate."

"Before dinner?" Lily shrieked.

"Yes, why not before dinner?" Rowan grabbed the two women by the arm and they marched out of the library as a threesome.

Chapter 47

Rowan had a call from Matilda to let her know her interview was scheduled for nine Friday morning.

"Is that the search and screen committee's first interview of the day?" Rowan wondered.

"Well, I can't really say, Rowan, but think about the time of day and make your own conclusion," Matilda answered.

"Can I ask you one more question, Matilda? Please? Please?"

"You can ask, not sure I can answer."

"How many candidates are they interviewing? In total I mean?"

"Well, I'm not sure I can answer. But what harm would it do?" There was a long silence. "Three."

"Three! Oh my God. I'm one of three."

"We'll see you Friday morning at nine – sharp. Good luck. Good bye."

There was a day and a half to prepare. Rowan stood and pushed the chair under the desk. She stared out the window not able to focus her thoughts. *What will I do with myself for almost two days?* Her heart pounded in her chest and she was light-headed. She wrung her hands together. Rowan didn't hear Lily walk into the office.

"Miss Daly?"

Rowan turned on her heel. Her head jerked back. She took a deep breath and held it for a moment. "Yes, Lily."

"Are you feeling well?"

Rowan worked on breathing naturally. "Yes, I just received the call. My interview is nine a.m. Friday. I'll be the first. There are only three candidates."

Lily rushed toward Rowan and grabbed both her hands. "Hurray!"

"I'm worried I won't be able to sleep. I've never been on a job interview in my life."

"Never?" Lily asked.

"Never. What am I going to do?"

Lily stood up straight trying to look directly into Rowan's eyes. "You're going to do what any self-respecting woman would do. You're going shopping. You'll need a new dress, and shoes, maybe treat yourself to a haircut. A little make-up will help, but I know your aversion to make-up."

Rowan held Lily's face in her hands. "You are so sweet. You're right. Can you cover the library this afternoon?"

"Of course."

"What color dress do you think I should buy?"

"A soft yellow with matching shoes. Yellow is a good color for you."

"You think so?"

Lily smirked and left the office without shutting the door.

§

All day Thursday Rowan thought back on her career. It was clear to her that ever since Florence hired her in Union Hall to work as a pack horse librarian she was destined for this job. In the last ten years she introduced many innovations at Frost Library and her reputation with faculty was exceptional. Thursday evening Rowan laid out her clothes to be ready for the morning. Once she was satisfied she was ready she took a few minutes to review a few points she needed to make during the interview. *What if I don't get the job?* Rowan gasped for air and she clenched her fists. *That just can't happen. It's my fate to be the director of Frost Library. If I don't get this job, I'm going to quit – never work in a library again. I'll sell ice cream at the drug store.*

Rowan turned on the radio and listened to several of her favorite radio programs to distract herself from doubtful, destructive thoughts. Burns and Allen gave her belly laughs, Gracie was so innocent. Following Burns and Allen she listened to the ABC Mystery and as usual couldn't figure out who killed Mrs. Baily. Rowan made herself herbal tea and let the night sink in the darkness. She heard the soft chime of the clock tower ring ten when she slipped into bed. The tea relaxed her enough she drifted off into a light sleep but forgot to set the alarm.

Rowan rolled over in bed and glanced at the clock – seven a.m., plenty of time for her toast and a warm bath. She dressed and brushed her hair fifty times. A fresh haircut made her hair shine. She looked in the mirror, smiled and winked.

Rowan walked into Matilda's office at eight-forty-five. Matilda expected Rowan to be early.

"New dress?"

"Yes."

"Very becoming."

"The committee is using Dr. Hutchins' office for the interview. I will escort you into her office promptly at nine. Can I get you anything? A glass of water maybe?"

"No thank you."

Rowan's hands trembled as she waited to walk into the interview. She put both feet on the floor squarely in front of her and took long, deep breaths. She let her mind go blank and follow her breathing. Matilda touched her shoulder and motioned with her hand to get up. Matilda walked in front of Rowan and opened the door to Dr. Hutchins office.

Rowan had been in Dr. Hutchins' office many times but today it was strange. To the right three men sat at a large oak table. The man in the center puffed on a pipe filling the room with a blue, fragrant haze. A single chair sat just a few feet away from the men at the table.

"Please, sit down, Miss Daly," the smoking man instructed.

The smoking man wore a stiff white shirt with a red necktie and matching handkerchief in his suit pocket. He kept his suit coat buttoned even though he was sitting at the table. He fiddled with the glass ashtray in front of him and laid his pipe carefully in the tray. A manila file was on his left and a pad of yellow paper with an expensive looking fountain pen sat on the pad.

"I am Mr. Howard, of the Jefferson County Howards. I am a Trustee with the Berea College Board of Trustees.

To my left is Dr. Ballard with the English Department, a distinguished professor of American Literature. To my right is Dr. Sapper with the Agronomy Department, he is a distinguished professor of crop sciences. Today we are interviewing for the position of director of the Frost Library. We have received and reviewed your resume and the five-hundred-word essay you submitted. You can expect the interview to take approximately one hour. We anticipate making a recommendation to Dr. Hutchins to-morrow. Do you have any questions?"

"No sir." Rowan sat forward in the chair and smoothed her dress.

Mr. Howard led the questioning. "I take it Frost Library is the only college library you have worked in?"

"Yes, sir."

Mr. Howard scribbled on the pad. "You were hired after receiving your baccalaureate degree here at Berea?"

"Yes, sir."

Mr. Howard picked up his pipe, scraped tobacco into the ash tray and set it back down. "Were you interviewed for the job?"

"No, sir."

Mr. Howard winced. "How did that come about?"

"I don't know, sir. Miss Pruett, the former director called me into her office one day and offered me the job. I had worked in the library all four years of college. I was very familiar with library operations. I graduated number one in my class for Library Science."

Mr. Howard squirmed in his chair. He turned to look at Dr. Ballard and then Dr. Sapper. "Gentlemen. Do you have questions?"

Dr. Ballard spoke first. "Miss Daly, I seem to remember that Frost Library was the first department to host the Second Wednesday events. Didn't you organize the event for the library?"

"Yes, sir."

"If I recall you had a special display on the history of the Tuskegee Airmen and Colonel Mitchell attended," Dr. Sapper recalled.

"That's right. One of the students working at the library knew Captain Mitchell personally and her father persuaded Captain Mitchell to attend. The library didn't have funds and her parents paid for Captian Mitchell's travel to attend the event."

Dr. Ballard adjusted his glasses on his nose. "Didn't Captain Mitchell also give the presentation of the Christmas convocation that year?"

"Yes, sir."

Dr. Ballard smiled. "So that's how that came about. I've always wondered. Nice work, Miss Daly."

"Gentlemen, I have a few critical questions." Mr. Howard said. "You were promoted to associate director of the library a few years ago?"

"Yes, sir."

"Did you interview for that position?"

"No, sir."

Mr. Howard wrote more notes on his pad. "When you were promoted, was that the first time the library had an associate director position?"

"Yes, sir."

"How did that come about, no competition, for the job I mean?" Mr. Howard inquired.

Rowan brushed hair out of her eye and wished she had worn a barrette to manage her hair. "Well, I'm not sure.

Miss Pruett's administrative responsibilities grew, and she wasn't able to devote as much time as she wanted to library development. I was given responsibility to curate displays, develop a program of regular presentations, manage the collection and develop the archive."

Mr. Howard scratched notes on his pad, picked up his pipe and set it back in the ashtray. "So, let me understand this. You have worked at Frost Library for ten years, been promoted to associate director and never been required to compete for the position."

"That's correct, Mr. Howard."

Mr. Howard leaned forward in his chair and looked directly into Rowan's face. "Did you expect you would be elevated to director of Frost Library without competition, Miss Daly?"

"No sir. I didn't have any expectations." Rowan stiffened and looked directly back at Mr. Howard.

"Now then, Miss Daly. How old are you?" Mr. Howard asked an obvious question.

"I am thirty-five this year, sir."

"Now, Miss Daly, your surname indicates you are of Irish heritage. Is that correct?" Mr. Howard asked.

"Yes, sir."

"Are your grandparents also of Irish descent?"

"Yes, sir."

"When did your people arrive in America, Miss Daly?"

"Mr. Howard, with all due respect I am not sure how my heritage is relevant in this job interview. I am not familiar with the family history of either my mother or father."

Mr. Howard narrowed his eyes and crossed his arms.

"Well, I believe that concludes this interview. Gentlemen, do either of you have questions?"

Dr. Sapper spoke first. "I agree that Miss Daly's heritage is not relevant to this interview and want to go on the record of opposing questions of such a nature, Mr. Howard."

Mr. Howard turned to Dr. Ballard. "Do you have anything to say or perhaps a question?"

"I agree with Dr. Sapper, a candidate's heritage is not relevant to this search and screen committee and I commend Miss Daly for commenting on it."

Mr. Howard threw his pen down on the pad. "As usual, I am in the minority at this university. As a trustee of this institution, I have the right to ask any question that I choose and get an answer. This interview is concluded. Miss Daly, on your way out tell Matilda to escort the next candidate in."

Rowan stood up and paused before leaving. "Thank you for the opportunity to compete for the position of director of Frost Library. I am confident you will make a fair decision based the merits and experience of each candidate." She turned on her heel and marched out of the room.

"How did it go?" Matilda asked.

Rowan's face was flushed, tears blurred her vision. She ran out of the building all the way home.

Chapter 48

*T*he next morning Rowan walked to the library as usual. She took several boxes she found in the basement left over from her move into Florence's – now her home. She wanted to be professional and begin clearing the office of all her personal things. There was a knock at the door and a student she didn't know handed her an envelope. "What is this?"

The student hunched his shoulders. "I don't know. I was told to deliver it to you first thing – from Dr. Hutchins."

"Thank you, young man."

Rowan ripped open the envelope with a handwritten note: "Please come to my office as soon as you come in to work today." signed Dr. Hutchins. Rowan folded the note and stuffed it into the envelope.

Matilda was not at the reception desk so Rowan went directly to Dr. Hutchins' office and knocked loudly.

"Yes, come in. Oh, Rowan I am so happy you are here early. Let's talk. I understand your interview yesterday was contentious."

Rowan crossed her arms across her chest and rolled her eyes. "I don't want to work anyplace where my age and heritage is questioned in order to do the job."

"Please, Rowan, don't be angry with me. I understand your indignation but don't make the mistake of directing it toward me. I called you in to let you know you will have a second interview this afternoon at one."

Rowan stepped back nearly losing her balance. "Oh. All right then. Thank you."

"I suggest you use your time this morning to prepare yourself for the interview."

Rowan left Dr. Hutchins office dismayed, running her hands through her hair. She scolded herself for not asking Dr. Hutchins why she was given a second interview. She found it impossible to focus. Rowan walked throughout campus for at least an hour and then went home to change clothes. Rowan took a long hot bath with bubbles to calm herself and regain her composure. Rowan chose a deep red blouse, tan trousers and matching shoes, the yellow dress may have been a mistake – it was ordinary. She tried to eat a peanut butter sandwich and an apple but couldn't finish. The clock in her kitchen chimed twelve-thirty. Rowan walked with quick, deliberate steps to Dr. Hutchins office arriving ten minutes before the interview.

Matilda didn't hear Rowan walk in. "Excuse me." Rowan whispered. A broad smile grew across Matilda's face. "Good to see you back, Rowan. Go right in. The search and screen committee is convened."

When Rowan entered the office, Dr. Sapper and Dr. Ballard stood to greet her. Mr. Howard remained seated with his head bowed.

"Would you like a seat?" Dr. Sapper offered.

"Thank you, no, sir. I want to make a statement. I don't want to work for any college or any other organization where they care about my age or my heritage. Every day I come to campus I believe in Berea's motto: 'God has made of one blood all peoples of the earth.' I am sure you are an important and powerful man. I also don't understand why you asked if I competed for the jobs I've held at Frost Library. I have worked there fourteen years, including my time as a student. I earned those jobs. I never asked for a job; Florence, that is, Miss Pruett, promoted me. You work at a bank, don't you Mr. Howard?"

Mr. Howard looked up but couldn't look Rowan in the eyes. "Yes."

"Do you promote people in your bank, Mr. Howard?"

"Of course."

"Have you been promoted, Mr. Howard?"

Mr. Howard smiled and stroked his beard. "Yes, several times."

"What is your title at the bank?"

"I am vice president for Business Lending and Development." He sat stiff.

"Did you compete for the job as vice president?

Mr. Howard cleared this throat several times and whispered, "No."

The air was heavy with silence. Dr. Sapper and Dr. Ballard looked across Mr. Howard at each other with raised eyebrows.

Mr. Ballard put his pencil on the table, folded his hands and looked directly at Rowan. "Is there anything you would like to add, Miss Daly?"

Mr. Howard kept his head down and didn't give Rowan eye contact. "You're wearing pants." he mumbled. Rowan stepped next to the table, planted herself directly in front of Mr. Howard. "What did you say?" Rowan sneered.

Dr. Sapper leapt out of his chair. "Now Rowan, we asked you here today because we wanted to learn more about your vision for the library. Your essay outlined several ideas and we wanted clarification. Please, sit down. We are here to listen, aren't we, Mr. Howard?"

Mr. Howard hunched over and said nothing.

Rowan backed up and sat down. She took a moment to compose herself. "I don't want Frost Library to be a museum where books are collected and gather dust. The library needs to be an integral part of a student's education."

"Can you be specific?" Dr. Ballard asked.

"I have drafted a new mission statement for the library. 'Frost Library is a teaching library that works with students to develop critical thinking and life-long learning skills. It works with faculty to support research and academic publishing.'"

Dr. Sapper scratched his head. "Mmmm, interesting. What does that mean?"

"For example, I would like to work with faculty to develop a course for incoming freshman on college life, how to use the library, study habits, how to write a term paper and whatever topics the faculty believe would be useful in making the transition from high school to college. I could have used it in my first semester. After receiving mid-term grades when I was a freshman, I was ready to pack my bags and go back to Pike County, riding the circuit as a pack horse librarian."

Dr. Ballard tapped his pencil on the table. "So you plan on working in conjunction with faculty, if hired as director, that is."

"Exactly. I also feel strongly that Berea College must welcome the entire community. Berea is a wonderful, liberal town. I have made many presentations in churches, the community center, even peoples' homes on topics such as the Tuskegee Airmen based on the library's display."

Mr. Howard kept his head down and didn't respond. Dr. Sapper and Dr. Ballard looked at each other and widened their eyes. Dr. Ballard leaned in and put his elbows on the table.

"Intriguing ideas, Miss Daly."

"Mr. Howard, do you have any questions of Miss Daly?"

"No."

"Well, thank you for sharing your thoughts with us, Miss Daly. The search and screen committee needs to deliberate now. You will be notified of our decision through Dr. Hutchins," Dr. Sapper explained.

Rowan cleared her throat several times. "I didn't mean to be impertinent earlier, gentlemen."

"You are a spirited young lady, Miss Daly, nothing wrong with that. Do you have any final thoughts you would like to share with the committee?" Dr. Sapper asked.

"Thank you, Dr. Sapper, I do. Since Miss Pruett hired me over fifteen years ago as a pack horse librarian in Pike County after my husband died in a mining accident my life path has led directly to this job. Everything I have accomplished and the challenges I have overcome make me ready to step into the job as director of Frost Library. I have devoted my life to helping others through the power and magic of literacy. I honestly believe I am the right person for the job at the right time. Thank you for your time."

Rowan stood and shook hands with Dr. Sapper and Dr. Ballard. Mr. Howard turned away and refused to shake hands.

"Gentlemen, let's take a break to get tea before we begin our deliberations," Dr. Ballard suggested.

Chapter 49

$\mathcal{A}$ week passed and Rowan was not notified the Search and Screen Committee had made their recommendation yet. She became more nervous as each day passed and doubt grew in her like the summer tobacco crop. She avoided Lily and Elisha, trusting they knew what needed to be done to keep the library open. Each day she closed her office door as soon as she arrived. The office became her prison. As each day passed doubt evolved into mind-numbing fear. She was certain her bombastic display during the second interview was self-destructive. Thoughts of all her days at Berea over the last ten years swirled through her mind. She imagined working in the five and dime store to support herself. Maybe she would be forced to sell the car and home Florence willed her. The pack horse librarian program was dismantled ten years ago so she couldn't return to Pikeville. Maybe she could search for a job in a county library or she could search for a job at Pikeville University if she still had the desire to be a librarian.

Lily rapped on the door so loudly she didn't hear

Rowan tell her to come in. Rowan opened the door. Lily was waving an envelope in her hand. "It's from Dr. Hutchins – open it, quick."

Rowan took several steps back as she removed the envelope from Lily's clenched hand. She took her time to find a letter opener in her desk and sliced the envelope open. "If you are available, I would like to meet with you at 11:00 a.m."

Rowan handed it to Lily.

"Doesn't say much," Lily said.

"Thank you, Lily. What time is it?"

"Quarter till eleven."

"Good, I won't need to wait."

Rowan walked with her shoulders straight back and her head held high.

§

"Matilda?"

"No need to knock. She's expecting you."

Dr. Hutchins stood when Rowan entered her office. She shuffled through papers on her desk and then handed one of the sheets to Rowan. Rowan's hands shook so much she couldn't focus on the words. She sat down and placed the letter on Dr. Hutchins' desk, smoothing it out with her hands.

With the recommendation of the search and screen committee and with the approval of the Board of Trustees, I am appointing you as the director of Frost Library, effective today. You will receive an annual salary of $2075 and be granted faculty *status. A contract will be provided for your signature within seven days of the date of this letter. Congratulations.*

Dr. Francis S. Hutchins.

The letter slipped through Rowan's hands and fluttered to the floor. She grinned, threw her arms straight up and shouted "Yes!" She bent down to pick up the letter and read it out loud three times in a row.

Dr. Hutchins leaned back in her chair and took off her glasses to clean them. "Rowan, you honestly appear to be surprised."

"Oh Dr. Hutchins, I am, I am. The decision took so long I was convinced I didn't get the job. I was coming in today to withdraw my name."

Dr. Hutchins leaned forward and put her glasses back on. "I'm glad you didn't; it would have been embarrassing, wouldn't it?"

Curiosity consumed Rowan. "What took so long?"

Dr. Hutchins leaned in closer and whispered so low Rowan had to scoot her chair to the edge of the desk. "Mr. Howard was furious you were granted a second interview. Your speech about prejudice personally offended him. He refused to accept Dr. Sapper's and Dr. Ballard's recommendation to hire you. He insisted the hiring be approved by the full Board of Trustees. It took a few days to schedule a meeting. They met yesterday. Each search and screen committee member was given ten minutes to make their presentation. The Board was horrified to learn Mr. Howard objected to your hiring because of your age, Irish heritage, and what he called preferential treatment for other library jobs. The Board unanimously voted to hire you. After the vote Mr. Howard resigned and stormed out of the room.

"I think it's time for tea. Matilda!"

Rowan fell back into her chair and brushed her hair back with both hands. "To be honest, in the last few days I convinced myself Berea College was going to abandon me after ten years. My entire life I have felt abandoned – by my father, then my mother's death, my grandma's death before I graduated from high school, Eli dying in the mine accident and Florence dying from leukemia." Rowan held her knees and legs tightly together and couldn't look at Dr. Hutchins.

Dr. Hutchins tilted her head back and leaned back in her chair. "Of course, I cannot comment on your life experience to this point. However, I hope you have learned that Berea College is your home, we are family. This family will never abandon you, Rowan. Let's finish our tea. Don't worry about coming into work tomorrow. I will inform Lily and Elisha you will be in on Monday."

A faint smile crossed Rowan's face. "Thank you."

"I read the notes from the interview and I want you to proceed with your plan to transform Frost Library into a teaching library, with consultation from faculty, of course. Any further questions?"

Rowan kept her head bowed. "No, Dr. Hutchins."

Dr. Hutchins stood and extended her hand. "Welcome to the faculty of Berea College. I am expecting a lot from you, Rowan Daly."

"Thank you. I will strive to do my best." Rowan folded the letter and slipped it into the envelope. She forgot to close the door behind her when she left.

Chapter 50

Rowan finally slept that Thursday night, letting all her pent-up emotions drain away and exhaustion set in. The sun had been up for an hour when she woke the next morning. After breakfast she felt the urge to drive to Marion County to visit her mother's and grandmother's graves and drive by the farm she was raised on.

Rowan felt this was a time in her life to reflect on the past and understand how she was able to get the job as the director of a college library at the age of thirty-five. When she was honest with herself, in many ways she had been fortunate in her life even though many of the people she loved left her long before they should have.

§

The hour drive was uneventful until she reached Gravel Switch and couldn't remember where the cemetery was located. There was only one cemetery in town so it shouldn't have been difficult, however, it was now seventeen years since she left town, never returning. She stopped at Penn's General store to ask directions. While there, Rowan picked up a few garden tools and a flat of marigolds for the graves. Rowan drove up and down the narrow road through the cemetery, she couldn't remember where the graves were located. In those many years her memory faded. She pulled over onto the grass and rested her head on the steering wheel. The horn went off and Rowan jumped in her seat. Rowan tugged at her hair. *Why can't I remember?* She jumped out of the car and slammed the door behind her and started to walk. Then she spotted a magnolia tree that was familiar. As she approached the tree, Rowan saw three grave stones next to each other. Her mother, grandmother and grandfather were buried together in the far corner of the cemetery at least twenty yards from the access road. The promise of perpetual care had been broken. The graves were covered in weeds and appeared like they had not even been mowed this year. Rowan pulled the weeds and piled them just outside the cemetery grounds. She used her spade and hoe to create a flower bed, stretching across all three graves and planted the marigolds. She stepped back to admire her work and silently thanked Dr. Sapper for teaching her about gardening.

She sat crossed legged at the foot of the graves.

"Mama, I'm sorry I haven't been back before this. I'm ashamed.

"Mama, you won't believe how my life has unfolded. I'm a librarian. Not just any librarian, I'm the new director of Frost Library at Berea College – me, Mama! Eli died in a mining accident in New Hope. I pray he's in heaven with you. I'm sorry, we never got married but I loved that man.

I've been afraid, Mama, afraid of being abandoned. Everybody I've loved has died. Most of the time I feel alone. I just learned I'm not alone. There are people who care for me very much. Oh, I wish you had been here to share my life with me. I don't want to be afraid anymore." Rowan swayed, felt dizzy and her heart raced out of control. She put both hands on the ground to balance herself, then took several deep breaths and exhaled slowly.

"I'm ok, Mama, I am. I'm going to give back, like all the people who have helped me. I'm going to throw off the blinders I've worn. I have a wonderful life, really." Rowan bowed her head and silently recited the only Bible passage she could remember. "The Lord is my shepherd; I shall not want..."

Rowan touched each of the headstones and left the cemetery to find the homestead where she grew up.

As she drove her memory kicked in and she found the farm. The house she grew up in was gone. In its place was a small cottage-style home with a red steel roof. The animal barn was also torn down, replaced with three, wood tobacco barns. All of the fields surrounding the house and barns were tobacco. The plants stood about two feet high this time of year. Rowan understood farmers who planted a cash crop they could rely on rather than trying to live off a few hogs, chickens and vegetable crops. It was clear to Rowan that her past, as she remembered it, no longer existed except in the confines of her memories.

When she drove back to Berea, she had a fleeting thought of continuing to drive east to visit Hazel in Pikeville. It would be at least a four-hour drive and she would need to find a place to stay overnight. She couldn't impose herself on Hazel and her family. As she drove she tried to remember the last letter she received from Hazel, it must have been at least three years ago and Rowan couldn't remember if she wrote back to her. Driving east on highway 21, Rowan turned south toward Berea College. Driving to Pikeville was only a momentary thought.

She visited Sutter's nursery on the outskirts of Berea and bought three goldenrod plants for Florence's grave. Rowan had not visited the gravesite since the brief interment service. The surface of Florence's grave looked as fresh as the day she was buried. Rowan stood back to decide the best placement of the plants. *One at either side of the headstone would look nice.*

She placed the containers on the ground before digging the holes. If she placed the third plant in front of the stone it would cover the inscription. *Well, Florence, I didn't think that out well. I have an extra plant.* She set it off to the side and dug two holes. She brought a watering can to soak both plants. Rowan watched the water puddle up underneath the plants and slowly sink into the ground. As she watched a thought flashed through her mind. *Florence, I'll plant the third goldenrod at home right underneath the front room window. I'll see it every day.*

Rowan stood back to admire her work then bent forward and laid her head on top of the gravestone. The top of the stone shimmered with tears. She steadied herself with both hands. *Oh, Florence, I miss you. I hope you would be proud of me. Two days ago Dr. Hutchins gave me a letter, I'm going to be the director of Frost Library. During my interview I was accused of privileged treatment because I didn't compete for my other jobs at the library. Can you imagine? One person on the search and screen committee had the audacity to question my age and Irish heritage. He forced the entire board of trustees to review hiring me. He lost, I won and he resigned. I've spent some time reflecting on my life. Without you I wouldn't have a life. You taught me how to change people's lives through literacy.*

Rowan made herself comfortable on the grass beside the grave. *I still marvel that you chose me to be a pack horse librarian. I'm happy that we had a few months to learn more about each other, share a few laughs, and grow our friendship. We have so much in common. We both lost the men we loved at an early age before having a chance to build a life together. We both attended Berea College. We both were left without family. We share the calling of working as librarians.*

Rowan stretched her legs out to catch the warmth of the mid-day sun. *You are the dearest friend I will ever have. You taught me to not fear being abandoned. I owe you my life. Living in fear can paralyze a person. Fear is a roadblock to living a meaningful life. I have worn blinders for too long.* Rowan brushed tears from her cheeks with a handkerchief. *No more living with my head in a shell like a turtle. I may not see you every day but I keep you here, deep in my heart. Thank you, my friend.*

Rowan stayed a few more minutes in silence, letting all the memories of their last months together drift through her mind.

Chapter 51

Saturday afternoon Rowan tucked her memories away to focus on the future. She took a long bath and considered how she would spend the rest of her day. The best thing to spend time on was to prepare for work on Monday and outline her plan to transform Frost Library into a teaching library. She was glad she had taken the time to reflect on her life journey.

§

Sunday morning Rowan found a yellow tablet and several fountain pens and sat at the dining room table to scribble down her thoughts. *I need to strengthen the mission statement I presented during my job interview.* She wrote down the first thoughts that came to mind, read them over, and tore off the page, scrunched it up and threw it on the floor. As the morning went on, the pile of rejected ideas grew on the dining room floor. From the ether Rowan came up with a three-point mission:

Frost Library Teaching Mission
1. Teach library research skills through seminars,
   classes and workshops.
   - To be required for all incoming freshmen.
2. Work with faculty to develop research guides for
   specific courses.
3. Create a reference desk where students can drop
   in for help at any time.
   - Will require development of a research librarian.

When she finished, Rowan noticed the sun begin to set. She had worked through the day, forgetting to eat lunch. She gathered up the crumpled papers on the floor and tossed them in the trash. Her stomach grumbled. Rowan warmed up some soup and cut herself a thick slice of sourdough bread and plopped herself in front of the radio for the evening.

§

Monday morning Rowan woke early to have time for a bath before walking to the library. She walked to work with a bounce in her step. She carried a small box with items she wanted for her office to personalize it for the first day. The most important item was a picture she and Florence had taken last Christmas in front of the Christmas tree.

Rowan walked into the foyer and found Lily balancing on a chair, blocking the entrance to her office. "Lily!"

Lily swayed back and forth, nearly tumbling to the floor. She snapped her head back to see Rowan. "Oh, Miss Daly!"

"What are you doing on that chair, young lady? You know it isn't safe. Get down. Please."

Lily stepped down and reached up as high as she could with a white cloth to dust off the brass office sign: "Library Director – Miss Rowan Daly."

"Isn't it perfect?" beamed Lily.

Rowan's mouth fell open. "It's perfect."

"I wanted it to sparkle for you, Miss Daly."

"You are very kind, Lily. Now, I would like you to be my first guest this morning. I have something to talk with you about. I have a few blueberry scones; would you like one?"

"I'll put the chair away and be right back. I'd love a blueberry scone. I love anything with blueberries. Should I worry that you want to talk to me on your first day?"

"Not at all." Rowan placed a scone on a napkin for Lily and put one on her desk, cutting it in half. She took a moment to think about how to talk with Lily.

Lily was back in just a moment. "Lily, as part of my job interview I made a proposal to develop Frost Library into a teaching library. It is a way to integrate the library more with the academic programs. I have been told by faculty that many students, especially incoming freshmen, need to learn about how to use the library to support their studies, how to write research papers, locate materials and other skills." Rowan took a few bites of the scone to let Lily absorb what she was explaining.

"I have an idea for a new type of librarian. I call the job – Reference Librarian."

Lily shuffled her feet and stared at the floor. She thought to herself, *I'm graduating soon in library science and never heard of a reference librarian.*

"Lily, you appear to be puzzled." Lily shook her head. "Well, this is a new idea. It would be a person, located here in the library, available to students to answer questions and guide them on how to use the library. It seems to me it would be beneficial if the reference librarian would be someone their age. I feel it is more likely students will be comfortable working with a librarian close to their age."

"Mmmmm." Lily nodded her head.

"Graduation is less than a month away, and I know you will be finishing at the top of your class in library science, I've checked. I would encourage you to consider applying for the reference librarian position."

"Oh, Miss Daly!" Then Lily bowed her head and kicked her feet back and forth on the floor.

"What's wrong, Lily, I thought you would be excited."

"Well, my Daddy would like me to move back to Lexington and get a job in the public library. He's on the board of trustees there."

"Do you want to move back to Lexington?"

"I love living in Berea; I can be myself here."

"Of course, it's your choice, but I'm not ashamed to try to convince you to stay. We have worked together well these past four years, and you are the perfect person to develop the role of reference librarian."

"Thank you, Miss Daly."

The End

Author Biography

Rex Owens published his first novel in the Irish Troubles Series, Murphy's Troubles, in November 2013, the second, Out of Darkness, in June 2015, and the third, Dead Reckoning, in April 2018. His fourth novel, The Life and Times of Rowan Daly will be published in May 2021. UW Madison writing instructor Christine DeSmet describes his writing as cinematic.

Rex is very active in supporting local libraries. He serves as the President of both the Sun Prairie Public Library and the Dane County Library Service. He is also the discussion leader for the Wednesday Afternoon Book Club which meets monthly.

He supports authors as the host of the award-winning radio talk program My World and Welcome to It, which airs on the first and third Monday every month at 10:30 a.m. CST. The interview program is live streamed at: www. sunprairiemediacenter.com.

To learn more about Rex's work visit: www.rexowens.us. To connect with Rex, you can e-mail him at rexowens00@gmail.com

§

If you enjoyed this book, please leave a review on your favorite website.

Thank you,

~ Rex